THE CRIVABANIAN

Odan Terridor Trilogy: Book Two

Savannah J. Goins

Copyright © 2019 Savannah J. Goins

Published by Mason Mill Publishing House 2019
Indianapolis, Indiana

Cover art by JD&J Book Cover Design at JDandJ.com

All rights reserved. No part of this publication may be used or reproduced in any manner whatsoever without the prior written permission of the publisher, except for brief quotations in written reviews.

ISBN: 978-0-9986455-5-1

This is a work of fiction. Any similarities between characters and situations within to real persons or places are coincidental. For more information, visit savannahgoinsbooks.com

This book contains brief, vague flashbacks of sexual abuse. Many people who have experienced this in their past have found this story to be cathartic and helpful in their growth and healing, but discretion is advised for readers sensitive to this theme.

Ofwen Dwir

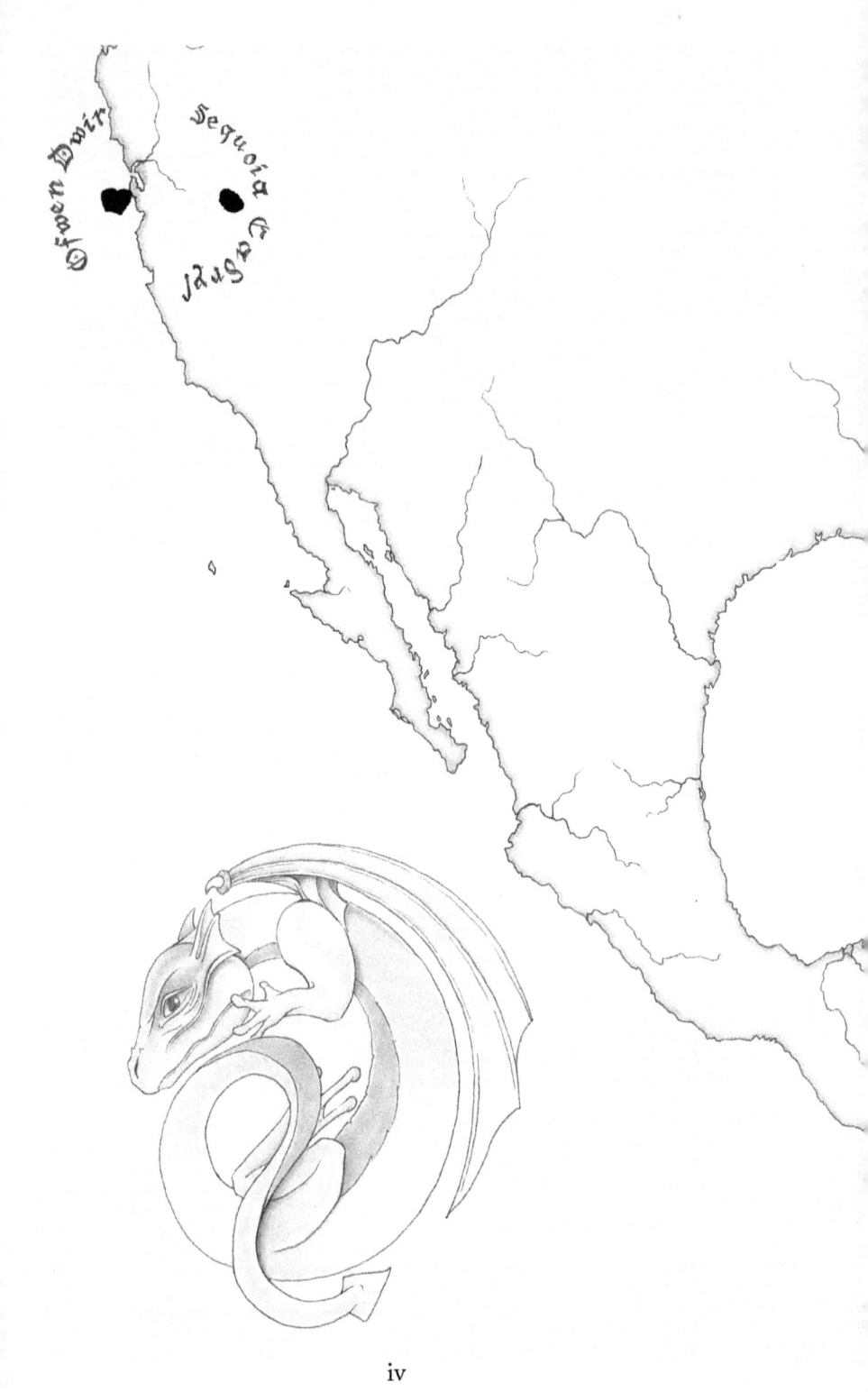

Sequoia Caeryn

Sor Odan
Ferrisios

Arborin
Boalsius

See page 262 for glossary and pronunciations of places and names

My heart pounded, confused, afraid, wanting to believe, and full of adrenaline.

A deafening, blinding roar rippled through the air from behind me. It vibrated the whole forest, knocking me to my knees.

The two Gwythienians stopped fighting and backed several paces away from each other, searching the sky.

I followed their gazes.

A dark shape against the sun. Flapping wings. A Gwythienian for sure. But who?

THE CRIVABANIAN

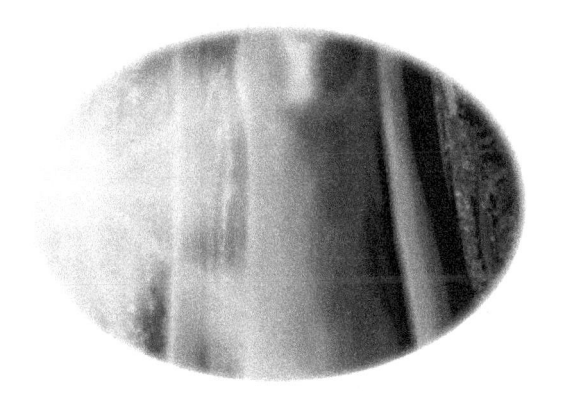

CHAPTER ONE

*F*ire danced off the curved wall in front of me. Something shuffled behind me, casting a shadow in the firelight. Pointed ears stood erect on the creature's head, but that was all I could see from its shadow.

Keeping one eye on the silhouette, I ignored a pestering itch on my leg and reached for my necklace. I may need to turn invisible fast—best to be prepared.

But it wasn't there. I patted down my neck and chest to be sure, but it was true. My heart pounded. The necklace was gone, and I was wearing a different shirt than the one I'd worn for the past couple of weeks.

Which meant no invisibility, and worse, if Tukailaan had the stone, it meant he would be even more eager to kill me than before so he could take over Possessorship. Fear sank through my gut. Where was Gaedyen?

"Tell me, young Veritamyk, should she not wake up, how would we handle that situation?" a husky voice asked, making me jump. I held my breath, hoping the swinging of the hammock I was on wouldn't give me away.

The itch on my leg persisted. I slowly shifted my arm and stretched my fingers between the coarse mesh of the hammock toward the spot.

The shadow shifted. "We'd need to bury her, for human tradition."

Neither voice was Gaedyen's. Neither voice was Tukailaan's, either.

"No, no, Veritamyk." Husky Voice sighed. "I didn't ask you what we would do if she *died*, I asked what we would do if she *didn't wake up*. Pay attention, please."

"Oh, right." The ears drooped slightly. "Administer a rousing draft."

I carefully pulled my arm back and tried to fit all of me under their tiny blanket.

"Good. What ingredients would you mix to create it?"

The shadow ears perked up at the praise, and Veritamyk's words nearly blended together. "Equal amounts of pickled branchbark from the fir tree and squeezed blue fruit juice—for the caffeine. Plus one summer berry per every three grams—two if they're out of season and canned specimens are the only option—and a pinch of the shaved-off orange flakes from the roots of the oldest, tallest ferns."

"Very good. Now, how many times would we need to double the recipe for this patient?"

I frowned. Did they really have to comment on my size?

The small voice paused, and the ears shifted and overlapped on the wall as the head turned to send me a sidelong glance. "At least twenty times?"

"Do not ask me, Veritamyk. I asked you. It's your job to find the answer. It's only a human's weight you must guess; it isn't as if it were a disgusting Gwythienian's." He spat the word as if it were dirty.

A loud grunt, followed by a heavy thud, interrupted Veritamyk.

"There he goes again." Veritamyk groaned, the pointy-eared shadow rising and disappearing from view. "Don't worry about it. I've got him."

More shuffling, then the husky voice said, "We're almost out of yellow moss root. I'll gather more. You stay here and mind these two."

"Yes, Dyn Meddy." A door opened, slammed, and the yellow-and-orange lights shone on the wall again.

But the pointy-eared shadow didn't return.

My heart raced even faster. Where was he?

I squeezed my eyes shut, not wanting to lose my chances of further eavesdropping, and listened closely for movement. Several seconds of nothing had me squinting open one eye to check the wall for shadows again. A pair of large eyes stared right back at me.

"Ahhh!" Jerking backward, I tumbled off the hammock and landed on rock-hard ground, sending fire through my nerves. "Ow."

"Sorry! I'm so sorry," Veritamyk said. Balancing easily on the swinging hammock, he stood about two feet tall and was covered in short white fur in front that faded to gray on his sides and back. Brownish-black markings covered his white face, and black pointed ears stood erect and slightly too big on top of his head. A tuft of black fur swooshed down from his forehead and tapered to a point between his eyes—like bangs.

He dropped to all fours and peeked over the edge of the hammock. "I didn't mean to scare you. I was monitoring your vital signs, just trying to gauge whether you were still in pain." The creature held a little black hand out to me, as if to help me up.

"Well yeah, I'm in pain *now*," I snapped, gingerly prodding my ankle.

The creature jumped into the air and...*expanded?* It was like his sides stretched out as he glided past and landed behind me.

A moment later, a pair of tiny hands lifted me back into the hammock. *Did that little guy just pick me up?* I thought of the creatures Gaedyen had told me about—the ones too strong for their size. Crivabanians, I think. Was I in Sequoia Cadryl? Sequoia Cadryl was close to Ofwen Dwir, which was the last place I remembered being.

"If you wouldn't have flown off the hammock at the sight of me—which is very rude, I might add, I'm offended—you *wouldn't* be in pain." Crossing his arms, he arched a brow, his swoosh falling into his eyes. "You had just enough pain control to keep you from feeling anything unpleasant, while also allowing you to wake as soon as possible. You've been out for days, human. That's too long. Not good for the health."

Up on the hammock, he looked like the kind of animal that would cower in the presence of most other beings. But this little fuzzbucket had his fists on his hips and a spark in his eye.

"Since you're finally awake," he continued, "I'll give you something more appropriate for the pain." He wagged a finger at me. "But absolutely no more flying off the bed. Humans aren't meant to fly, and your injuries would thank you if you'd just accept that."

He was so tiny and, well, *cute*, that it was a bit hard to take him seriously.

"Okay…" I lifted an eyebrow.

"Lie back down. You need to rest those muscles after straining the heck out of them."

Bossy little turd. I crossed my arms and remained sitting.

He ignored my defiance and jumped higher than he should've been able to, widening again, the sides of his body stretching to his ankles and wrists. He soared to the far side of the room, out of the firelight's reach.

"How are you able to do that?"

"Do what?"

"Like, *expand* and float on the air."

"Oh, that." He bounced back into view and raised his arms, displaying the furry membrane that connected each side to his wrist and ankle. "I have these things—kind of like wings, except cooler." He smirked. "When I stretch them out, I can glide through the air. Can't actually fly though, so they aren't *technically* wings. But they're still cooler. My name's Veritamyk, by the way. You can call me Veri. And you are?"

"I'm Enzi." *Shoot, maybe I should've given him a fake name.*

"That's an unusual name." Veri chuckled, leaping up and gliding back to the far side of the room. He landed on the other side of the fire, tossed the corner of a stiff, green curtain out of the way, and disappeared.

I frowned. "Not as weird as yours."

Glass clinked and liquid sloshed.

"What're you doing back there?"

"Mixing all kinds of delicious goodies for you."

Hmm. "How'd I end up here?" *And more importantly, where's Gaedyen?* If he'd died and I'd never been brave enough to tell him how I felt…well, maybe it was better that way. *Am I really that much of a coward?*

"You were passed out—thought you were dead at first—face in the ground, looked like you'd fallen from high up. There was a huge skid mark, like maybe you two had crashed in some kind of vehicle—something bigger than you. But whatever it was, it was nowhere to be found. Trust me, I looked."

My heart leaped. "Us two?"

"Yeah, you and the other human."

My face fell as fast as an Adarborian flies. "Other human? Was anyone else found with us?"

"No. Should there have been?"

"No, I guess not. What's the human's name?"

"Don't you know him?"

"I don't think so."

"Interesting. Do human men normally pass out naked in the woods with women who don't know them?"

My jaw dropped. "What? Naked? I wasn't naked, was I? Is he on the other side of that curtain? Let me see his face." *As long as it wasn't somehow Caleb... Of course it couldn't be...*

Veri laughed. "Yeah, he's still passed out back there. Won't sit still. And no, you were dressed. Though your clothes were nasty. And, more importantly, you weren't bleeding as badly as he was. You were bruised to heck with five fractured ribs, but you weren't bleeding out. Unlike your mysterious friend."

Then what had happened to Gaedyen? He *couldn't* be dead. We had a mission. We had to find out what happened to the rocks and what in the world it had to do with Dad. I couldn't do that without Gaedyen! This wasn't my world. I didn't know where to go next.

I took a deep breath. Gaedyen would want me to be sensible, not to focus on all the things I *didn't* know. *So, what do I know?*

I was in Sequoia Cadryl, the realm of the Crivabanians. Those who live *within* the trees, unlike the Adarborians who live *among* the trees. Wasn't their Gift supposed to be insane strength? Veri must be one of the extra gifted ones. What were those called? *Cadoumai* or something?

Veri pushed through the curtain and returned, his small feet pitter-pattering on the wood floor, holding a small glass full of sloshing blue liquid.

"Now this won't taste like a sprinkled chocolate doughnut, but it'll be worth it."

Sprinkled chocolate doughnut? How does he even know what that is?

Grimacing, I slowly reached for it. My fingers closed around the cold glass just as the bitter fragrance hit me.

"Now, drink up."

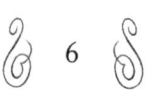

I frowned. *Demanding little thing.* Could I trust his strange concoction? I mean, if they wanted to kill me, they could've done it already.

He hopped onto the hammock, pressed a small black hand against my fingers, and directed the glass toward my face, smiling encouragingly. "Just try not to inhale as it goes down."

Pinching my nose, I poured the liquid in, trying to bypass as much of my tongue as possible. Then I coughed so hard I nearly dropped the glass.

It tasted like burnt bugs and bad breath. But seconds later I felt relaxed, yet still coherent. Not like when Shaun's stuff had knocked me out, or when the nurse had placed an anesthetic mask over my face years ago. This was much better. The pain ebbed away, and a light awareness that I still shouldn't move around too much tickled the back of my mind.

"There. What'd I tell you?" His fists were still planted on his hips, Superman-style.

I cocked my head, wincing at the glass. "What'd I just drink?"

"A tincture for relief of neuromuscular and somatic tissue pain. One that doesn't cause drowsiness. Way better than the stuff in your human hospitals."

Neuromuscular? Where'd this guy get his vocabulary?

I arched an eyebrow. "How do you know how to make something better than what they have in human hospitals?"

"I am apprenticed to Dyn Meddygaeth, an advanced healer. He knows everything there is to know about medicines and treatments and bandaging. He taught me that one." He nodded toward the empty glass, then plucked it from my hand and headed back to the curtain. "How about some cocoaberry tea? To get rid of the taste?"

"Uh, sure. What was in that?"

He hurried back on two legs this time, cupping a mug of steaming brown liquid in his little black hands.

"Various herbs…" He hesitated, throwing me a sidelong glance. Then he shrugged. "And certain anatomical bits of bugs." He grinned, pushing the tea at me.

My stomach heaved. "Ugh, gross!" I grabbed the tea and sniffed, eager to get rid of bug aftertaste but hesitant to drink anything else this creature gave me.

He counted off on his fingers, "Wings of the blembledinger beetle, rose-red wasp antennae, the abdomens of—"

"Okay! Stop right there." I held up a hand in his face, then risked a swig of the sweet-smelling tea.

"You asked." He shrugged, grinning.

The tea tasted like mint and chocolaty coffee. *Coffee!* I closed my eyes and swallowed the rest in a couple of huge gulps. A citrus aftertaste clung to my tongue and I licked my lips.

"Ah! That was delicious! Can I have some more?" I offered him the empty mug.

He took it but frowned. "That was all I had. You humans drink a lot more in one sitting than we do. I'll make more as soon as I can, though."

I tried not to sulk. "Okay. Thanks." I glanced down and noticed my clothes. I'd been right earlier—they weren't mine. Green twine straps held up a loose bit of fabric trying to be a tank top. I touched the scar on my neck and followed it to the neck of the tank top. I'd never shown this much of it before. Following the neckline, I felt another two puckered lines not covered by the fabric. My heart pounded in my ears, and I started sweating.

The shortest pair of shorts I'd ever seen barely covered the tops of my legs. My not-smooth, not-muscular legs. Nobody had any business seeing this much of me. "And where the heck are *my* clothes?" I glanced around for something to cover myself with.

"Bloodstained beyond the point of salvageability, I'm afraid. We burned them. Tell me about your battle scars." He had the nerve to look *excited*.

"Seriously? You *burned* my clothes? Those clothes have been with me through too much to just be burned. Do you have any idea what I went through to get those stupid *pants?* And they had so many wonderful pockets. And who *dressed* me? And I don't have to explain my scars to *anyone*. Don't you people have any respect for privacy?"

Veri waved off my concerns. "Take a chill pill, Enzi. Your clothes were so torn up, they would've been worthless even without all the bloodstains." He tossed his swoosh of bangs out of his eyes. "Whose blood was that? There was more blood all over your clothes than one human body has to lose."

He stared into my eyes, pressing me for an answer. I didn't want him to think I was a mass-murderer or something. But what was okay for him to know? If I gave these people any information about our quest, I might not be safe without Gaedyen. And he might not be safe when he came looking for me. If he ever did.

If he was even alive…

I opted for a change of subject, hoping to buy some time. "Veri, where's my necklace?" I tried to hide the shaking in my voice. If Tukailaan had it, Gaedyen and I and countless others were in real trouble.

Veri cocked his head. "You weren't wearing a necklace when we found you."

Oh no.

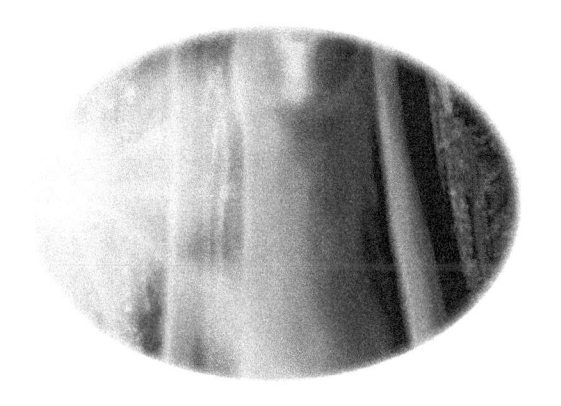

CHAPTER TWO

I didn't know whether to be more afraid that Veri could be lying or that he could be telling the truth. If they had found my necklace and suspected what it was, well, I had no idea what that meant for me.

But what if he *was* telling the truth? Could the mystery man know where it was? Or maybe Gaedyen grabbed it and flew off to save the world, leaving me in Tukailaan's clutches to distract him.

It would have been the smart thing to do, to save more lives in the long run—even if it would've cost mine. Did I mean so little to him?

And why hadn't Tukailaan killed me? And the bow! It was so important to Aven. She'd entrusted it to me. I hadn't even had a chance to learn to use it, and I'd already lost it.

If Gaedyen didn't have it, Tukailaan did. I cringed, remembering his sharp claws. The fact that I was still alive meant he could do nothing with the rock yet. As soon as he realized the rock wouldn't work for him, he'd come for the kill. Since he knew I was the Possessor and not Gaedyen, I was in even more danger of being Gwythienian chow than before.

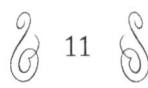

My head throbbed with each unanswered question, the dull prodding steadily escalating to piercing jabs of pain. Could Tukailaan find me here? Perhaps I'd be safe as long as he didn't know the way in. If I asked how to enter the realm of the Crivabanians, that would give away that I knew more than the average human should.

I closed my eyes and pressed my fingers to my temples. "If I'm not supposed to feel pain right now, why do I have a headache?" I hoped this would get Veri off the subject I wasn't thinking clearly enough to risk discussing yet.

One eyebrow remained raised, as if he knew I was hiding something. But instead of pursuing it, he answered, "You've just gotten yourself worked up. Headache pain is different than pain from lacerations and bruises. But you can't mix anything with what I gave you, so just lie down already and stop worrying about clothes and necklaces and all that, and you'll feel better. But it'll only work if you give yourself a break and think about something that isn't distressing. Can you handle that for a few minutes?"

"Sure." I just wanted to be left alone so I could think in peace.

He nodded, turned, and hopped to the floor. The back of his head was dark like his swoosh of bangs, but it faded into a stormy gray covering the rest of him. He padded toward the door. Lightly leaping from the threshold into a smooth glide, he soared into the dimness, black-tipped gray tail sailing after him.

The same questions repeated themselves in my mind—I couldn't help it. My imagination was working overtime against my will to show me in gruesome detail every horrible thing that could've happened.

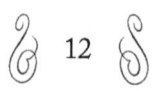

I felt my mop of usually messy hair and found it to be brushed smooth, free of leaves and twigs. My new clothes were scanty and my feet were bare, but these creatures had taken care of me.

The headache decreased a bit. Huh. The little fuzzbucket was right. It worked.

Bits of light streamed down on me, leaking through the cracks in the ceiling, falling on my nakedness. Caleb approached me in slow motion, leering.

A face flickered behind him, a reptilian face. Gaedyen! But it wouldn't come into focus. It was there, but only barely. Fading.

I wanted to scream his name, to beg him to help me. He was right behind Caleb—why didn't he knock him out?

But I didn't want him to see me like this. Should I call to him? He was gone in a flicker.

"No! Come back!"

But it was too late. Caleb was too close, and I couldn't escape.

"Good morning, Sunshine!"

I bolted upright, shooting pain instantly reminding me why that wasn't a good idea.

"Shut *up*." I collapsed backward. "Ugh, why do you have to be so loud! What do you want?" I ripped the pillow—made from that stiff green fabric—from under my head and held it over my face.

"I told you, you've spent too long sleeping. Yesterday I gave you pain medicine that wouldn't make you sleepy, but it sure didn't help you stay awake, either. So today you're getting something else."

Yesterday? I'd slept that long?

"So. *Enzi*, huh? How'd you get such a weird name?"

I rolled my eyes. "It's short for Mackenzi. My dad's name is Mack. My mom named me after him." *Maybe I should call her again and let her know I'm okay. Whenever I see a phone again.*

"Still a weird name." He grinned, then backflipped to the foot of the bed and leaped into the air. A moment later he was across the room, climbing a huge shelf full of glass containers. Light from an open door streamed in behind me, illuminating the part of the room I hadn't been able to see in the firelight.

I turned to get a glimpse out the door. Sprawling green ferns surrounded the bases of large red-brown trees, and the air itself had a greenish tinge to it. I inhaled the fresh, humid air. Wherever that door led was a place I wanted to go. It was so green!

"Let's go out there." I breathed in the fresh air again, this time noticing an unpleasant smell. "Also, I need to shower." When Veri didn't answer, I turned to see why.

He'd climbed down the shelf and was combining the contents of a couple of containers over a small cup.

I grimaced. *My morning meds?* "Hey, are you putting anything gross in that?"

"You betcha."

"Ew! Then I'm not taking it."

"Okay." He chuckled. "Just wait till yesterday's wears off. Then we'll see."

Rebelliously I crossed my arms, wincing as they pressed against my chest with too much force.

I masked the pain with a stoic expression. Today's nastiness was a thick green liquid. None of me hurt bad enough to chug *that.*

I looked away, toward the cheerful scenery outside.

"Yeah, we'll see." He snickered, turning back to his mixture. "So that human you don't know...I think you should take a look at him. Just in case," he said over his shoulder.

"If that will get me out of drinking the bug soup, then absolutely."

Veri didn't acknowledge my words. "He has a tattoo on his shoulder—*had* one anyway. Whatever happened damaged the tattoo so badly I can't tell what it used to be."

I frowned. Gaedyen had a shoulder tattoo...I shifted my feet, bumping my sprained ankle. Surprisingly, sharp pain soared up my leg. "Ouch!" I blurted before I could stop myself.

"See?" he said smugly. "What'd I tell you?"

My ankle screamed, but I still wasn't sold on the green stuff. What other grossness might be in this new concoction?

Veri sighed. "Look, here's the thing. Dyn Meddy said that if you take the medicine, and you let me re-splint your ankle, I can give you a tour. You want to go outside, don't you? Then we can settle the question of the other human. Come on, whaddya say?"

Sitting and worrying about Gaedyen wasn't doing any good, so I might as well.

"All right, fine. On one condition. Can you bring me something delicious to eat after drinking this? And some cocoaberry tea to wash it down?" I snatched it from him, grimacing. "It smells like it has a bad aftertaste. Plus, I'm starving."

"Sure," he agreed. Again, he jumped toward the door and into the air with arms and legs outstretched, catching the slight breeze and riding it out of sight. That was kind of a cool trick. How come everyone but humans got to fly? *So not fair.*

He returned shortly with fresh bread smeared with something creamy. It smelled mouthwateringly scrumptious. I swallowed the green goo in two mouthfuls, quickly biting off bread to follow it. The taste lived up to its aroma.

When he handed me water, I looked in to it for a moment before taking a sip. Could I see Gaedyen in the water if I looked hard enough? I tried to concentrate on him and where he might be. But either I was still incapable of seeing through water, or he wasn't near any at the moment.

Veri lifted an eyebrow. "It's not poisoned, Enzi."

Anxious not to blow my cover, I took a quick sip.

Soon, the pain ebbed as it had the day before, and Veri exchanged the empty cup for a mug of cocoaberry tea. The citrus flavor followed the minty chocolate and erased the nasty bug soup taste.

As I sipped the tea gratefully, Veri crafted a splint for my ankle out of sturdy sticks and strips of the greenish fabric.

"You guys use this stuff for everything, huh? What does it come from?"

"It's made from plant fibers. And you humans use way more than you should. You people are ridiculously huge. And no fur! What an idea."

Fair enough. So that's why they barely gave me enough to cover myself. I'd use a lot more than their tiny little bodies would. At least they weren't mad at me for not being able to shrink to their size like the Adarborians.

"There," he announced, brushing his hands together dramatically. "A real work of art, if I do say so myself. Have a try; see how it does."

I stared at him. "Won't the medicine take away the pain? How will I know if it's working?"

"The medicine will prevent the pain itself—the feeling of something hurting. But it doesn't erase your brain's ability to detect when something is wrong. You'll know something's not right, but it will be an awareness, not stabbing pain."

I pushed off from the bed, bearing all my weight on my good leg, and slowly evened out the burden, waiting for the "awareness" Veri described.

With my weight evenly distributed, I still felt no such sensation. I stepped forward with my good leg, allowing my bad one to take all my weight. Bad idea. I turned the step into a limp and balanced on my good leg. It was a typical response when experiencing something painful, only I didn't feel pain. It didn't feel like someone was rubbing rocks together with my bones, as it had every step of the way before.

"See? Right twice in fifteen minutes. You should really start listening to me."

I grinned with him this time, amazed. "Still though, if I have that feeling, doesn't it mean I shouldn't walk on it? I don't want to make it heal slower or something."

"Precisely. That's why I'm going to carry you. The splint is just there for protection in case you bump in to anything. It's not for walking yet." And he jumped onto the side of the bed and scooped me up in his tiny arms before I could protest.

He leaped lightly to the ground and padded toward the door.

"Doesn't this hurt your back?" I asked. "Seriously, just because you *can* carry something a hundred times your size doesn't mean you should."

"Pfft!" He laughed off my concerns. "This is our Gift. The Gift of my people. We have more strength per micrometer than you humans, or even the Gwythienians. Carrying you is no problem. Come to think of it, I could probably carry a full-grown Gwythienian. Those are these savage dragon things no one really likes." His chest puffed out with pride.

Savage? I hoped my face hadn't given anything away.

Greenish light shone through the doorway, a promise of fresh air and tree breezes. I couldn't wait to get outside.

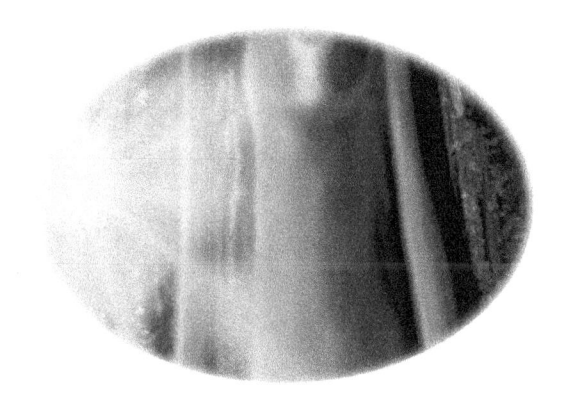

CHAPTER THREE

A whisper of warm air fluttered through my hair as Veri carried me outside. Tall, thick ferns spread over the forest floor, frequently covering the bases of trees. The ferns were all taller than Veri, and many were probably taller than I was.

The trees were crazy huge, too. The closest tree from where we stood must have been six feet thick. And the next was twice as wide as that. They grew several feet apart, leaving plenty of open forest floor for walking.

It was an odd perspective to be carried so close to the ground. With each of Veri's steps, I feared hitting my butt on the dirt and leaflitter. But he managed to hold me up high enough that it never happened, and before long I trusted him.

Something felt strange about the way the light glimmered all around us. I tried to gauge how high the trees really were. They stretched what had to be hundreds of feet toward the sky. Sunlight filtered through their many branches, but it was so far away that the light was green by the time it reached the ground. No yellow in sight.

As Veri carried me away from the infirmary, I glanced over his head to see what it looked like from the outside. It was a gigantic tree trunk—the largest yet. It must've been twenty feet wide, at least. And it rose many stories before even one branch came into view. I couldn't see how high it went after that.

"The infirmary is a tree, too?" *That would explain the curved walls.*

"That's right," Veri replied.

"Wow. I had no idea trees could get that big. How high up do the rooms go? I mean are there, like, staircases up to other levels?"

"Of course. It would be a huge waste not to use all the space. There are many redwoods here, but there are many Crivabanians, too. We all need places to live."

"But trees keep growing. What does that do to the structures inside?

"The trees in Sequoia Cadryl are different—special. Our lives are tied together, so as we grow, so do our trees. Young Crivabanians carve out their own place from the bottom level of whatever tree has grown enough to allow it. They hope to get nice neighbors upstairs, or they'll have to carve out their own section of the spiral connection, too."

"Wow."

"My cousin is the luckiest Crivabanian ever. He moved in under a bakery."

We neared an even bigger tree, its rich, russet bark the color of cinnamon and pumpkin stems in the fall. "How old are these things? And how long does it take for another layer to grow thick enough for someone to build in?"

"I don't know exactly how old they are. Hundreds at least, maybe thousands of years old. It takes a good couple of years for a tree to grow enough to be ready for a new layer of habitation."

"Wow."

"Yeah, it's kinda cool. Less cool when you've lived here forever, but you know."

"Which tree do you live in? Do you have your own place yet?"

He laughed so hard he almost dropped me. "Heck, no! I'm the oldest of my siblings—and there are a lot of us—so I'm stuck at home helping with the kids. It's really not cool. The best part of the day is when I come to the infirmary to learn from Dyn Meddy."

"Does he have other apprentices?"

"Nope. Only lonely me. My age group is a bit…low in numbers. I was the only one with interest in medicine. So I'm apprenticed to him. Have been for two years now."

"Wow! So you're going to be a doctor, then? Or technically a veterinarian?"

He laughed. "Yeah, something like that."

"So you know how to make wonky concoctions, like you did for me. What else do you know?"

"How to splint a broken bone, what ingredients to put into various salves for various injuries and ailments, where to find those ingredients. Things like that."

We passed five more gargantuan trees as we walked, each one bigger than the last. They had small hints of habitation on their thick trunks. Miniature windows—holes in the wood with shutters on the outside or thick curtains on the inside—fluttered in the breeze. Under many of the windows, little garden boxes grew moss and mushrooms instead of flowers.

I stared in awe at the disappearing height of the tree, windows and doors scattered as high as I could see. "How many of you can live in one tree?"

"Oh, I don't know. A few hundred, probably. We tend to have a lot of kids, and we cram them all into one layer, no matter how big the family. In that tree over there, for example, there are more layers than you can see. Twelve or more before the branches start. Each one has at least two family members in it, most of them up to twenty."

"Wow. How many siblings do you have?"

"Seven. Two sets of twins."

My eyebrows shot up. "I can't imagine having so many siblings. How do your parents pay for it?"

"It's not *that* many, really. Our family is on the smaller side."

"Holy cow."

He eyed me. "You must not have many siblings if you think seven's a lot."

"I don't have *any*. And where I come from, people usually don't have more than like three or maybe four at the most. Usually one or two."

"Such small families!"

I caught a glimpse of a gray-and-white face peeking down at us from one of the windows. I smiled and raised my arm to wave when the curious expression turned into a glare and disappeared behind a mossy shutter. It made me wonder exactly just how upset the locals were about my presence.

"Veri? I'm feeling a bit like this is hostile territory. Are you sure this is a good idea?"

"Of course it is. All my ideas are good ones." He smirked.

I rolled my eyes. "All right then. Where's this idea of yours taking us?"

"Just a brisk stroll in this crisp morning air to refresh your grouchy human spirits."

I snorted. "Okay. And where is this brisk stroll headed?"

"Back to the infirmary. You got your fresh air, and now it's time for the other human to get his."

"Good. About time I finally see his face. Hey, are you really sure you found us together? It just seems bizarre…"

"Yeah, I'm sure. Are *you* sure you don't know him?"

I shrugged. "I won't know till I see his face."

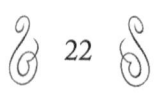

"Hmm. So how exactly did you end up out there, anyway? All torn up and bloody? With so much blood caked on your clothes?"

Heat rushed into my face. I only had two seconds to come up with something before it would be obvious I was lying. *I'm no good at this…*

"I'm not really sure. It's like…like I have some blank spaces in my memory." I winced. True, but too obvious?

"What's the last thing you remember?"

What was a safe last memory to have in this situation? "I remember walking outside my apartment"—*And then being kidnapped!*—"Someone had questions about…about something. It's all kinda fuzzy."

"Hmm." He dragged out the sound as if he sensed something suspicious.

I kept quiet. *Better not to risk making it worse…*

"Hopefully we'll find out more once he wakes up."

"Are you sure he will?"

"Oh, yes. His body took a lot of hits, but Dyn Meddy's confident he'll make a full recovery. He just needs time to heal."

I hadn't dreamed up Gaedyen and everything else, had I? If I'd woken up in a human hospital surrounded by other humans, I could worry about that. But not here. The guy…it couldn't be Caleb. Of course not. He was too far away. Though Tukailaan in the form of Tony had shown up unexpectedly. Shaun? I should be so lucky. And unlucky.

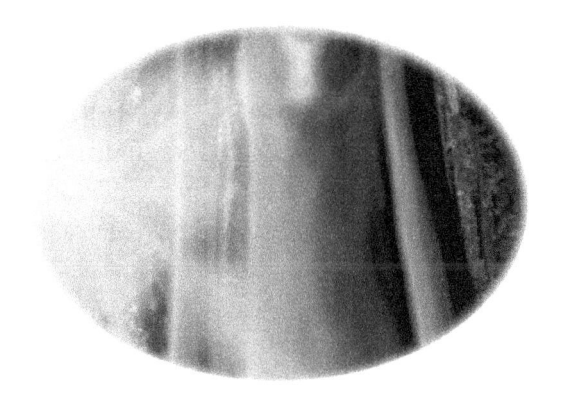

CHAPTER FOUR

*A*s we approached the infirmary, my eyes followed the giant tree's copper-colored trunk as far up as they could. It disappeared before I could find the top.

"Oh, you forgot to take me by the showers."

"We don't have showers, Enzi. What does this place look like, the Ritz?"

I rolled my eyes. "You don't have showers? Fine then. The *baths*."

"Don't have bathtubs either."

I stared at him. "Then how do you keep yourselves clean? How'd you get all the blood and dirt off me?"

"Easy. We groom ourselves. You know, lick the fur clean."

I grimaced. "You didn't lick me while I was passed out, right?"

He rolled his eyes. "Grooming another person is rather an intimate thing in our culture, so Dyn Meddy and I cleaned you up with wet cloths."

Scrunching my nose at the thought of the two of them cleaning me, I was relieved that at least they hadn't done it with their little tongues.

"Okay, so then you forgot to take me to where the clean rags are kept."

"There are some in the infirmary."

"And where can I sponge-bathe myself in privacy?"

"In the infirmary, I guess. I'll leave for a while, and you don't have to worry about the guy. He should be asleep a little longer. Probably."

"All right." I sighed. Not as private as I was going for, but I'd take it. I really needed to get clean.

Veri carried me up the little steps and through the door, then set me on the hammock. A rustling noise came from the other human, and we both looked toward him. The curtain was drawn back—maybe Dyn Meddy had been in to care for him? He stirred, then kicked and flailed his arms, nearly toppling off the bed.

Veri leaped on him. "Hey! Wake up, dude. What's wrong with you? Wake up!"

The tan man flung Veri off him, back through the open door.

"Hey! Don't throw him." I rose from the hammock, bearing weight on my good leg, peering out the door for any sign of Veri. "He was just trying to help."

A puff of gray and black glided toward me from outside and landed on my shoulder. Relieved, I turned back to the human, who'd stopped rustling.

Terror gleamed from his wide brown eyes, then relief washed over his face. And I couldn't believe it.

Shaun.

Every beautiful, tan bit of him. His muscles bulged even more than when I'd seen him last. Had he been working out? His biceps were as big around as a football.

My heart thumped at the sight of him. And then plummeted—I was practically naked, my scars and my fat way too visible. And to top it all off, I still smelled like unshowered traveler. I wrenched the curtain off the wall and threw it over my shoulders. Spotting my naked legs, I tucked them closer inside the makeshift blanket. *Stupid Crivabanian shorts.*

"Hey!" Veri scrambled onto my head to avoid being smothered. "What did you do that for?"

Shaun dropped his head into his hands. Slumping onto the heap of blankets, he asked, "Are we in Sequoia Cadryl?"

I narrowed my eyes at him. "Yeah. How'd *you* know?"

Veri dropped onto my blanketed shoulder. "And all that thrashing was *really* unnecessary."

Shaun raised an eyebrow at Veri and let out an exaggerated sigh. "Thank you for housing and healing us, Crivabanian. How long have I been incapacitated?"

"Five days. You *were* welcome, until you knocked me into next week. Now I'm not so sure." He puffed out his furry chest, fists on his hips.

Shaun tensed. "Is there…any news? Anything interesting going on, outside of here?"

I raised an eyebrow. "Dude. We're inside a tree. Does it look like we get channel thirteen?"

He glared at me. "Not—" He glanced sidelong at Veri. "Never mind. I feel strange. What medicine have you given me?"

"Our best healer saw to your wounds. They're healing, but you'll need to take it easy for a bit. Even with accelerated recovery, it'll take a while for everything to return to normal. Your body took a lot of damage."

Slowly, Shaun turned to look over his left shoulder, and finding the bandage there, he ripped it off. His mouth parted slightly at whatever he saw. I could barely see a couple tendrils of the mark—like a cracked eggshell—sneaking over his shoulder, like Gaedyen's mark. *Do they have the same tattoo?* He slammed the bandage back into place, wincing.

"What'd you do that for? Now, I'll have to rebandage it." Veri crossed his arms over his chest. "You can't just go around wasting materials like that, dude." And he leaped off my hammock toward the storage shelves. "You stupid humans have already used up way too much. Hardly helping your case here."

I took the opportunity to hiss a question at Shaun. "Where's Gaedyen?"

He looked askance at me and shook his head.

I followed his eyes to Veri, who was still too close for an actual conversation. "Hey, Veri? Shaun looks kinda dehydrated, don't you think? Maybe he should drink some water, too. And probably some of that cocoaberry tea."

Veri's ears flicked up, and he glanced at us. Hanging on to a shelf with one hand and gripping more green fabric in the other, he gave Shaun a shrewd-eyed once over. "Stick out your tongue."

Shaun frowned. "What?"

"Stick out your tongue. Like this: Ahh." Veri stuck out his tongue at Shaun.

Shaun glowered and stuck out his tongue slightly.

"Yeah, you're right. He is dehydrated." Veri dropped to the floor and pulled open a drawer. Reaching inside, he fished around and drew out a handful of items. After a brief inspection, he slammed the drawer.

"You." He pointed a finger at Shaun. "Don't touch this stuff until I get back." He sat the items on one of the shelves and then he leaped into the air and out the door.

A breeze ruffled my hair as the door shut behind Veri. I looked back to find Shaun watching me. My mind felt slow as molasses under his gaze.

"How much do you remember?" he asked.

Frowning, I narrowed my eyes. "I remember Gaedyen went into the ocean to look for Ofwen Dwir, and then Tukailaan showed up and grabbed me and flew away, nearly squeezing me to death. I think I remember Gaedyen bursting out of the ocean at some point while that was going on, but it's fuzzy. That's it. So where is he? And how in the world did *you* end up here?"

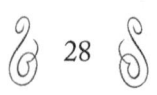

"Gaedyen did emerge just in time to stop Tukailaan from killing you. But Tukailaan still got away with the...*necklace*. Gaedyen needed to go after him, so he called me to look after you. I got a bit beat up on the way."

Gaedyen's alive!

Relieved, I exhaled, steadying myself on the hammock. At least he hadn't died fighting Tukailaan as of the last time Shaun had seen him. But he'd left me. Anger and some soft appreciative feeling warred within, chasing out the relief. So he'd rescued me from Tukailaan, but then he went off on his own to continue the adventure?

I tried to make myself be reasonable. He hardly could've taken me, passed out and bleeding to death. And he needed to fight Tukailaan. Maybe I'd only ever been a part of this because I was the Possessor of their rock, and Gaedyen hadn't needed or wanted me for anything else.

Clenching my fingers in the folds of the blanket, I tried not to tear up. "When did you last hear from him?"

"When he left you with me and I tried bringing you here."

"Do you have any idea how he's doing now? Whether he's okay?"

"I think he is all right for the time being."

That was good. But he'd left me. *Am I that useless?* "So what happened to you?"

He kept his lips sealed.

Another cool breeze filled the room, bringing Veri with it.

Saved by the fuzzbucket. Figures.

Veri retrieved the bandaging things from the shelf and pattered toward Shaun's hammock. "Now don't go wasting this one. Once it's against the skin, it releases soothing ointments that prevent infection and inflammation. They're very difficult and expensive to make. And they last for three days, and you wasted the one I just put on this morning. So leave this one *alone*."

Veri hopped onto Shaun's hammock, roughly tugged his shoulder forward, and stepped behind him. As he gently peeled the ruined bandage off, I winced at the damage. Pinkish scar tissue formed thick, uneven lines, with a huge scab off-center. It looked like it'd been healing for a few weeks instead of just a couple of days. But I couldn't imagine how much that had to hurt. I could barely see the black lines of the strange tattoo under the scarring.

Veri's quick little hands had the bandage in place before I had much time to gawk at the wound. Instead I found my eyes wandering to the smooth skin stretching over his exposed biceps.

When I glanced at his face, he was looking at me. *Oh crap! I'm sure he really needs my help on that ego...*

I glowered back, knowing that looking away quickly would just make me look guilty. He quirked a small smile.

Then that thing he did to my stomach—the melted cartwheel thing—it came over me, catching me by surprise. This time, I couldn't help glancing away.

"What happened to your shoulder?" I asked, busying myself with straightening the covers over me.

"I fell."

I raised an eyebrow, hoping my disbelief would mask that feeling that was still there, bubbling under the surface. "That's all?"

"Yes."

I crossed my arms, scowling at him. "Sure." If he was anything like Gaedyen, begging for an answer when he was clearly not going to give it wouldn't help.

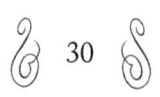

Despite the jolt Shaun was unknowingly capable of sending through my stomach, I envied him where Gaedyen was concerned. Gaedyen made me feel warm and safe. Imagining all the adventures the two of them had seen—and would experience once I was back in the regular world and out of their lives—sent jealous claws wrenching at my gut. He and Gaedyen were more than Gaedyen and I were. And I couldn't help wanting to be the most important part of Gaedyen's world.

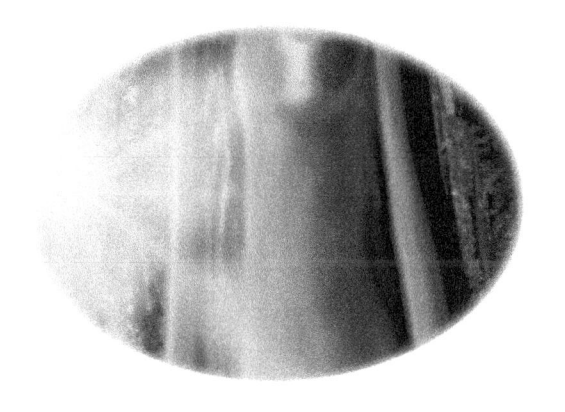

CHAPTER FIVE

It was hard to fall asleep, knowing Shaun was just a few feet away. And I still needed to wash the stink off myself. And I needed better clothes. I hadn't gotten the chance to remind Veri about that before he'd left for the night. I hadn't really wanted to draw attention to it by asking in front of Shaun.

I envied his being so much more a part of this world than I was, but I was also attracted to him. I wanted to ask him how he and Gaedyen had met. How they'd become friends. I wanted to know what Gaedyen was like when he was a "hatchling." But with Veri running in and out all the time and Dyn Meddy making an occasional appearance, there was never a safe moment to bring it up. I didn't want to risk getting us in trouble for being associated with Gwythienians. I wasn't sure why the Crivabanians disliked them so much.

The blankets rustled softly as Shaun breathed steadily. It was a dull and comforting sound. I missed Gaedyen's slower, deeper breathing. I missed being safely concealed against him, under his wing, feeling his warm middle pressed against me. Back and forth with each breath. It was lonely here, without him. But at the same time, not private enough.

How was Shaun able to fall asleep so easily?

I tried to focus on the monotonous creak of the hammock as it swayed with Shaun's breath.

There was movement at my back, like comforting breathing. Gaedyen? No, it was too small. A human? Shaun? My face heated. I turned to see who was so close…and my stomach dropped to my toes.

Dark eyes gleamed against pale skin, black hair askew.

Caleb.

I tried to leap up, but my body was unresponsive. I needed to get to my feet, to run! But I was helpless to escape as he raised himself up from behind me.

Tears trailed down my hopeless face faster than I could move. It was over. I couldn't do anything but endure.

I didn't want to endure.

But I didn't have a choice…

"Enzi!"

A voice that didn't belong in that scene called to me.

But Caleb didn't stop. He kept shaking me. He had me by the shoulders.

"Get off me, Caleb!" I sobbed, pushing weakly, trying to shove him away and run for it. My ankle could deal.

"Enzi? It is me, just Shaun. No one is trying to hurt you. You are in Sequoia Cadryl. With the Crivabanians."

Disoriented, I tried to catch my breath. *Just a dream, only a dream.* "Oh. Did I wake you up? Sorry." I rubbed the sleep out of my eyes, straining to see his face in the darkness.

"No, no, it is fine. No need to worry about it." But he didn't go back to his own hammock. I couldn't see his eyes, but I felt them on me.

"What is it?" I asked.

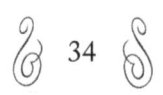

"What…what was happening?"

I frowned. "I don't have to share the details of my nightmare with you."

"You were having a nightmare?"

"*Obviously.*" I rolled my eyes, even though he couldn't see them.

"Oh. Should I not have disturbed you?"

He sounded embarrassed, as if he'd offended me. "No." I sighed. "No, I'm glad you woke me up. I didn't want to…to finish that nightmare."

"Okay." An awkward pause, then he pushed himself off my hammock. His own creaked with his weight a moment later. It swung less and less as time passed, until it was just barely creaking again. Peaceful.

I stretched out, wishing I could forget my stupid dreams. My feet reached to where he'd been sitting, the curtain I'd hijacked as a blanket still warm from his body heat. I hadn't realized how cold I was. I shuffled myself all the way down to where he'd been sitting, scrunching into a fetal position in the spot of warmth to absorb as much as possible. It would fade in a few moments, but I didn't want to waste it.

Wincing, I hoped he hadn't noticed how much I needed a shower.

The next day, I insisted on cleaning myself before doing anything with Veri. But when I asked for a change of clothes, Veri informed me the outfit I was wearing was the only lonely one in existence.

"But the fabric is special. It's very similar to the bandages. Your clothes won't get dirty—well, unless you fall in mud. They're made of plant fibers, like I told you, and they're sort of alive still, in a way. Microorganisms live in the material and metabolize things like sweat and blood and stuff, so they won't get stinky like normal human clothes."

I frowned. "Why in the world would you invent something like that when you don't even wear clothes?"

He shrugged. "The material is used for bandaging wounds and keeps things clean. And we didn't invent it; we discovered it. The plants already existed in nature—we just found a way to use their properties to our advantage."

"Okay," I whispered, glancing at Shaun. "Let's keep it down. I don't want him waking up until this is over."

Rolling his eyes, Veri retrieved a couple of mixing jars filled with water.

"No soap?"

"Sorry, we don't have any here."

"You've got to be kidding."

"Why would we need it?"

"Fine. Hand me those."

Over the next several minutes, Veri stood on my hammock, holding up the curtain, while I awkwardly washed myself the best I could without totally taking my clothes off. The hardest part was doing everything sitting down. But Veri wasn't tall enough, even on the hammock, to hold the blanket high enough for me to stand. I shushed him every time he made a noise, afraid it might wake Shaun.

When it was finally done, my skin practically glowed compared to before. *I'm never going another day without a bath.*

"Happy now?" Veri dropped the blanket, fists on his hips.

"Yes."

"Good. Let's go."

Veri checked my splint and then carried me out for a stroll. A few minutes in, he set me against a tree and went behind it. He emerged a moment later, carrying a richly carved bow and quiver.

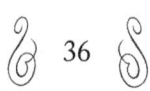

Aven's bow! My heart leaped out of my chest. It hadn't been lost, and it was in one piece!

He held it out. "Is this yours?"

I wanted to claim it, but I couldn't. I was supposed to be a normal teenage girl lost in the woods. Not a girl who traveled with Gwythienians, knowing about magical rocks and realms and carrying special Adarborian weapons.

"I don't believe I've ever seen that before."

The lie hurt. I wanted to snatch up Aven's gorgeous gift, but it wouldn't work with my story. A Gwythienian and an Adarborian were clearly etched on it. I couldn't think of a believable way I could own it. It was too valuable a gift not to claim, but I couldn't risk it.

"Huh. That *is* interesting. Considering it smells exactly like you."

Crap! Crivabanians have sensitive senses of smell too, huh? I hoped my eyes weren't giving me away. "That's weird. Why would it do that?"

He cocked an eyebrow. "You tell me."

"I don't have anything *to* tell you." I tried hard to stare straight back into his eyes. "What exactly is it? A bow of some kind?"

"'What is it? A bow of some kind?'" He imitated my voice in a snarky, whining tone. "Pfft! You're ridiculous. I don't know how you got this or why you're so intent on denying it, but I *know* it's yours. You're a horrible liar." He took a little hop forward, holding the bow out to me.

I reached out to hold it for myself. "It's very beautiful. What kind of wood do you suppose it is?"

My attempts at distraction earned me nothing but a dramatic eye roll. But it wasn't like I'd asked about their liryk or anything like that.

"Enzi, look. I don't know your story, and I'm doing my best not to pry, but your bits of history are inconsistent. I've known since the beginning that you knew more than you should about us. You were willing to accept talking animals too easily. I already know something's up. So you might as well just claim it if it's yours. I won't require its story in exchange. You can just take it."

Play dumb and offended? Or admit the truth and risk he might be bluffing? Whatever I'd done for him to guess something was up, I'd likely do it again. More lies would only make it worse. So I'd accept it. But I still wouldn't outright admit anything. "I accept your gift, Veri. Thanks."

His fists landed on his hips as his eyes did another trip toward the sky and back. "You're hopeless, you know that?"

"I don't know what you're talking about." What a dumb thing to say. I obviously did. "Where'd you find it?"

"Close to where we found you. We were checking the area for any other dying humans."

So we must be close to where Gaedyen and I parted ways for him to search for Ofwen Dwir. Close to where Tukailaan found me...

I shivered. Would he return to finish the job?

"How close are we to where you found me?"

"A few miles away. Why?"

That's way too close for comfort. I hoped any scent trail of mine had washed away by now. Even so, it could be easy for Tukailaan to find me.

"Does this...*place*"—I almost said *realm!*—"have any kind of protection?" I hoped that wasn't completely obvious, but I had to know.

"Yeah." He narrowed his eyes. "Why? Are you in danger?"

Forcing myself to look right at him, I said, "Not at the moment." It was technically true. Sort of. Seeking distraction, I ran my hand over the textured surface of the quiver, wondering what stories it told. Wondering again why Aven had it, why it was empty—useless—and why she had a bow and empty quiver when Adarborians fight with blow darts and poison?

Ornate engravings covered the mahogany surface, and it was heavy. I hadn't gotten the chance to use it yet, what with us flying straight to the beach near Ofwen Dwir then almost dying right after Aven gave it to me. And Gaedyen wasn't here to make rymakri for me to shoot. What good was the weapon without him?

"And despite it belonging to you, you don't know what it is?"

"Well, it looks like a bow. Like for shooting arrows."

"Yeah, *obviously* it's a bow. But do you know what *kind* it is?"

"Well if you're so eager to tell me what *you* think it is, why don't you just do it?"

"This is a weapon made especially for humans to fight alongside those overgrown lizards I told you about earlier, the Gwythienians. Remember? This was made for a human-Gwythienian fighting pair."

"What?" Human-Gwythienian fighting pairs? How was that possible? It must've been a long time ago, before the rocks…

"See how heavy the bow is? How thick both the curved wood and the taut string are? Normal bows aren't like that. This was made to shoot something heavier. Sticks bitten to a point by a Gwythienian—that's how they make weapons—and then tossed to a human companion to fire at an enemy. Or something like that anyway. It's really old. Or at least it should be. Hmm… come to think of it, it looks a lot newer than it should. Strange. Anyway, it's way too heavy for you to shoot worth a darn."

"Thanks." I frowned and narrowed my eyes at him. I wished Aven would've had time to tell me more about the bow before we fled. And it was made for a human-Gwythienian pair? Now, *that* was interesting. Not that it mattered now.

Something still confused me. "But if it was made for that, why was there a quiver at all?"

"What do you mean?"

"I mean the human would have to use the rym—ahem"—I cleared my throat, hoping to cover the mistake—"the bitten sticks quickly, so why the quiver to store them in?"

Too late, I realized what I'd done. I definitely should not know Gwythienian saliva breaks down wood after making it harder. His satisfied smile said as much.

I should've kept my big mouth shut.

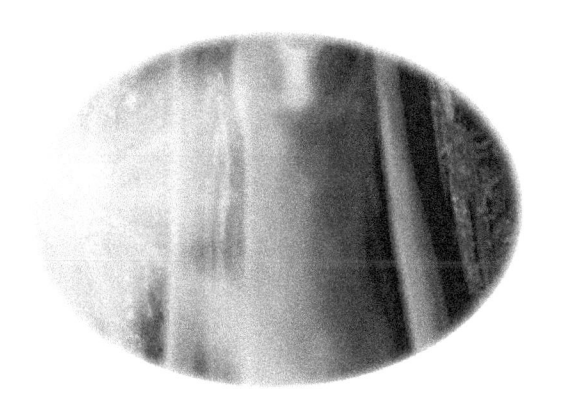

CHAPTER SIX

"An interesting question! *Very* interesting." Veri cocked his head with an I-totally-just-caught-you smile. My heart raced. How to reply? But he didn't press me.

Instead he made a show of inspecting his tiny forepaws. "Too bad you're probably not up to giving it a try right now."

I rolled my eyes. "Yeah. Too bad." But in all honesty, I did kinda want to shoot it. I mean, it would be nice to have a weapon I was better at than throwing knives. And it was from the ruler of a world unknown to the rest of my kind. That was freaking awesome.

I was glad he'd seen through my lie and let me keep it instead of claiming it for himself. It was cool, but I wouldn't be able to conceal it in the normal world, so it wouldn't offer me much protection against Caleb. But against Tukailaan…

Tukailaan could come after me at any time. I needed to be prepared. It would be better if Gaedyen were here to make rymakri as I ran out, but even if I had to make my own sharpened sticks, at least I had the quiver. So that was something.

I thought about how Gaedyen had wrapped his arm around me to guide my fingers over holding the knife correctly, how he'd held my arm to show me how to throw without moving my wrist all wrong. A shiver trembled down my spine, leaving a tight ache in its wake. *He left me.*

A subject change had been well in order for several minutes. "Hey, Veri? Can you make medicine to prevent nightmares? Or just dreams in general?"

The suspicious smile faded to a frown. "No. There *is* a recipe for such a thing, but it's highly addictive. Dyn Meddy chose not to teach me how to make it yet. Though I, too, would like to have such a thing on hand at times. I'm sorry, Enzi."

So he has bad dreams too? "No worries. Thanks anyway."

"All right. Back to the infirmary for lunch."

That night, as I lay in bed listening to the sheets rustle with each of Shaun's breaths, I tried to turn invisible.

It didn't work.

Gaedyen had told me I'd eventually be able to do it without touching the rock. But apparently I wasn't good enough yet. That slippery wall I needed to break through felt bigger. Vast. Impossibly huge. And smooth as glass. No fingerhold for miles.

It'd always been physical contact with the rock that allowed me to find a crack in the hard surface and break through the wall to invisibility. Without the rock, I was out of luck. For now.

What was Tukailaan doing with the rock? Had he figured out yet that it wouldn't work for him? Was he planning to search for me, to try harder to kill me?

I closed my eyes and focused again.

Gray, impenetrable nothingness.

I tried again.

Nada.

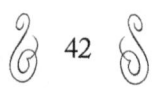

I rolled over, burying my face under the pillow. Would I ever figure this out?

Sawdust scratched my back with each movement. I screamed, "No! No, Please!"

The barn cats yowled along with my broken sobs.

"Shut up!" He hit me again.

Where was my rymakri? My clothes? I'd made them all appear before, why couldn't they show up now?

He stopped. I wanted to puke, to throw up in his slimy face.

There was a choking noise, but it wasn't coming from me. I dared raise my eyes to his disgusting face…and found him *choking. I slid away from him, grateful for the distraction that had his hands on his own throat instead of mine.*

What was happening?

The choking got louder—turned into screaming. Caleb thrashed around on the sawdust floor, but the sound of rustling blankets met my ears.

Blackness surrounded me, and the thrashing and panting were coming from the other hammock.

Was Shaun being attacked?

Blindly, I ran for him in the dark.

"Hey! What's going on! Who's there?" I hoped shouting would either surprise an enemy or wake Shaun, whatever needed to happen. I jumped on his pile of thrashing blankets and yelled.

"Shaun! Shaun, what's going on? Are you okay?" I felt around for his neck, checking to see why he was choking. Strong hands grabbed my arms and held me still. *His* hands.

"Shaun, it's just me, Enzi. You were thrashing around like you were being attacked."

He lowered his arms but didn't let go. I held my place, unsure of how awake he was.

"What happened? Was it a nightmare?"

His voice shook. "If that is what you call it when something horrible feels real but then you wake up and it is as if it happened in another place, as if it only happened in your own history, despite how many others were involved...."

Hadn't he ever had a nightmare before? "Yes, that's a nightmare, Shaun. Is this the first time you've had a bad dream?" I tried not to sound too incredulous.

"No. Not the first time."

"Oh."

That discussion over, I suddenly became very aware of our bodies. I was practically straddling him, one leg on either side, my wrists still encircled by his huge hands.

For the briefest flicker, I relished the warmth and longed to crawl under the covers with him and go back to sleep. For the tiniest fraction of that flicker of time, I almost did. But when I realized what I'd been thinking, I popped off him as if his skin burned mine and jumped into my bed so fast that even an Adarborian would've been proud.

I wanted to say something to break the awkward silence instead of leaving it hanging. But nothing came to mind. My heart throbbed in my ears too loud for me to concentrate.

"Enzi?"

Heat rose to my cheeks. My name sounded delicious on his lips. Why was I being like that? That was ridiculous..."Yes?"

"Thank you. For making it stop."

"Just returning the favor."

The blankets rustled as he turned over. But they didn't resume the steady pace of his sleep-breathing. His breaths were uneven—jagged. He was still awake. What horrors now stole his rest?

Without the comforting sound of his breathing to calm me, it was ages before sleep returned to me.

"Are you sure this is the best idea?"

Veri seemed intent on carrying me again, somewhere farther than we'd gone before. Yeah, he was a creature that was supposed to be unnaturally strong, but could that really be okay for his back?

"Oh, come on, Enzi. Strength is what I'm good at. I'm what we call a Cadoumai, remember? That means I'm extra strong. So I've got this. Like I said, I'm probably strong enough to carry a whole Gwythienian. You're easy." He hauled me off the cot. I glanced back at Shaun, but he appeared to be still asleep. I hoped it was with better dreams.

"Okay, so where exactly are we going, Mister Ego?" I asked as Veri walked through the door and took off in a new direction. I thought of Gaedyen's size and seriously doubted the little poof could carry him.

He grinned up at me. "To the only place we are never supposed to go."

That piqued my interest. "Oh? Why aren't we supposed to go there?"

"Dyn Meddy likes to keep it sort of sacred, I guess. And he has a point. It's the site of an accident that wiped out a third of our people...and I am not disrespecting their memory," he added quickly. "It's just that we have such a shortage of forbidden places to sneak off to around here, I have to take what I can get and tread lightly."

"What happened to them?"

"You'll see."

He was quiet for the rest of the walk, perhaps giving the dead respect in preparation for visiting their quiet, undisturbed grounds.

We passed several inhabited trees, some with frowning faces poking between curtains or through shutters. It gave me the creeps, being so surrounded by a community who didn't want me there.

I glanced at the leafy branches several yards up, focusing on them instead of the grouchy locals. Thick leaves obscured the sky overhead—just a beautiful canopy of green, filtering the orange light of the sun into relaxing, naturey hues. I could get used to that.

"Wow. These trees are just so huge!"

"Thank you, Captain Obvious." Veri laughed, rolling his eyes.

My heart did a sad little flop at the sound of the nickname I'd given Gaedyen when his bossiness reminded me of Captain von Trapp. *Captain.* I frowned at him. "Whatever."

He chuckled.

Soon we came to a tree that looked dead. Its leafless branches drooped, its bark a lighter, sickly color and flaking off. As we passed, the back of it was blackened and charred. Up ahead, similar trees mixed with healthy ones. But the dead became more numerous until, a few minutes later, charred skeleton trees surrounded us.

The light was sharper—less green—here. Some vegetation crawled up from the ground, but no leaves decorated the trees. They were all dead, nothing but splintery limbs reaching grotesquely outward, the sun peering through their giant corpses with a grayish tinge that glared off the shiny charred bits.

And then there were more fallen trees than upright ones. Long, dead trunks crisscrossed across the ground, some tangling with still-living trees. The uneven stumps of broken branches decorated some of the trees. Was that a rymakri under the leaflitter?

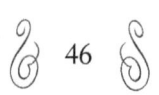

In the midst of all this was some kind of wreckage. All I could make out at first was a lump of twisted metal, but as we drew nearer, the tail of a helicopter poked up from the pile. A faded yellow mark stood out on the side. It seemed familiar, but I wasn't sure why.

"So all this from a helicopter crash? But, Veri, you said there was protection around here. The helicopter shouldn't have gotten in. Shouldn't it have bounced off or something?"

"That's not exactly how it works. The barrier exists around our realm, but not in a physical way. It's like a laser alarm system, sort of. There's a layer of old magic surrounding the realm, and if someone on the outside gets close to it, it sends a signal to their brains persuading them to go the other direction. It isn't something they'd notice. But it has no effect on inanimate objects with no mind to be misled."

"Wow. A lot of your people were hurt in the crash?"

He set me down in view of the site as he answered. "Yeah. That was…a really bad day. And as I said, Dyn Meddy made a rule that no one can get too close. It's too bad it fell here, in the younger part of the forest. If it had been just about any other place, the trees would've been too big for the helicopter or the Gwythienians to take out so easily. The shortest tree stumps, the last ones that were destroyed in the fight, are the wall—the line we aren't supposed to cross."

My heart raced. *Gwythienians were involved in this? Too risky to ask outright…* "Has anyone ever crossed that line before?"

A mischievous grin curved his lips into a childish smile. "*I have.*"

I humored him, hoping to distract myself and appear normal despite my curiosity. "Oh yeah? And what happened?"

He stuffed one hand into his stomach.

"Whoa! What…?" I stammered, confused by the apparent flesh pocket.

He rolled his eyes again. "It's a *pouch*, Enzi. You know, what non-sentient marsupials carry their babies around in? Crivabanians have pouches. No need to look at me like I just pulled an arkencain out of my ear. Sheesh."

"What? What's an arkencain?"

He raised an eyebrow.

"No, really, I've never heard of that before."

"Right." He crossed his arms, his eyebrow even higher. "It's this type of magic weapon that an old race—the Arkensilvers—used to make. They were a race of creatures like giant silvery-black foxes—even greater than the Cathawyrs, whom I'm sure you *also* haven't heard of. But they died out years ago. Anyway, I was going to show you this."

He opened his palm, revealing something small and bright. For the briefest moment, I thought it could be one of the missing rocks—but it was a twisted piece of metal, sparkling in his hand as if polished.

"I found this in the wreckage." He tipped it into my outstretched hand. "As far as I know, no one else has actually gone inside."

I held up the metal. "Why'd you go in there if you're not supposed to?"

"It was several years ago—I was a little kid. Someone had gone missing there, and I hoped I could find her if I just looked hard enough. I got this scar from it." He held out one arm and pulled his fur out of the way. Under the flattened hairs, a jagged ridge of skin about an inch long rose above the surface. "I slipped while checking it out, and a broken part caught my skin."

He seemed proud of it. *I should probably say something.* "Cool?"

"You're lucky you don't have fur all over. It's easy for you to show off your battle scars." He pouted.

I frowned. "*You're* the lucky one. You aren't forced to show yours off if you don't want to."

"Don't you want to?"

Hugging myself, I looked away, avoiding his eyes. "No."

"Oh. That's strange."

"So did you? Find the person who'd gone missing, I mean." I felt bad asking, but we needed a new conversation topic.

A cloud passed over his face. "No. And when my mom came looking for me, she refused to cross the stumps. She must have hoped I'd been a better child than I was—that I wouldn't have gone there. That was when I figured out I could get away from people here. I don't visit too often, especially since my apprenticeship started, but sometimes, when I need to get away, I know no one will bother me here. No one knows it's sort of my place."

I wondered who he'd lost, but I didn't want to be too pushy. I eyed his pocket instead. "Doesn't it get uncomfortable? I mean having a piece of metal in there, with the pocket being, like, your skin and stuff?"

"No, it's not uncomfortable. But the more I carry, the heavier I am, and that makes gliding difficult."

"The more you carry? You have other stuff in there?"

He got that self-conscious look again. Gripping the edge of the pouch, he pushed it away from his body and peered into it. "Well, a few other knickknacks. Pocket knife and stuff. Mostly interesting things I've found around here."

"Why do you carry them all with you? Couldn't you just leave them in a hole in a tree like normal squirrels do?"

"Oh *no*"—he wagged his finger at me—"you did *not* just call me a squirrel!"

"Yeah, I did, *squirrel*," I teased back. "Now, stop avoiding my questions!"

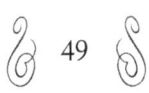

"I'm *not* a squirrel. I'm a Crivabanian, a member of the realm of Sequoia Cadryl. Very *unsquirrely*, thank you very much." He sniffed, fists planted on little hips again. "And I keep my things with me because, as I said, I have several younger nestmates, and if I leave anything anywhere near them, they will play with it to death."

"I see."

Though I didn't, not really. I didn't have younger siblings, or any siblings. Unless Mom has been lying about that too. *Will I ever be able to call her again? What will happen to her if I don't? She sounded so awful last time we talked—sleeping at the police station waiting for a report on me and everything. I hope she listened to me and stopped doing that.*

"What's it like, having brothers and sisters?"

"Annoying as heck," he grumbled. "And why are we talking about my brothers and sisters, huh? Don't you want to have a better look at the crash site?"

"Won't we get in trouble though? If we get caught?"

"*If* we get caught. Which we won't. I never have." He scooped me up in his little arms before I could protest.

"Yeah, but you're a lot stealthier than me. And you can hardly be stealthy if you have to carry me around."

He ignored me. As he carried me in silence, I focused on the pile of twisted metal at the center of the trees ahead. It had been black once, I guessed, but now it was scratched and faded. That bright yellow pattern on the side stood out more and more the closer we got. It looked like some kind of insignia. The top was rubbed off, but I could make out a half circle at the bottom and a few other meaningless lines.

The image seemed so familiar, but I couldn't place it. Maybe it was a brand of helicopters available for hire for tours of the area?

"Did a storm take it down?" I asked.

"No," he replied gravely. He shifted his hands and held me above his head.

"What happened, then? And why are you carrying me over your head?"

"I'm walking like this to avoid stepping on any bones, Enzi. Everyone possible was found and buried, but things fly off in explosions. I never know what might be on the ground in front of me here. I have to be really careful. That's the main reason that Dyn Meddy made it off limits—to protect us from the gruesome possibility of finding ourselves standing on our loved one's missing fingers or someone's charred skull. Carrying you like I was, I can't see directly in front of me."

"That's...disturbing."

"Yeah."

We reached the wreckage, and he set me in the floor of it, on what had once been the ceiling. Seat stuffing hung above me.

Veri hopped over me and jumped up to hang upside down by his tail from the controls. "Anyway, remember how I told you about those things called Gwythienians?"

I gulped. "Yeah."

"They did this—killed so many of us. If I ever meet one..."

Denial washed through me. *No, they wouldn't do that. At least, Gaedyen wouldn't. Would Padraig? Tukailaan probably would. I don't even know any others. Maybe they would.*

"Two Gwythienians had some kind of falling out."

Yep. Two Gwythienians could definitely take out a helicopter.

"So they fought, right in front of the humans in this helicopter. They didn't even try to hide, even though they could probably turn invisible. That's one of their gifts, like our strength. But only some of them are good at it. Anyway, Dyn Meddy can tell the story better, so I'll stop there for now."

"What? No! What happened?"

"You'll just have to wait for the next time Dyn Meddy tells it."

"When will that be?"

"At the next Divinado Legendelor."

"At the what-what?"

"It's like a night of storytelling. We recite poems and legends and things."

"Oh. Do you sing?"

"Nope. Just words and intonations, no music."

I wished they would sing. I missed singing. And music. I never got to hear the Gwythienians sing. Would I ever get to hear that? Gaedyen's voice in song? "So when's the next Divinado…story night thing?"

He grinned. "In a few days."

"How long is a few days?"

Veri dropped from the controls and scooped me up again. "I don't know the exact date. Time to get back. You'll be due for more medicine soon."

I crinkled my nose. But my ankle had begun tingling, which meant he was right.

I nearly bumped my head as Veri stepped out of the helicopter. And then all of the sudden, I went flying up into the air, scrambling to grab the wreckage before crashing. I missed and slid down the side, landing hard on my butt.

"Veri? Are you okay?" He'd just thrown me into the air!

"Sorry," he said, tiptoeing into view. "I slipped on some wet leaves. I was trying to keep you from landing hard, but that clearly didn't work. You okay?"

I rolled to my knees and brushed myself off. That helicopter was pretty dirty, faded with a layer of pollen and grime. I glanced at it to see what color was under all the dirt my butt had just wiped off. I'd slid over part of that mark. I brushed off the rest of pollen and crud to get a better look at it. A collection of curves and lines emerged from under the dust. They formed a strange shape I'd seen somewhere before.

My heart dropped to my toes as the fear I'd felt last time I saw it crept back in.

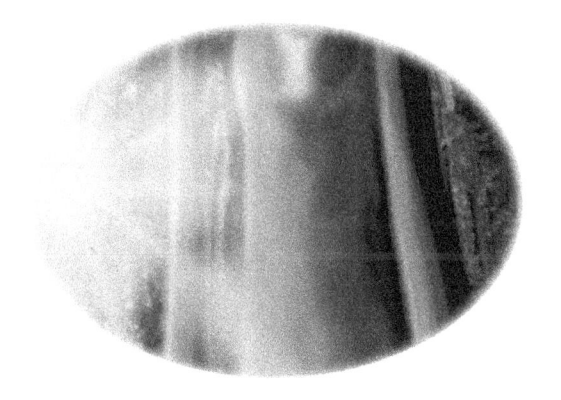

CHAPTER SEVEN

I wracked my brain for the answer. For the reason it hit me like a sucker punch.

A circle in the middle, divided into quarters by lines. At the top, sun rays and a star. Below, a straight line over a squiggle. My heart pounded in my ears. *Why does this seem so familiar?*

"What're you looking at?" Veri popped up next to me, following my gaze. "Oh yeah. That's the symbol of the military group the helicopter belonged to." He glanced at my face, frowned, and darted a look toward my ankle. "Are you in pain?"

"What? No, I'm fine. Let's go."

"Enzi, what does this symbol mean to you?"

Crap. I should've blamed it on the ankle. "Um, nothing. I didn't know it was military until you told me just now."

Planting his fists on his hips, again, he frowned and tapped his toe.

"Oh, toe tapping is a thing with you now too?"

Silently, he rolled his eyes and scooped me up above his head again.

I hoped he couldn't hear how loud my heart hammered. The military. The symbol. Flying monsters capable of ripping off limbs.

What happened to my dad—This had to be where it happened.

Shaun lay with his ankles crossed and his arms folded behind his head, staring at the ceiling.

I'd worked myself into a headache again, trying to sort out the facts. Now they just seemed even more muddled than before. My brain needed a distraction. "What are you thinking about over there?"

He jumped a little. I must've pulled him from some far-away thought. "Oh, nothing much."

I closed my eyes, pressing my finger and thumb to my forehead. "That's what people say when they don't want to share their thoughts."

When he didn't reply, I turned to see if he was asleep.

He smiled and inclined his head as if in agreement, still staring off into space.

Sighing, I shifted so my head was at the foot of the hammock. "Fair enough."

The silence droned on, my headache pounding along with it. "Do you miss your human family?"

"I do not have one."

"Everybody has *some* family, even if you don't know them."

Nothing.

"What about Gaedyen? Are you, like, brothers?"

His brow furrowed. "Sort of, but not exactly."

Cryptic. "Are you ashamed of his parents too? Everything they did?"

"Yes."

"But you'd still rather count *them* as family than your human family?"

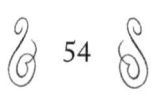

He exhaled, running a hand over his face. "Not exactly."

"Why is a straight answer such a struggle for you?"

"I have good reason. If you knew, you would understand."

I sat up and stared at him. Was I making headway? "Then tell me so I *can* understand. Please?"

"I cannot."

"Is there anything you *can* talk about?"

"You are much more beautiful than those two girls who were going to steal the necklace."

Whoa. What? Heat rushed into my face as I became extra conscious of my exposed skin. I pulled the curtain blanket closer around me. He couldn't really mean that, could he? My headache pulsed harder as I wondered whether he was just trying to get my attention off his secrets.

I struggled against Caleb's weight, but there was nothing I could do. I silently cried, wishing I was anywhere else in the world.

A shadow moved behind him. Another man. Taller, darker.

Shaun?

I didn't want Shaun to see me like this either, though. Should I beg for help?

Before I could make up my mind, the shadow writhed away into nothingness. I'd only imagined it.

"No!"

The knife made an appearance again. I should've known better than to scream.

"I have some good news for you! Dyn Meddy thinks your ribs have healed enough to take the bow for a practice shoot, if you feel up to it."

About time I started preparing to defend myself against Tukailaan. "Yes! Let's try it out." I glanced at Shaun. He was out cold. He probably needed plenty of sleep to heal.

Veri grinned. "I was hoping you'd say that."

"Except we don't have a Gwythienian to make rymakri for us."

"Yeah, I see that. Bow and quiver accounted for, but no arrows. Some archers we are, huh? Seems as though we do need a Gwythienian. Interesting point. When did I tell you that their arrows are called 'rymakri'?"

He narrowed his eyes at me, and my stomach jolted—had he mentioned that word? Or was I not supposed to know about that? I was too afraid of saying the wrong thing to think clearly. "You must have. It's not a normal human word. So what are we going to shoot then?"

He narrowed his eyes, raised his eyebrows, and smiled at me. "Yeah. Mm-hmm. Don't worry about projectiles. I've got us covered."

I was supposedly not ready to walk on my own yet, even with the splint. So Veri carried me, but I was hoping to walk myself back after shooting practice.

"So, Master Fuzzbucket"—I cracked myself up at the nickname—"are you going to teach me how to use this thing properly?" I traced a finger over the wooden curve of the bow.

"Something like that." There was a smile in his tone. "I have to teach myself first, though. I've never shot one of these things before. And you can lose that nickname."

I snorted. "Then how the heck are you going to teach me how to use it? And we'll see about that." I was fully committed to using the name as much as I could now.

"It can't be *that* hard."

Smirking, I predicted disappointment after his first attempt.

He located a place he deemed appropriate for target practice and set me next to a thick tree trunk. I leaned against it, stretching my legs out in front of me and lacing my hands together behind my head in anticipation of the snarky little squirrel's failure.

"All right, these are the rules."

"Rules?"

"That's right. The redwoods are our homes. We live in them and grow with them. It would be disrespectful to cut their branches or shoot at their trunks. So when you're shooting, be careful not to shoot a redwood. The pines, like that one straight ahead, are okay. They are a soft wood, so their wood will be easier to pierce, but we'll be doing it with their own branches, which are soft wood too. Also, you probably can't tell, but we're near the edge of Sequoia Cadryl, near the invisible barrier. That's because we don't want to accidentally hit any Crivabanians. So always aim for a non-redwood and always toward the edge of Sequoia Cadryl. That way." He pointed.

"Okay. And where are the 'projectiles'?"

Reaching behind him, he brushed a cluster of ferns to the side, revealing a pile of long, straight, recently sharpened branches. "Told you I had us covered."

I nodded. He sure did.

He pulled the bow off my lap, hefting it in one hand. "It sure is a beauty." In a flash, he swept one of the sharpened branches—longer than his whole body—off the ground and strung it. Pulling the cord and bending the wooden part to an incredible degree, he let loose, releasing an intense *thwang* from the cord. An instant later, a dramatic crunching sound emanated from somewhere farther ahead than I could see.

My mouth dropped open, and my arms fell to my sides, partially in awe of what he'd just done, and partially in exasperation that it'd been so easy.

"What the heck, man! How did you ace it on your first try? You're not even tall enough to hold the bow straight. And that makeshift arrow of yours wasn't even that sharp. You were kidding, right? About never having shot a bow before?"

He grinned from ear to ear, more than a little pleased with himself. "I wasn't lying, Enzi, this *is* the first time I've shot a bow. I'm just that good." He made a show of dusting himself off as he sauntered the few steps back to me.

I wasn't having that, at least not without a chance to try it myself. I probably wouldn't be anywhere near as good as he was, but Tukailaan would be coming, and I needed to be prepared.

So I shifted my weight, balanced on my good foot, and stood, steadying myself with one hand on the tree. "Bring me that thing." I adjusted so my left shoulder, on the same side as my bad ankle, leaned against the trunk, leaving both my hands and arms free. *Kind of awkward.*

He pranced over, still smiling, and handed me the bow and another sharpened branch. As I took them from him, I noticed he'd carved a thin, straight line on the back of each makeshift arrow, where the string was supposed to go. Gripping the bow with my left hand, I pulled back on the string, sloppily trying to hold the edge of the stick against it. I pulled back steadily, noting with distaste that the bow wouldn't bend half as much as it had for Veri.

Frowning, I aligned my eye with the stick and its future path. I focused on a tree twenty feet ahead and let loose. Leaves rustled, but no wood crunched. So I'd missed. And I couldn't see where it'd landed. Veri dropped to all fours and skittered off.

"I found it!" he shouted. A moment later, the stick appeared above the ferns a good three feet to the right of the target, green fronds swishing as Veri weaved through them.

I frowned.

"Hey, don't worry!" He grinned, bounding back into view. "It doesn't count when you can't even stand up straight. Today is just for funzies."

He had a point. I *had* been in bad shape since even before Aven had given the bow to me. I'd sprained my ankle and bruised every inch of skin days before we reached Maisius Arborii. But what good would I be if I couldn't manage unless I was in perfect health? I needed to be able to shoot Tukailaan if he came after me. Where was the best place to shoot a Gwythienian?

"Let me try again."

Wordlessly, Veri returned the stick and hopped back a few steps, clear of the bow. Once again, I raised it, pulled back, lined up, and let it fly.

It shot to the other side of the tree this time, even *more* off course. Veri leaped up to fetch it. My frown deepened, and I tightened my grip.

Veri reached me, stick in hand, and asked, "Do you want to try again?"

I snatched it from his tiny hands. Once more I took aim, let loose, and…missed.

"But look!" Veri shouted when he found it. "It's closer this time."

He was grinning like a chimp when he handed me the stick for the fourth time.

My frown melted slightly as a glimmer of hope sparked inside.

We spent the rest of the afternoon like that. I shot the poor excuses for arrows, and Veri retrieved them, offering encouragement with each bad shot and praise with each improvement.

Eventually, Veri pointed out that he'd made his amazing shot at an angle, due to his being a good deal shorter than the bow. He suggested it couldn't hurt for me to try it. So I did. It didn't help.

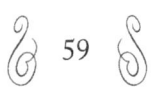

When we finally stopped, my good leg was so stiff and my shoulder so numb that as soon as I tried to move, I would have crash landed if Veri hadn't caught me. But I'd managed to hit the tree three times. Never quite where I was aiming, but still, I made contact. I'd broken one stick and shot another so far in a burst of frustration that Veri couldn't find it. I was honestly kinda proud of that one. *Maybe I'm not completely hopeless.*

I did miss the smooth feel of the rymakri in my hand, the strange value of a weapon you could only hold for a short time before it was gone forever. I wanted to keep up my rymakri practice, but these sticks Veri carved were much too light and thin. And I didn't think it was because of the soft pine wood. Gaedyen had made weapons from all different kinds of wood on the way down from Odan Terridor. My guess was whatever chemical reaction from his saliva that made it hard enough to pierce wood also made it heavier.

Would Gaedyen ever come back and make me rymakri again?

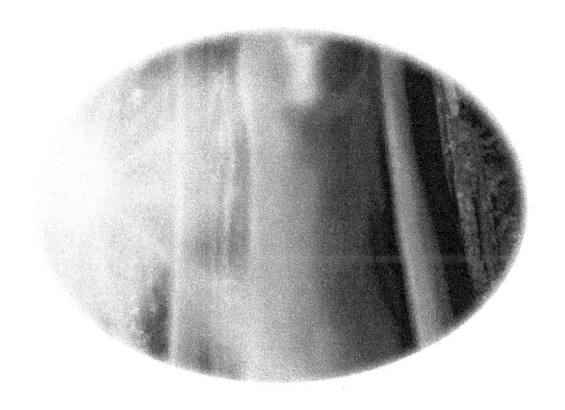

CHAPTER EIGHT

"How are you feeling?" I asked Shaun as I prepared for another day of shooting practice. I was back to nearly perfect health—walking on my own and standing without having to lean against anything—now that I'd been in Sequoia Cadryl for several days. And I was slightly better with the bow. Sometimes. I was better than I'd been with throwing the rymakri, and Veri always managed to find some little compliment to encourage me, which was nice.

"A bit improved, thank you," said Shaun.

I frowned, unconvinced. Something was up with him. Back home, he'd been either annoyingly cheerful or cryptically urgent. He hadn't gotten any less cryptic, but he was strangely mellow—didn't seem to have the same range of emotions. Maybe it was the Crivabanian healing mixtures.

Pushing himself up with an arm to support his head, he opened his mouth as if to say something when Veri leaped through the door and landed on my hammock. "I've got a surprise for you guys! Someone found a ton of blue fruit. It's only ripe a handful of days out of the summer. You'll love it. I'm going to get some for us."

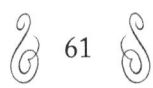

He was gone again before I could thank him, gliding out on a warm breeze. My stomach growled at the thought of something tasty.

Shaun regarded me. "How was shooting?"

"It was fine. I seem to be improving." *Nowhere near good enough to have any chance against Tukailaan, though.* I sat on my cot, then swung my legs up to lie down instead. "You know, I'm still really curious, how *did* he get in touch with you that day?"

Shaun sighed. This wasn't the first time we'd had this conversation. He was good at wiggling out of my questions and never giving me a straight answer. "I told you, it is complicated to explain. Please just forget about it. What matters is you are safe, and though Tukailaan has the rock, he cannot Possess it."

"But I can't figure out your relationship. You're not brothers... are you like...*together?*"

He huffed a laugh. "No. We are not together. Not in that way. We are too alike."

"Why do you talk like him? It makes you sound so formal."

His eyebrows shot up. "Is that something I do? I did not realize—"

"There! You did it again. You said 'did not' instead of 'didn't.' That's not how people actually talk, which makes me think you must've been raised in Odan Terridor, like Gaedyen. Am I right?"

"It is true I grew up in Odan Terridor, yes."

"How did you survive? If Padraig is all against humans and wants to kill them off and everything, why did he let you live?"

"I managed to avoid him a great deal."

"Why is a straight answer so hard for you?"

"Enzi..." He sighed again, looking down. "Please. Just trust me. If I say too much, there is a chance it could hurt you one day, unnecessarily. And I would never wish to cause you pain. If you can leave it alone now, you will be so much better off."

"That just makes me more anxious to know. Why are you always so cryptic?"

"What is your favorite color?"

This was going nowhere. *Why does he have to be so stubborn?* "You're just trying to distract me. You don't care what my favorite color is."

"Actually, I would like to know."

I debated whether to answer. What even was my favorite color? It used to be purple, because the stone had been the one thing I liked about my appearance. But now…"Reddish, I guess." *Reddish-brown. The color of Gaedyen's skin.* It still made me mad and hurt that he didn't need me to help with the journey anymore, not since I'd lost the stone. And at the same time, I was worried about him. But that color meant a warm, safe place. It meant the only friend I'd had in years. And it meant flying on the wind, through our own air that no one else but us could breathe.

"Red like blood?"

I shook my head. "No. Red like…" I wasn't about to tell him. He had some kind of claim on Gaedyen I didn't understand. It was none of his business how I felt about him. But what else could describe the color? "Sort of like the leaves in the fall, when they change color." They were pretty enough, yeah, but they meant the world was about to turn cold and miserable. They meant the heating bill was going to skyrocket, at least whenever the heat actually stayed on. They meant I would crave coffee even more than usual and be even less likely to afford it.

"That is a nice color."

"Yeah, thanks. So what's yours?"

"Gray."

Was he serious? "Gray? Like winter?" I shivered.

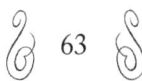

He just smiled that knowing smile, as if he knew some joke only he understood. "No, not like winter. Gray like phantom mist rising from the water early in the morning when no one else is up yet and you have the world to yourself. Gray like the sky across from the horizon, the place no one thinks to look. The secret gray no one else notices but is truly the most beautiful in its silence."

I stared at him, eyebrows raised. "Well that was kind of poetic."

His grin widened. "Can I take that as a compliment?"

Something about his face looked like Gaedyen. Was that really possible? Was I just projecting some craziness because I wished something that wasn't? It made my heart hurt. "What? Oh, sure."

Smooth muscles rippled as he shifted to lie on his back. Why did I have to notice? Why couldn't I just keep on being mad at him? As hurt as I was about Gaedyen's leaving, it felt wrong to be ogling Shaun when I would be hurt by Gaedyen being attracted to someone else. I didn't want to be a hypocrite.

But he was so nice to look at.

Gaedyen wasn't even here. I might never see him again.

"Ugh! Why'd he just leave me, Shaun? Why? I can't believe him."

"I thought you would appreciate that he left someone to protect you. He did not leave you completely alone."

"Seriously? Quit defending him. Just forget about it." Of course he'd be on Gaedyen's side.

"Enzi—"

"Let's just stop talking, okay?" I shouted.

"Dang!" Veri exclaimed, gliding into the room with a grin. He dropped a basket on the ground and landed on the edge of my hammock. "What did I just walk in on? Got any good comebacks?"

"Don't encourage him." I glowered at Veri. "Didn't you just hear me tell him not to talk to me?"

"Fine, then. Dude, don't talk to the lady while she has her little hissy fit—"

"What? Hey!"

"Just out of curiosity, what *would* you have said to her, had she given you permission to speak?"

"I thought I was 'kind of poetic,'" Shaun said to me. Then to Veri, "If she is determined to think badly of someone who is just trying to help her, that is her decision."

I turned from them to face the wall. *Way to make me sound like the bad guy here.*

"So who's this mutual friend?" Veri ventured, plucking a blue fruit from his basket and handing it to me.

I stiffened. Did Shaun know Gwythienians weren't liked here? To keep quiet about what Gaedyen was? My heart skipped a beat. Should I interrupt him? No, too obvious. Unsure of what else to do, I took the plumb-sized blue fruit from Veri. Its skin was slightly fuzzy like a peach.

"Just a friend of Enzi's. And sort of a friend of mine too. I do jobs for him when he needs help."

I was relieved but still pissed at him. "Some kinda jobs you do," I mumbled, thinking of how he'd knocked me out and kidnapped me.

"Well, you *have* benefitted from each of them, have you not?"

I snorted, searching my arsenal for an angry retort, and I realized to my disgust he was not wrong. I *had* benefitted each of the times I'd met him. Well, I guess the first time was debatable, since that'd started it all. Actually though, the *very* first time I'd met him, when I was only dealing with human-world craziness, he'd fought off my high school nemesis and opened my car door for me. That, too, had been a good thing. I'd only managed to hold on to the rock as long as I had before learning its value because of him.

But I could hardly admit that now. "How do you always know where to be when I'll need something?"

The smile on his lips as he prepared to answer once again reminded me of Gaedyen. It was the sort of look he'd get when he knew the answer to my question but enjoyed keeping it to himself too much to share it with me.

"I am just that good."

Blue jelly burst from my hand, splattering the front of my shirt and shooting Veri in the face.

"Hey! Stop ruining valuable deliciousness." Veri wiped the blue of his face and licked his fingers.

Ignoring him, I glared at Shaun. "Fine, then. What's that tattoo on your shoulder mean?"

Shaun's face went blank. "It does not mean anything important. Just forget about it."

Veri had been watching our bickering with rapt attention, but his interest faded now. He glanced around the room, apparently unperturbed by the awkward silence.

Why does he have to hide everything from me? Ugh! He's so frustrating.

"I know what you need," Veri blurted, bursting into the air. He stuffed the basket full of valuable deliciousness under some equipment and retrieved the bow from where it leaned against the wall. He scampered back across the room with it. "When in a bad mood, shoot something."

That didn't seem like an ideal philosophy, but I grabbed it from him and jumped out of the hammock, not caring that I'd already been shooting for hours today. I marched out the door, the light pressure of two small feet landing on my shoulder.

"What do you keep humoring him for?" I demanded once we were a safe distance from the hut.

"Why'd you give him such a hard time?" he countered. "He saved your life, at great personal risk by the sound of it, and before that only helped you."

"He keeps so many secrets from me. Plus, he kidnapped me."

"Yeah, you mentioned that. I thought you got lost in the woods?"

Scoffing, I rolled my eyes. "I did. As a result of being kidnapped. It's complicated."

"Isn't that what people say when they don't want to tell you something?" He sighed. "You know, if you aren't ready to talk about it, that's fine. You don't have to tell me. Not now, or ever, if you don't want to."

The stubbornness deflated right out of me. Well if he was going to be like that…but no, I still couldn't tell him. Maybe it was hypocritical of me to keep things from Veri when I was so annoyed with Shaun for doing the same to me, but it might be too compromising. And that line could totally have been a reverse-psychology strategy to get me to break down, as I almost had.

Was I being a hypocrite? Veri didn't understand my reasons, but that didn't make them any less valid. The fact that Shaun actually might have a good reason didn't make it any less frustrating.

"Thanks for understanding, Veri."

"Yeah, I do. You still shouldn't be a jerk to Shaun, though. He cares about you."

"You are the most obnoxious squirrel in the world."

"You can be a bit obnoxious yourself sometimes."

"Whatever." Restless energy rippled through me.

When we finally reached the place where we kept our sticks for shooting, I grabbed one, aimed, and let loose. The stick grazed the side of the tree and dove into the ground a few yards off.

I stomped over and rounded the wide tree. A flash of light blinded me, and a moment later three humans came into focus. I froze. Two adults and one child stood just beyond the grounded stick, and they were staring right at me, a camera on a strap hanging around the woman's neck.

"It's okay, Enzi." Veri stilled on my shoulder. "They aren't really looking at us. Remember the border around Sequoia

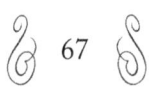

Cadryl? They can't see through it or hear us. They're looking at something else that isn't really there, and they're about to realize they'd rather go in another direction."

All three wore brown hiking boots. The man sported a huge backpack, and the woman had a little bag for extra lenses and flashes draped around one shoulder. The girl held a shiny, black, elongated crystal-like object, examining it intently.

Veri gasped, his hands over his mouth and eyes bugging out.

"What is it?" I hissed, glancing around us and reaching for another stick, just in case.

I followed his eyes to what the girl was holding.

He rubbed his fists over his eyes and looked again.

"What is it?"

"It…" His voice trailed off.

The woman reached for the child's hand. The little girl clutched the object in one hand as she reached for her mother with the other. They skipped off in the opposite direction as if nothing was amiss.

"Veri," I asked, "what happened? Are you okay?"

"I thought I saw something. Yeah, I'm fine. It couldn't have been what I thought. I just have arkencains on my mind since we talked about them the other day."

"You thought you saw an arkencain?"

"I couldn't have. They've all been destroyed."

"You never told me what an arkencain is."

He took a slow, deep breath. "An arkencain is a bit like a rymakri, a weapon to throw. But they're smaller, and the Arkensilvers poisoned them with cursed magic. A pack of Arkensilvers used to live in this area, but if they'd left any arkencains around, we would've found them. They're historically a set of five. So it couldn't really have been one just by itself."

I shrugged, hoping he was right.

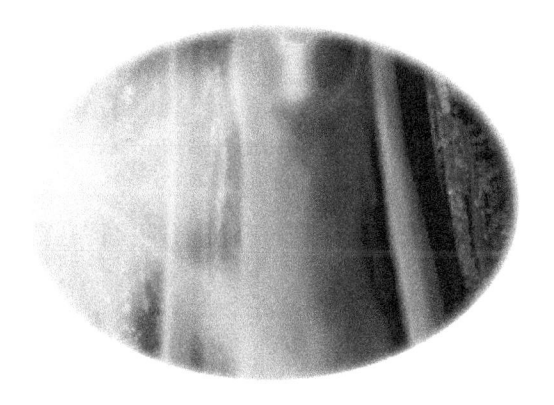

CHAPTER NINE

"*E*nzi, I am sorry about our disagreement yesterday. I hope you will forgive me for being rude." Shaun sat on his hammock and adjusted to avoid leaning his bad shoulder against the wall.

"*You're* apologizing?" I was the one who'd started it; if anyone should apologize it was probably me. But I was still annoyed at him, even if he did have a good reason for his secrecy.

"For the outburst, yes."

"But not for taking Gaedyen's side over mine?"

"It is not about sides. I am sorry, though, that it bothers you so much. I wish it did not. But while he is not here to defend himself, I feel I must speak up for him."

"Why is that?"

"Well, you say he did a horrible thing in leaving you, and you hate him."

"I never said I hate him. But it was a horrible thing."

"Horrible to leave you in the care of creatures who excel at healing? Horrible to leave someone with you to explain things so you would know what happened? You may not have said you hate him. You did not need to. It is very plain."

"It was horrible of him to leave and go on adventuring without me. As if I couldn't handle it or something."

"Trust me, he knows you can handle anything. He really wishes he could come back, but he is not able to yet."

I shot upright. "You've talked to him? When? Let me talk to him! I just want to know he's alive. I promise not to throw a tantrum at him. I'll save it."

His face fell. "I am sorry, Enzi. I do not have a way for you to talk to him."

"But there's a way for you to talk to him?"

"Not really."

I threw my hands up. "Then how the heck do you know what he's thinking?"

"I just do. I know him well."

"Well that's just great. Next time you two have a telepathy session, tell him he's an asshole and I *do* hate him."

"Well look who's up." Veri glided through the door.

Shaun turned to him, glowering. He started to cross his arms, then dropped them into his lap as if remembering his injuries.

"Dyn Meddy has decided to decrease the intensity of your medications, Shaun. You're healing at an acceptable rate now." Veri grinned from the corner of the hammock he'd landed on. "You'll have to come shooting with us. Maybe even tomorrow. I'll talk to Dyn Meddy about it."

Wide-eyed with horror, I tried to send Veri a stealthy death glare. I did *not* want Shaun seeing me fail at shooting. That was such a horrible idea. I missed more often than I hit, and hardly any of the ones that hit actually stuck.

Shaun cleared his throat and grinned at Veri, who chose to ignore me in favor of a less icy expression. "I would love to try shooting a bow. I have not tried before."

"Have you ever thrown a rymakri?" I challenged.

"Oh yes. Many of them. By far my favorite weapon choice."

"Cool." *Oh great.* Even more reason for him not to come shooting. He'd been throwing rymakri for years, just like Gaedyen. Of course. And I'd only been at it for what? A few weeks? And it'd been at least a week and a half since I'd touched one, maybe longer. I did *not* want to compare our rymakri-throwing abilities. One more way to look like an idiot in front of the hottest guy I'd ever seen and the only guy in the world who'd ever talked to me.

Yup.

I turned to Veri, hoping his all-over-the-place mind would have some cheerful subject change ready to burst out before Shaun could challenge me to some kind of rymakri competition—if those were even a thing. But he was already looking at me. And I could've sworn that for just an instant, his eyes narrowed. His usual grin was back in place a moment later, leaving me wondering if I'd imagined it.

"Well. I'm going to grab us some lunch. Try not to kill each other while I'm gone. I'll be back in a few minutes." Veri leaped off his perch and glided out.

The gust of wind that flew in right afterward had me leaping up to shut the door. "Man, it's chilly out today." I sat on my cot, pulling the curtain-blanket over me. With a shiver, I tucked my feet in.

When I looked up again, Shaun was leaning toward me, his arm outstretched, passing me his blanket. "Here. I am not cold. Have mine too. If you want."

Gaedyen. He was like Gaedyen again, offering me his wing that first time in the cave outside of Odan Terridor. I missed that wing so much.

I pulled myself out of the memory. "Thanks, Shaun."

I tried to smile, but it wasn't convincing. He smiled back though, so it must've been worth something. And dang! All Veri had given him to wear was a pair of too-short pants made from the same material as my strange clothes. The fabric only reached just above his knees. He sat with one leg folded and one stretched out, both of them dark and muscular.

That feeling shot through my stomach again. As my eyes slowly grazed his sculpted chest and neck, across one beautiful arm reaching toward me, I realized that arm was still handing me a blanket. With a start, I ripped my eyes away and snatched the blanket from him, almost toppling from my hammock.

"You are welcome."

I heard the smile in his voice, so I risked a quick peek at his face. He arched an eyebrow, a smile playing about his lips. I made a show of how much more time consuming arranging a second blanket could be.

More awkward silence.

"Have you ever heard the Gwythienians sing?" I asked.
"Yes."
"Really? What does it sound like?"

He lifted his eyes away from mine, as if searching for the words. "Like nothing else in the world. There is a natural harmony to it. A ring. A sort of...echo. I do not know what human-world sound to compare it to. Though, the point is to be united, and I was always on the outskirts. I did not get to enjoy the community of a song. But it is glorious. I am sure you would enjoy hearing it."

It ached to know I might never get the chance. "Can you sing one of their songs for me?"

He looked as mortified as Gaedyen had when I'd asked him the same question.

I rolled my eyes before he could get the words out. "Ugh, never mind. I should've known. You guys are ridiculously similar. How long have you known each other?"

"Many years."

I frowned. "Could you be a little more vague?"

"Somewhat longer than I have known you."

I snorted. "I wasn't being serious."

He chuckled. "I know." His soft smile sent that feeling through my stomach again. Why did he do that to me? Did he know he was doing it? Judging by his eyebrows a moment ago, he might.

"You know," I said as I changed the subject, "you talk like you belong to Odan Terridor, but you say you had to hide while you were there to be safe from Padraig. How can you speak as if you're a part of it if you were never accepted?"

He glanced down for a moment, then back at me. "That is a difficult question. The more pressing matter is when we can leave."

Ever avoiding personal questions. "Okay."

Another gust of chilly air swept into the room, and I pulled the blankets up farther around me just as Veri landed on my head. "Veri! Get off me, you fuzzbucket. And shut the door. It's cold."

Without a word he dropped a basket into my lap and backflipped toward the door. With a creak, it finally shut against the wind.

"Look what I brought you."

In the basket there were several items of varying shape and size. "What's all this?"

"Lunch."

"Cool. Is there more of that blue fruit?"

Veri wagged a finger at me. "I don't know. You've been wasteful of valuable deliciousness. That kind of behavior is not tolerated here. Blue fruit is too tasty."

Lifting a brow, I said, "Okay, well, now that I'm not in the middle of a fight with Mr. Secretive over there, can I have another chance at valuing the deliciousness?"

He eyed me suspiciously. "I don't have any with me today, but as for tomorrow…we'll see."

Shrugging, I pulled out one of the packets and opened it. Between two slices of something resembling pita bread, there were thin slices of tomato, lettuce, and avocado. At first, I was disappointed there was no meat. I wanted fish or something. But then I caught a delicious whiff of some kind of sauce or dressing. I bit into the sandwichy thing and savored the zesty flavors, wishing for a little lemon juice and oregano.

Veri tossed one at Shaun. "Dig in!"

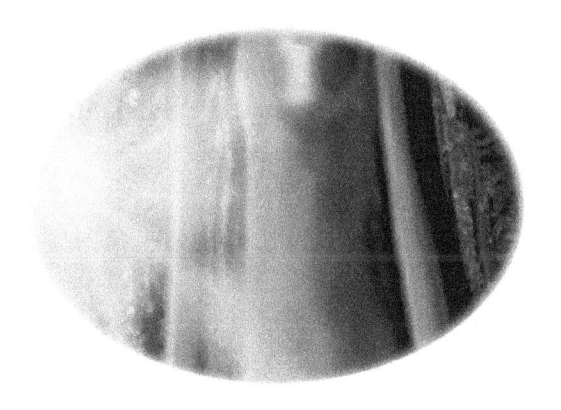

CHAPTER TEN

The next morning, Dyn Meddy wouldn't let Shaun more than ten feet outside the infirmary. After a positive afternoon recheck, he allowed us to take Shaun for a longer walk. He and I strolled to the shooting place, Veri scampering and chattering between us the whole way. But we were under strict doctor's orders not to let him touch the bow. Shaun limped, favoring his left leg.

I hoped my stiff walking went unnoticed. I didn't want him to see my skin jiggling with each step. *My old cargo pants and T-shirt would be amazing right now.*

On the evening of the next day, Dyn Meddy gave permission for Shaun to carve sticks for us while we shot, but he was not to risk his shoulder on the bow.

Shaun sat down against a tree, and Veri handed him his pocketknife and leaped away to gather sticks for him to sharpen. I hefted the bow, blushing at the idea of Shaun having to see this. It was going to be embarrassing.

A few minutes later, Veri returned with an armload, and I was holding the first of the carved sticks Shaun made, wondering how someone could make scraping bark off a stick look so...

like something I wanted to keep watching. The way his dark, muscled wrist flexed with each swipe of the blade against the wood...it didn't help that he still had nothing to wear besides his wonky shorts.

I was about to make a total fool of myself. In front of *this* guy.

Wincing, I glanced away, avoiding their expectant gazes.

"And...go!" Veri punched the air.

Planting one foot in the ground and leaning forward on the other, I stretched the bow and aimed at the target Veri had carved into a pine tree. *This is practice to stay alive if Tukailaan finds me. This is not something I'm doing to impress Shaun.* I let out a breath and then released the missile. It soared to one side of the tree and off into the distance.

Shocking.

Veri popped into the air, gliding after it, side flaps stretched to catch the breeze.

I dared a glance at Shaun.

"Want another one?" He offered a freshly stripped branch.

"Sure, thanks." *Now I can embarrass myself again. Woot.*

I waited until Veri was out of the danger zone, then shot another one. That one at least had the dignity to scrape off a bit of bark as it sailed past the target tree. *A little closer.* That was something.

"Better!"

Shaun's voice. I tried to hide the smile I felt creep to my lips. He'd noticed I got closer and complimented me on it. That was...nice.

Veri tossed me the one he'd retrieved and waited for me to shoot before getting the last one.

Once again, I aimed, released my breath, and let loose. A satisfying, solid *thunk* met my ears as I lowered the bow to stare openmouthed at the stick protruding from the tree.

"Woohoo! Nice one, Enzi." Veri jumped up a nearby tree stump and paused at my eye level, holding out one hand for a high-five. I high-fived him back, grinning and hoping my arm didn't jiggle and my scars weren't too noticeable from that angle. Shaun smiled when my eyes found his, and I felt proud to do something right while he was watching, but also a little embarrassed. I wasn't sure why. Glancing down, I fumbled with the bow.

"That was pretty awesome. Well done, Enzi," said Shaun.

He was still grinning at me. I looked away for a moment, clearing my head and trying to remember what he'd said besides my name. "Sorry, what?" I searched his eyes, heart racing.

"I just said that was an awesome shot."

"Oh, thanks." I tried to smile at him, then quickly glanced down. What was I thinking? If he was a Shimbator, he'd be in even more trouble in Sequoia Cadryl than we already were as humans. I needed time to process this, then I'd ask him. I'd demand an answer. When Veri wasn't around, just in case.

Out of the rest of the shots I made that afternoon, only one managed to hit the tree, and it didn't stay stuck. It just plunked against the trunk and fell to the ground. My spirits had significantly dropped from their high point.

"Hey! I have an idea." Veri burst from a branch, backflipped, shot a stick in mid-flip, and landed lithe as a cat on another branch.

Show off.

"How about you guys do your rymakri-throwing thing? You can use these sticks. I mean if you're just throwing stuff, you don't need both arms. So Shaun could do it too, instead of just you."

I froze, darting a look at Shaun, then tried to undo the look before Veri noticed. Judging from the expectant smile on his face, he hadn't. I thought fast, afraid of letting on too much.

It would be better to play it smooth, to go with it and not act weird. Don't be noticeable, just agree.

"Yeah, that's a *great* idea!" I hoped I wasn't overdoing the enthusiasm. "What do you think, Shaun?"

"I am up for it." He lifted himself from the ground, biceps flexing. Bits of that mark peeked out of his bandage, and I couldn't wait for the wrappings to go so I could have another look. I wanted to ask him about it and see how similar it was to Gaedyen's. He'd probably be as vague as Gaedyen, but it was worth a try.

He'd shaved down several small branches, most of which were now sitting in the quiver on my back. I pulled out a couple and tossed them to him. He caught them and took position to my right, facing the same target tree, easily hiding any apprehension he may have felt at Veri's bringing up the rymakri.

"All right, here's how we're going to do this." Veri bounded up to my shoulder and seriously placed his little fists on his hips. I couldn't help smiling at him. Too funny. "Both of you get ready to throw. I'll have you throw one at a time so we can keep track. Shaun, you go first."

Shaun held his shoulders straight, as Gaedyen had taught me, but his feet were all wrong. Then he leaned back almost as if he expected someone to catch him, then stumbled and looked surprised when no one did. And his fingers around the blade... they were close to how Gaedyen had taught me to hold mine, but not quite the same. His thumb stuck out.

Finally he found his position and held his right arm back, readying to throw. His arm whipped out and pitched the stick and...he *missed*.

"I suppose I am a bit rusty." He smiled at me and took a few steps back, giving me plenty of room.

I frowned. Hadn't Gaedyen taught him how to throw?

I positioned my feet as Gaedyen had instructed and, paying special attention to not letting my wrist turn wrong, I flung

78

the stick at the target tree. I was rewarded with a solid *thunk*, though the stick didn't stay embedded in the wood. Still better than Shaun.

Shaun clapped. "Well done!"

I squinted at him. He seemed happier than he should be about this. Had he let me win? I didn't need that!

"Thanks. Want another try?" I tossed him another stick, and he missed again. Maybe he was missing on purpose for Veri's sake. I missed the next one on purpose just in case, then another by accident.

Veri was a good sport and went searching for our sticks each time we ran out.

"Oh!" Shaun crouched, and I stepped toward him to see what was up. He rose and turned, holding something out to me. A small, round bit of brown was already leaving a shimmery, slimy trail across his palm.

"A snail? Oh, gross! Put it down."

Shaun grinned so mischievously, I held up my hands and took a step back, half expecting to be pelted with slime. Instead, he opened his mouth and popped the snail right in.

My jaw dropped in horror. Surely he hadn't just eaten a snail? A raw, *live* snail? I stepped to the side and looked around him, hoping he'd chucked it over his shoulder, but nothing.

"Oh, man." I covered my mouth, feeling nauseated. "You did not just—"

"He sure did." Veri glided to my shoulder, grimacing with his ears all droopy.

A loud *crunch*, followed by several smaller munches, interrupted me.

"Oh, man!" I winced and stepped farther back. "That is seriously disgusting."

"Really bad taste in snackable items," Veri agreed.

"Well, it certainly was not anywhere near as good as the ones in…that I have had before, but it was decent." He smiled that teasing smile again.

My stomach responded with its usual flip-floppy somersaults. Shouldn't his eating a snail make that less likely?

The snail. The leaning back, almost as if he expected a tail to be there to help him balance. How stupidly he held his thumb, as if he'd never had a thumb in his way while throwing before. The mysteriously knowing things about Gaedyen's current feelings and intentions.

Are Shimbators really real? Am I looking at one?

"Okay. Let's get back to the infirmary." I hurried away before he could eat any more nasty bugs. He laughed, limping behind me.

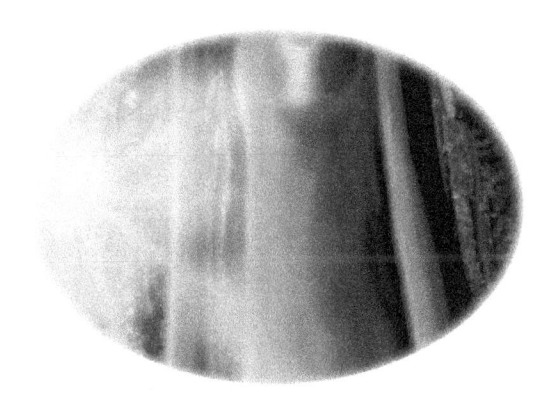

CHAPTER ELEVEN

The next morning, I woke up with Tukailaan on my mind. The truth was, even with weapons practice, I just couldn't get good enough to win a fight in a few days. And he might show up any time. I'd be a sitting duck. So I should really try harder on the invisibility front. Gwythienian Possessors could do it without physical contact with the rock, but I didn't know how long it took them to reach that point. Maybe it wasn't the fact I was a human that was preventing me. Maybe it was time. I'd only been Possessor for…how long? Did it count from when Mom first gave me the necklace? Even then, that was short by Gwythienian lifespans.

Scrunching my eyes closed and clenching my fists, I searched the mental wall for a crack. There were none to be found. What if I could make my own? If I could mentally rip through a crevice, perhaps I could also create the crevice in the first place. *But how…?*

I tried to hurl thoughts at the wall, but they bounced off.

I tried mentally stomping on it, but that didn't carry any weight. A headache built behind my eyes, and moments later I was staring at the edge of the hammock, breathless and visible.

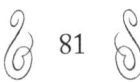

What was I doing wrong?

I tried again—and almost thought I had something—when the door slammed. I sat up in surprise, blinking to clear my head. The dull ache had escalated to a piercing pain.

Veri appeared in the doorway. "She lives!"

"Yeah, yeah. I'm awake, and you're a rude fuzzbucket." I stretched, my mind distracted with trying to analyze my attempts at invisibility.

Veri leaped onto the hammock and took my left arm. "Come on," he coaxed, pulling me up. "I carried you plenty of times. It's your turn to carry me today."

"Okay, sure." I shrugged. "Hop on. Are we going to shoot? Can I eat some blue fruit first?"

He climbed on my shoulder and gripped my shirt's fabric with his weirdly flexible toes. I stood and walked toward the door.

"Yes to shooting, and we'll pick some blue fruit on the way. If you promise to be responsible with it." He leaned around to eye me intently.

"Yeah, yeah." I shooed him away, turning to invite Shaun to join us, but the words stuck in my throat. Questions about him and Gaedyen and Shimbators and secrets flooded my mind.

"Wanna come, Shaun?" Veri's weight shifted as he faced my roommate.

I smiled, relieved Veri had asked.

Shaun smiled, eyes heavy-lidded. "Dyn Meddy said I overdid it yesterday and gave me extra medicine today. He said it would make me really tired, and I feel like I would probably fall down if I tried to walk." He looked nearly asleep once he finished talking.

"Okeydokey! We'll see you later then," Veri said. "Let's go."

I stepped out the door, strangely disappointed by Shaun's decision.

I was imagining how the day might've gone, how we might've had fun together, when Veri interrupted my thoughts.

"Wait, don't go that way."

"Why not?"

"We've been taking a short cut. Let's take the scenic route today. And that's where we'll find the blue fruit."

"Sure. Point me in the right direction."

Eventually, the dense foliage parted. As much as I enjoyed the greenish atmosphere of the dense forest floor, I hadn't realized how much I missed real, unfiltered sunlight until I saw it pouring through the gap in the trees above the stream. I hurried toward it.

"Calm down!" Veri complained as my increased pace set him to bouncing uncomfortably on my shoulder. He leaped off and soared around me.

Trees whizzed by as I ran faster than ever before, relishing the lack of pain in my ankle and whole body. Groups of ferns with purple berries thickened as we neared the stream.

Stopping at the water's edge, I leaned over it, basking in the delicious, warm rays shimmering off the stream and gazing at the beautiful pebbles at the bottom of the crystal-clear water.

I wonder if I could find Gaedyen in here.

If I looked for him, but saw Shaun, would that be proof that my Shimbator suspicion was right? He wouldn't have lied to be so blatantly though…would he? I stared into the water, tried to focus, and searched my head for a fracture in the wall. I squinted, concentrating as hard as I could. I willed him to be there.

But no fissure appeared, and no Gaedyen rippled beneath the surface.

Ugh! Why can't I do this?

Then I glimpsed my reflection. My eyes were brighter—more wild-looking. What other parts of me had changed while I'd been on this journey?

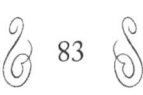

I stood to get a look at my whole reflection.

I was the same size I'd been the last time I'd seen myself. My legs were still thick, my arms too wide...I bent my arms and held them at different angles, judging them from different views. Was that a little muscle I saw?

Flexing one arm again, I leaned closer to the water. Yeah, it was still thicker than Carlie or Jillian's perfect barbie arms, but it was a lot stronger than it had been a few weeks ago.

Veri's little hands and feet landed on my shoulder as he appeared next to the face in the reflection. "Whatcha doin?"

"I think I'm realizing I've gained some muscle." I turned this way and that, examining my legs in the reflection and then looking directly down on them.

Relief and excitement washed over me. I looked...kinda good. It was too much to take in all at once. As I traced my finger over my collarbone, it hit the scar running down my neck. The uneven ridges felt strange compared to the smooth skin around it, making me frown. But I didn't have a single zit.

The longer I stared at my face, the more unsure I became about whether I was technically pretty. I still didn't look anything like Jillian or Carlie, but they didn't look anything like each other either, and they were both knockouts. Turning my head slightly, I wondered whether the scar stood out more or less now.

"Veri, am I pretty?" I blurted.

He snickered. "Well, judging by how Shaun looks at you, I would say you are more than just pretty. As humans go, anyway."

I whirled to face him, mouth hanging open. "He looks at me like...like *that*? Wait, what do you mean? What does he look like when he looks at me?"

He held up both hands. "Whoa, whoa, *whoa*, now! I'm not going to analyze his every expression for you, Enzi. He just looks at you like...well, like you are a very attractive member of his species, I guess."

Shaun looks at me like that? Maybe since he grew up in Odan Terridor, he was never around women so he doesn't realize I'm not one of the attractive ones. But, what if I am now? He did say I was prettier than them.

And the way he'd made me feel that day and several times since, the fluttery feeling in my stomach...I certainly knew how attractive *he* was. And he'd done a lot to help me, even though he'd kidnapped me. I would have him do it again if it was between that or never having this adventure. If it weren't for him, I'd be home, studying for finals and working at the greasy burger joint, hopelessly attempting to save for college and bored out of my mind.

I should worry about college. And bills and the school I still have to finish and Mom. But I can't do anything about them at the moment.

I had to admit it to myself. I did have some kind of feelings for Shaun. They were less comfortable than how I felt about Gaedyen, more like an overwhelming blaze rather than cozy, comfortable hearth fire. It was too much for me to deal with. Why couldn't my heart just tone it down a bit, be a little more manageable? I loved Gaedyen. But what if...but it just couldn't be. That would mean he'd lied just like Mom.

At least Shaun and I were the same species.

I wasn't over the pain of losing Gaedyen. But I couldn't help smiling at what Veri had said. Right now, it was just enough to know someone thought I was worth looking at.

"Whoa now," he repeated, "I thought you didn't like Shaun with how much you frown at him all the time. Besides, what about that mark on your neck?"

My lips tightened. Was he saying I wasn't good enough for Shaun? "What do you mean?"

He lifted one brow, swooping his bangs out of his face. "If it isn't a battle scar, then isn't it a commitment mark? You know, like that you're...*engaged* or something like that?"

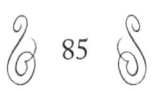

I scrunched my eyebrows. "What?"

"I think I heard that was a human thing, right?"

"What? No! Humans wear rings when they get engaged. They don't get a scar. Where in the world did you hear that?"

"Oh. Is it a Gwythienian thing, then? I can't remember. But isn't that what the mark on Shaun's shoulder is?"

My heart plummeted to my toes. Tattoos on Gwythienians meant they were engaged? Was Gaedyen engaged? *Oh my gosh.* But why would Gaedyen want his hidden? And Shaun's identical mark…

Were they both engaged? Were they engaged to each other, even though Shaun had claimed they weren't? Shaun did seem to know Gaedyen's thoughts.

Whoa.

"Enzi? Are you okay?"

"Yeah, fine. Just, um…waiting until you're ready to go shooting."

They were both more out of reach than ever before. But I needed to get over it. Fast. I needed to be ready if Tukailaan came back.

"Oh." He looked askance at me, unconvinced. "Then yeah, let's do that." Veri hopped onto my shoulder.

It didn't take long to reach the place. I still missed more than I hit, but even so I hit a fair amount. I remembered several days prior when I'd only hit the target three times. I had more than twenty hits today, somehow improving despite the distraction.

"Shimbators are supposed to have marks, too. I think."

My shot went way off course as the force of this new information knocked me off balance.

Veri eyed the tip of a sharpened stick, tapping the end lightly. "They're these shape-shifting things. I think they're extinct." He held the stick up to his eye, closing his other eye and staring down the length of the shaft. "We have some old stories about those things. Not very popular, though. We used to fear them because we'd never know their true form or where their allegiance lay. Some of us banded together to kill them off a long time ago." He blew off the tip of the stick and stood. "All right, let's call it a day. I'm bushed." Veri planted himself on my shoulder again.

Shimbators have marks? I hadn't seen one on Tukailaan or Tony, but I hadn't been looking for it. Could that mean...*Are they really the same? Did he really lie to me that bad?*

Well, how else would Shaun keep showing up right when Gaedyen disappeared? Was it possible? If any of the other realms didn't like Shimbators and had gone to the extent of killing them off, that could be why Gaedyen was so intent on hiding it.

"Uh, sounds good to me."

"Ready to get back to your man, huh?"

My face heated. "What?"

"He thinks you're *pretty*." Veri dragged the word out.

Did it matter? What if he was already taken? Or was he a Shimbator? "Knock it off. And don't you dare say anything like that in front of him."

"Sure thing. Oh, look! Blue fruit." Veri smirked at me, disappearing into the shrubbery. He came out with two pieces. "Here. Do *not* squash it this time."

I took a bite, and the tangy, slightly sour juice made me wince a little. But it grew sweeter as I chewed. It reminded me of strawberries and blueberries together, but better. I considered squeezing some of the juice at Veri just to annoy him, but I had to admit, he was right. That would be a waste of valuable deliciousness.

"How was shooting today?" Shaun sat up as we walked in, situating himself to lean against the wall.

"Enzi did a fantastic job! She hit a lot more than usual. Can't *imagine* what caused the boost in confidence." He looked dramatically at Shaun, then me, then back again.

I blushed, shooting Veri a death glare. *Now would be a good time to turn invisible.* I checked for a crack in the wall again, not expecting to find anything. But to my surprise, I found the smallest rift in the smoothness—a fingerhold.

"Nice job, Enzi." Shaun smiled at me, seemingly oblivious to Veri's teasing.

"Well, I'm going to go learn stuff from Dyn Meddy. I've been reprimanded for neglecting my studies. Catch you later." Veri leaped into the air and glided out the open door.

"You look happy today. I am glad."

"Oh, thanks." I awkwardly brushed some hair behind my ear, trying not to look like I was a million miles away, focusing on the crack in the wall.

"It is impressive you are making so much progress with the bow."

"Thanks." I smiled at him, then whirled around to straighten my hammock. The already-made hammock really needed straightening right then. Could I turn invisible in front of Shaun? Technically he already knew everything, so it wouldn't be a problem...

I wondered if he thought I looked good holding the bow? Or in general? If he even noticed. I wanted to focus on my invisibility, but there was no focusing with him watching me and making me nervous.

"I better help Veri find dinner. You know how he is. I'm really hungry. Be back in a minute." *Veri isn't even going to find dinner! What was I thinking?*

I ran out the door, trying to act casual. Leaning against the enormous trunk of the infirmary, I closed my eyes and found the fissure again. I focused on it, mentally clawing at it. And then, miraculously, I was through. I opened my eyes and looked down to see tree bark with no person leaning against it.

"Yes!" I tried not to be too loud, but I was too excited.

Where had Veri gone? He was supposed to be learning something from Dyn Meddy, right? I wondered if I could sneak up on him.

I walked through the ferns, a soft breeze ruffling my invisible hair.

Just when I thought I'd found Veri, the Crivabanian leaning on a branch in front of me turned to the side, and I saw his profile: shorter ears and lighter markings on his face. Not Veri. His ears twitched, as if he'd heard my approach and was waiting to see what he'd hear next. I stayed still as a deer, unsure whether this might be a mean one.

He faced forward again, but I couldn't see what he was watching. Clenching the fist that wasn't holding on to the tree, he let out an angry growling sound. In a flash he leaped up and raced toward me. Before I could duck, he was already flying past me, mumbling something about how they would pay for their betrayal.

Leaves and branches crashed against each other with the creature's retreat as I caught my breath and kept still. When nothing else happened, I crept forward to see what this guy had been staring at.

I almost fell right on top of them.

Dyn Meddy had his fists on his hips, watching Veri intently. Veri had a bowl-like object and a small, wide stick made of the same material, and he was pressing the stick into the bowl, grinding some mushy stuff.

Why was that angry Crivabanian spying on them?

"There you go. Use the mortar and pestle to release the juices. Then pour them out like that—no! No. Don't drop the skins, Veri. The skin of the berry is the part we want for this."

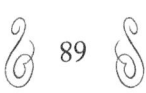

"Right, sorry." He carefully squeezed out the purple-black juice from the mush without losing the skin.

"Now, grind the skin even finer. Then we will put it out to dry and come back to it in a few days." Dyn Meddy carefully scooped his fruit skins onto a rock, then spread them into a thin layer with the pestle. Veri finished squeezing his out and then followed suit.

"Veri, how are you getting along with our visitors?"

This will be interesting.

"Very well. Humans are interesting creatures. I like them."

"Hmm. Have you noticed anything strange about them?"

Strange? Oh no. What's he figured out?

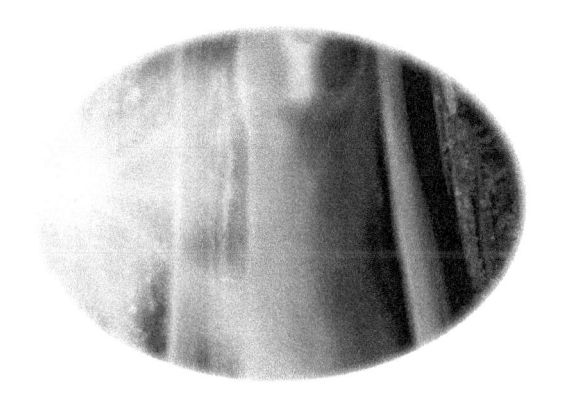

CHAPTER TWELVE

"Strange? Like what?"

"Strange as if they know more about our world than expected. Anything indicating they're more than normal, silly teenagers."

Veri's face remained comfortably focused on the task of spreading out the layer of fruit skins.

"No, I can't say I have. Other than the smell when we first found them. Probably due to their dire need for a grooming, I suppose. But nothing else. Why?" He looked up at Dyn Meddy with innocent, questioning eyes. "Have you noticed something? Should we be concerned?"

"You needn't be concerned, Veri. Just keep an eye on them. Keep them close to the infirmary, too. There has been some unrest…just don't take them out too far, and be sure to keep them in after dark. I want to do what's best for everyone, but if it comes down to what's best for some outsiders and what's best for our people, our people will take precedence. Just don't let that happen, all right?"

"Of course, Dyn Meddy."

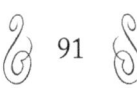

Dyn Meddy heaved himself off the ground. "I have other patients to attend. Repeat these steps for the rest of the fruit we gathered, please. I will see you tomorrow."

"Good night, Dyn Meddy." Veri sighed at the sight of all the fruit left to smash.

I tiptoed back toward the infirmary, thinking it was really nice of Veri not to tell on us. Maybe he was the one creature in the world I could trust. And he should know about their spy. But how could I tell him about that without admitting I'd been spying too? And that I'd only gotten away with that by doing something very abnormal for a teenager?

When I was far enough away and pretty sure no one could see me, I became visible again, then walked back to where Veri was still smashing berries.

I peered over a tall fern. "There you are. Need some help?"

He nodded vaguely. "Sure, thanks. You can bring me fruit from the pile and then spread it out after I smash it up."

I picked up a piece. "Veri…" I couldn't think of a way not to implicate myself and put Shaun and me in even more danger.

"Hmm?"

"I…I know Crivabanians don't usually sing, at least not for the Divinado thing. But do you ever sing on your own? Just because you can't help it?" That was the first thing I could think of.

He pressed the pestle against the mortar and ground the contents further. "Not really. Why?"

"It's just that I used to sing and listen to music a lot. I haven't in a long time. But I really miss it. I used to turn the music up all the way in my car, and I could sing as loud as I wanted without having to hear myself. I have a terrible voice." I smiled at him, feeling silly sharing all that. "I'm not much for singing when I have to hear myself. But I miss music a lot."

"If you teach me a song, I'll sing with you." He grinned.

"Hmm." I placed my handful of fruit on the rock. "Only if you promise to sing louder than me."

He laughed. "Deal."

"All right then…well…"

I searched for a good song to share with him. I thought of one I really liked, one only a few years old. It was a country song about the singer's Mercedes. It took a few tries to remember the words, and I totally failed at singing it for him. But somehow, he managed to pick up the tune, and by the second round, he was outshining me with his voice as much as he had with the stupid bow.

This had better not become a habit.

It had been ages since I'd cooked anything. Even longer since I'd seasoned anything. So when we passed a deserted market on the way to shooting after grinding up all the fruit, I went a little crazy.

"Why's it deserted? Shouldn't people be out selling their stuff, not just leaving it sitting around?"

"It's daylight."

I raised an eyebrow. "Yeah, prime time to be doing things. Since, you know, you can actually *see*."

"We're nocturnal, Enzi."

"What? But *you* do everything during the day."

"I was already somewhat adjusted to it because of how Dyn Meddy is about my apprenticeship. But I've adjusted more since you arrived."

"Why? Why not just make me stay up late and sleep in or something?"

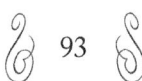

"Because you were sick and your body needed to be operating as normally as possible to heal quickly. If I'd changed your sleeping schedule, you would have healed more slowly. And for safety reasons."

Safety reasons?

"But if you're nocturnal, doesn't the sun hurt your eyes?"

"Not really. It can make my eyes tired after a while. But I drink a little mix every day that lowers my vision level so it's not so uncomfortable."

"But what if you're ever in trouble and need good eyesight?"

"The effects of the drink wear off after several hours. I have fairly normal vision again by evening."

"Hmm. Well anyway, I'd like to cook something for you as a thank you for the medical help and archery training. In my normal life, I'm a decent cook. But if the market's closed now, should we come back when it's dark?"

Veri's pleased smile morphed into a wince. "Um, Enzi, thanks, but remember how I told you there was a bit of resistance to Dyn Meddy's decision to allow you in?"

"Yeah. So?" I played dumb, not letting on that I'd seen that spy or heard his conversation with Dyn Meddy.

"So another reason we adopted your schedule instead of mine was to avoid the other Crivabanians. That's the safety reason. We come out during the day to shoot and walk around and all that because no one else will be up and about then."

"So if I went to the market, people would refuse to sell to me? Or worse?" I asked, as the ramifications clicked in.

"Yeah."

"But why do they dislike humans so much? Is it because of the helicopter crash?"

"Our bad history with humans goes further back than the helicopter crash. And grudges can be held for generations, unfortunately."

"But won't everyone respect Dyn Meddy's orders? He's the leader, isn't he?"

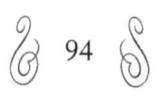

"Yes, he is. But he also has to take the Crivabanians' feelings into consideration. He didn't become and remain the leader for so long by ignoring their input. And a lot of our people are uncomfortable with your presence."

"But couldn't they just come out during the day and attack us or something?"

"Yeah, they could. That's always a concern. That's why we never go too far from the infirmary and only go between there and Dyn Meddy's home—it's sort of near where we shoot. The people have always respected him greatly, which is why there hasn't been an outburst yet. And why the other Crivabanians leave it at scowling at us from their windows. But it is precarious. We must be careful."

We might all be in greater danger if I don't tell him what I heard and saw...

"Veri," I cleared my throat, "when I found you grinding up the berries, someone else was there."

He narrowed his eyes. "What do you mean?"

"I mean I saw another Crivabanian on my way to find you. He was running away from where you were, saying something about paying for betrayal."

Veri rubbed his face with one hand. "Prinspur. He's the one riling everyone else up. I'll let Dyn Meddy know, but it's not a surprise."

"Oh, okay. So no shopping."

"No shopping *for you*. You can tell me what you want, and I can pick up the items."

"Fair enough. But I don't even know what kind of ingredients you have here…"

"How about I teach you how to make something. Like the bread and the sauce from the other day?"

I brightened. "Yeah, that'd be cool."

"Okay. Great. But we can't do it tonight. It'll have to wait for another day."

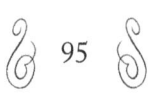

I frowned. "Why?" All I wanted to do was cook.

He smiled. "Tonight is a Divinado Legendelor."

"It is? So I can finally hear the whole story about the crash?"

"Yep. Though it's a sad story, so I wouldn't be too excited."

He'd lost someone in that accident. How could I be so thoughtless to get excited over something that'd hurt him? I'd have to hide how much I wanted to know what happened.

"Sorry, Veri, I—"

"Don't worry about it. Let's go practice with some moving targets. I bet I'll beat you by a lot." He grinned sideways at me.

I rolled my eyes. "I bet you will. But hey, how will I be safe at the Divinado thing? Won't other Crivabanians who don't want me here see me?"

He smirked. "Don't worry about that. I've got a plan."

We reached our shooting grounds, and Veri pulled our new *moving targets* out from behind a fern. They were bits of that greenish fabric, stretched taut over a crossed pair of sticks. We took turns throwing them, sort of like Frisbees, while the other tried to hit them before they ran into a tree. And Veri definitely beat me by a lot.

"All right, I've humiliated you enough for one day. Let's take a break."

I sat on the ground and leaned against one of the enormous redwood trunks.

"Enzi, I have a question about that song you taught me."

"Sure, what?"

"What's a 'starlet'?"

"That's like…an actress who's on her way to fame. Also a really hot girl that every guy drools over. And she has everything going for her in life."

"And that's what you feel like when you drive your Mercedes?"

I snorted. "No way! I've never been anything close to a starlet. And I don't have a Mercedes. Only rich people have those, dude. I drive a broken-down Oldsmobile with different colored fenders."

"Oh. So you didn't make this song, then?"

"No, of course not. A country music artist wrote it. I just like to sing it and pretend I'm her. Or not really her exactly, but someone who could sing those words and really mean them, you know?"

"Gotcha," Veri replied, and then seemed to be thinking hard. "You know, I bet Shaun thinks you're a starlet."

I laughed again, thinking of my new reflection. "Well, I am closer to being one than I've ever been before. All of this eating whatever I can find in the woods and running and climbing all the time really did my body good. I've never felt as physically strong and in control as I do now. That's pretty awesome. But still, I won't ever be able to sing that song and mean those words. There's too much else…it's hard to explain, I guess."

"You know what I think?"

"Do tell."

"I think you overcomplicate everything."

I laughed again. "Maybe so."

"I also think you're a starlet."

I smiled at him. A real, eyes-nearly-tearing smile. No one had ever said anything like that to me before. He was like the best of brothers. And his words warmed my heart.

"Thanks, Veri."

"You're welcome. Now let's go."

"I'll just be a second." Veri leaped off my shoulder and scampered up a tree. He'd told me we needed some for the sauce for the sandwiches, and they had to be from the very top. I wondered who'd discovered the leaves at the top tasted better.

The stream flowed nearby. I knelt by its edge again, willing my reflection to be replaced by Gaedyen's face.

Glaring at the water, I started from the bottom of the wall, searching for anything I could use to rip it apart. And then my mind found a change in the angle. Had I just found the bottom of the wall? Could I lift it instead of tearing through it?

I concentrated on lifting the wall instead of finding a crack. Maybe that would do it. I was almost on to something when ferns rustled behind me.

I jumped to my feet and reached behind me for a stick, but the quiver wasn't there.

Shaun's grinning face appeared in the dappled shadows of the trees around us.

"Oh my gosh! You scared me to death. Stop being so sneaky." I let out a frustrated groan.

He held his hands up defensively, still smiling. "Sorry." He sat by the water, and looking up at me with dark-brown eyes, he patted the ground next to him. I sat and folded my legs underneath me.

"So what are you upset about this time?"

"I'm trying to find Gaedyen in the water, but I suck. Some kind of Possessor I am. Can't do any of it right."

Shaun chuckled, leaning back on his arms. "You are too hard on yourself. You had an incredibly abnormal situation thrown at you, and you ran with it like a champion. That is something to be proud of."

Smiling slightly, I said, "Thanks. Did it ever bug you growing up with Gaedyen and not being able to do some of the things he could?"

"Here is a better question for you."

I frowned. *Never answers my questions...*

"What would you do if he came back?"

I turned to face him. "Is he coming back? Have you heard from him?"

"No." He gazed out over the shimmering water. "I was just curious."

"I suppose I might slap him in the face for leaving me."

Shaun chuckled again. "I guess he would deserve that."

"He would."

"Then what would you do?"

"I don't know. Something between another slap and a hug, I guess. Maybe run away and hide since I'm clearly not a good enough Possessor to be worth keeping around."

"He took you to Odan Terridor and Maisius Arborii. Almost took you into Ofwen Dwir. He would have if he could. And he brought you here with someone to keep you safe and someone to heal your injuries."

"Why are you always defending him?" I sighed and glanced away, knowing he wouldn't answer.

"Maybe because it is easier to defend *him* to you than to defend *you* to you."

I lifted an eyebrow and looked at him again. His eyes stared into mine, and he looked almost...*nervous? What could he possibly be nervous about?* "What do you mean?"

His eyes found the water again, but mine stayed on his face. "Maybe I mean I want to tell you what an awesome person you are. But apparently, I am not good at it because every time I try, you laugh it off or completely ignore it. I do not know what I am doing wrong. I just want to encourage you. I wish you could see yourself through my eyes, Enzi. You did not have to take all this—all of us—on, but you did. You did not have to leave everything you knew to help Gaedyen restore his reputation and save everyone from Tukailaan's wrath. But you did.

"You think those stupid girls I met that day are better than you just because of how they look. But you are wrong about that. Neither of them would have continued running hour after hour, day after day to keep up with Gaedyen and make it to Maisius Arborii in time. But you did. Neither of them would have made do with what food was available, or tried to contribute themselves, but you did. You thought you were weak, but look how strong you really are. And you think they are more beautiful than you."

Glancing down, he let out an awkward laugh. "See? You at least come up with something to say when I defend Gaedyen, even if you disagree. But if I say anything about you, you ignore me. I have seen you are troubled, and I know you have many things to worry about. But I want to help ease the pain and fear you feel. Perhaps I am just not saying it right."

I stared at the gentle water, not really seeing it, trying to process his words. He couldn't mean it. No one could mean that about me. Maybe some average guy, one day, but Shaun? No way. Not a tall, tan Adonis like him. But was I just doing exactly what he always thought I did? Did I really ignore him whenever he said nice things? How often had he said nice things I just assumed I'd imagined or mistaken his meaning?

"Shaun, I didn't mean to—" I looked up, but he was already gone. He was so sneaky! "Shaun! Come back!"

I jumped up and ran into the woods after him.

Reaching him, I grabbed his wrist. He turned, and I ran right into his chest. I looked up at him, and he had that look guys in movies always get right before they kiss the girl.

I backed up a step, my heart thudding in my ears.

"Shaun, I didn't mean to ignore you. I thought I was always mistaking what you meant whenever you said anything nice. I didn't think you could mean it like it sounded. I wasn't ignoring you, I promise. I just didn't understand."

"How else could I have meant it? Enzi, I…you mean a lot to me."

Whoa. Was he saying what it sounded like? Surely not… but I'd always thought that and apparently been wrong…I liked him too, but I still had feelings for Gaedyen, even if I was pissed at him. And even if he was saying what I thought he might be,

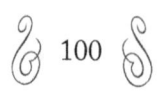

I was not relationship material. I wouldn't be able to be with him that way.

"Shaun, I'm not sure if I'm misunderstanding, but just in case, you should know there's someone in my past..." How could I explain without humiliating myself? But he needed to know I couldn't be the other half of a real relationship.

His wide eyes and slightly parted lips made something jerk in my stomach. Not a nice jerk—a painful one. As if I'd caused him pain and was feeling my share of it. And he looked as if I'd just told him I was in love with someone else, but that wasn't it at all. *Oh crap!* Could what I said still sound like that? I'd thought I might be in love with Gaedyen, but he clearly didn't feel the same, and I wasn't sure what I felt anymore either. I was talking about what Caleb did to my life. Had Shaun misunderstood me?

A moment later the usual charming smile was back in place. "That is great, Enzi. I am happy for you. I only meant I care for you as a friend, of course. I am sorry if I made you uncomfortable. That was not my intention."

"No, Shaun it's fine. I—"

"Dyn Meddy wanted me to return quickly. I am due for another bandage change. I will see you later."

As he walked away from me, that horrible feeling in the pit of my stomach grew. It grew until it was all I could feel. He really might have been about to say he...liked me a lot, or something like that. I'd just ruined it. And the truth was, I really did want to hear him say it. And I wanted to say it back.

Oh my gosh. Am I in love with Shaun too?

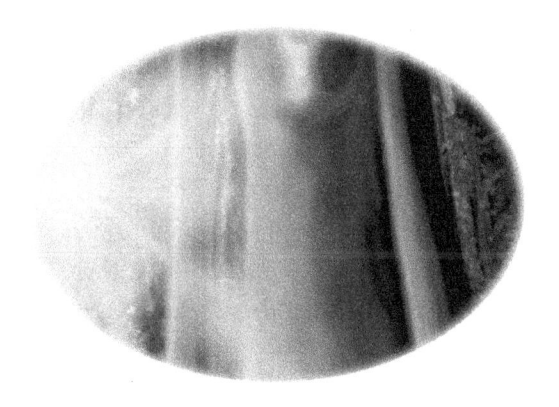

CHAPTER THIRTEEN

How could I have completely fallen for two people, one of whom wasn't even human? What was wrong with me? Why was I falling for people—and dragons—all over the place when I couldn't even be a normal part of any romantic relationship?

I walked back until the stream was sparkling at my feet again. Sitting, I dropped my face into my hands.

I'm a complete idiot.

Fern fronds rustled behind me. I turned, hoping and dreading that Shaun had come back. A small black-and-gray face peered at me from knee-level fronds. It scowled and disappeared again incredibly fast.

Before I could react, rustling came from above me. I glanced up in time to see a Crivabanian coming right at my face.

I screamed and threw myself to the side, scooting back, trying to get my feet under me.

"Calm down!" Veri frowned at me, fists on his hips. "What's gotten in to you?"

Shaking my hair out of my face, I got to my feet. I glared at Veri, still breathing heavily.

"What's gotten into me is you were just telling me how important it is to avoid all the other Crivabanians, and then you come falling out of the sky at my face, that's what. You scared me to death."

"Maybe we should go back to the infirmary."

"I thought it was the night of storytelling?"

"It is, but I don't know if you should be there. It could be dangerous. I hadn't fully considered the dangers if we were caught."

"But I need to hear that story, Veri."

He narrowed his eyes at me. "Why do you need to hear it?"

"Because it matters, okay? Please take me."

Veri frowned. "We'd better hurry, then. People will start gathering soon. We need to be well above them before they get close. Dyn Meddy could already be there, and if he is, all bets are off. And you'd better leave the bow. It will only get in your way."

I frowned. *I thought Dyn Meddy was supposed to change Shaun's bandage soon?*

"Sure." I *was* curious. The design on the tail of the chopper really had me stumped. It tugged at some memory, something recent, and I was fairly sure it had something to do with the whole rocks thing. And I had never in my life needed a distraction more than at this moment, after my awkward conversation with Shaun. "But aren't you going to keep me hidden somehow?"

He smiled, his eyes narrowing into that look that said he was up to no good. "We're gonna sneak you in."

My eyebrows rose as I placed the bow and quiver among the thickest group of ferns I could see. "How do you suggest we do that?" I could, of course, just turn invisible. But I couldn't tell him that. That would open up too many difficult questions.

His face broke into a sneaky smile. "Here's the plan."

Swarms of little gray figures milled around far underneath us in the limbs of pines and younger redwoods. I shifted my weight, trying to move my shin from where a broken branch jutted into it. Leaves rustled as limbs shuddered under my weight.

"Careful! Don't shake anything loose. If anyone looks up and sees us, that'll be really bad news. For both of us."

I blew a stray hair out of my face. This was Veri's brilliant idea: arrive super early and climb way too high in a tree. Wait a few hours till everyone else shows up. Listen to Dyn Meddy tell the story from a safe distance where no one could be upset about my presence.

Well. It was a good thing that flying with Gaedyen had made me more comfortable with heights. Not *that* comfortable, though. I tried not to look down—which of course, made my brain focus on exactly that.

And looking down was definitely a mistake. Suddenly the ground danced and wavered beneath me. My stomach felt like it was squeezing tight and exploding all at once—kind of like how Carlie described the moment going down a roller coaster to Jillian once—ages ago.

And it was super uncomfortable. Since this was so much higher than Crivabanians usually climbed, the branches were not well-kept. There were dead ones and broken ones, all jagged and pointing right at me. We'd been up here for ages, and I still hadn't found a way to get into a sitting position. I was too busy balancing and glaring at Veri for this horrible idea.

"Veri, help me out here. How can I get into a sitting position? This is super uncomfortable, and it sounds like we're going to be here for a few more hours. My feet are already going numb, and I'll fall for sure if I have to keep this up."

Veri snickered but directed me to a place a few feet over where there was a conveniently chair-shaped branch that Y-ed into a back support. As I carefully crawled to it, he skittered and glided through the branches around us. The trees shook ever so slightly as he frolicked around, making me more and more nervous.

"If you keep popping around like that, you're going to be the one to alert them. Knock it off!" I hissed.

He just chuckled and glided down to my now-situated shoulder. "Better?"

"Yeah. So what are we going to do until it starts? How long do we have?"

"I don't know. A little while."

"Can you tell me a story while we wait?"

"Tell you what. I'll trade you. A story for a story."

"But I don't know any stories."

He lifted an eyebrow ever so slightly. "I bet you know one or two." Hands on hips, he shot me a knowing look.

"What's that supposed to mean?" I hedged, though my heartbeat sped up a bit. Had I given something else away? Besides the rymakri, of course. Did he know what I was hiding? He at least knew I was hiding *something*.

"Do we have a deal?"

Ignoring my question...not a good sign. "Sure."

He nodded. "Okay, then. There's this one story, and, well... it always makes Dyn Meddy uncomfortable. People tend not to tell stories about this out of respect for him. He would never ban it or anything, but he is such a good leader, we give him the same respect he gives us. At least in circumstances that don't involve humans.

"There are...*things* in the world. A lot of things that are not common knowledge among humans. Things about the history of the realms. You see, there are other realms besides ours. Places with unusual sentient creatures..."

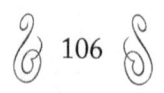

He eyed me pointedly, and I raised my eyebrows, putting on my best impression of never having heard any of this before.

"...and unusual magical objects. Long story short, there once was a set of rocks—one tied to each of the Four Realms—that helped keep the realms united. They're lost now. No one knows how these rocks came to be, but there are...*speculations*. Some believe they were each made from the right eye of the first Possessors. Others believe the first Possessors created their own rocks. But there is one other story.

"Some believe in the Cathawyrs, the Sky Leopards. Supposedly they are a greater race than any of the others, highly intelligent, with innate wisdom. It is said they live in the sky, somewhere above the clouds. And they can't die."

He looked excitedly at me, as if I were a little child believing his every word.

"It is said these beings were creatures of magic, and they stored their abilities and talents in objects like rocks. As the legend goes, they each made many rocks and stored skills in them they could extract for later use. But the females were more cunning than the males, and they made better rocks with better skills. Eventually only one male remained. When he died, there was no way to carry on the rest of the race. One of the females destroyed most of the rocks out of grief over the male's death, and then there was a great uproar over the lost rocks and who had really destroyed them. They ended up killing each other and ending their race. Supposedly."

My eyebrows rose. "That escalated quickly."

"Over the years, members of the other realms each found a rock with specific abilities, and each race embodied those abilities as time went on. Until now, when we each have specific gifts. But that's just one version of the story."

Pretending not to know as much as I did, I asked, "What other realms are there, and what gifts do they have?"

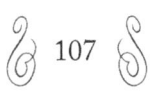

He gave me an eyebrow, and I questioned myself, wondering if I'd slipped. Again.

"You know our Gift is strength. The Gwythienians are able to walk unseen and sort of spy on other places through water. The Rubandors are giant salamander-ish things that live in the ocean. They use sonar-type abilities to find their way in the dark. Invisibility doesn't work so well down there. They communicate and find food and each other and stuff that way. And the Adarborians are kind of like fairies, but they have bird wings instead of butterfly wings. They can change their body size as needed."

"Wow. You guys are so much cooler than us boring humans." It was the honest truth. "So the story of how these rock things came to be…is it true?"

"Some say so. Really though, it's just a child's story. No one can remember that far back, and no one wrote down what really happened. At least, no one has found it if they did."

I remembered Gaedyen mentioning legends about great cats. But didn't he say something about there only being five rocks? Which one of them was right? Or were they both wrong? "I wonder what really happened."

"No one knows. But maybe we'll find out someday." He smiled as if he really believed it. "And you know, there's a rumor that one other rock, a rock with healing abilities, survived the great cat's grief and is still out there. That one has never been found. But I have a feeling it will be someday."

"Really? What gives you that feeling?"

"There is only so much Dyn Meddy and I can do with herbs and things. It's a lot, in a way. But it's not always enough. There *has* to be something out there that can *really* heal people. Besides, if I were a magic cat and could create a rock to store any ability in, I would store healing. Who wouldn't? It could come in handy so much more often than anything else."

What was with his obsession with healing? I mean, he was pursuing that as a career, but this seemed deeper. Maybe it had to do with whoever he'd lost in the past.

A glance at the ground revealed an ever-rising wave of Crivabanians climbing the trees. A few of them had bangs kind of like Veri's. One pulled a tiny mirror out of her pouch. She examined her fur style from both sides before slipping it back into her pouch.

I resituated myself, butt thoroughly numb where it rested on the branches. "Veri," I asked, "why do Crivabanians hate humans so much?"

"Another legend," he answered gravely. "Remember the fight between the Four Realms I mentioned before?"

"Of course."

"Well, some believe the humans were involved too. Some say one of the great cats came down from the clouds and drove the humans far away. There is evidence to support that's what excluded the human realm from receiving a rock. The humans were killing members of the Four Realms, especially Crivabanians, but not in fair fighting situations. They came after us in great numbers.

"While any one of us Crivabanians could hold our own against two or even three humans, our strength is no use against an arrow to a vital organ. And they skinned us, only taking us for our pelts to be made into fancy human clothes. Not for any good reason. Just to make money. Because our skin is very strong—practically impenetrable—and covered with soft fur at the same time."

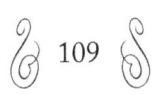

During our travels, Gaedyen and I had killed many fish. But we killed them to eat them, not for people to keep up with fashion. And fish weren't sentient like the Crivabanians. I couldn't imagine killing someone like Veri. He looked like an animal, and was in a way, but he was also a person. He was a living, thinking being with a sense of right and wrong. And my own kind thought it was okay to do that to them. I wasn't really that surprised at my own species. We humans do a lot of stupid things.

"Wow. That's horrible."

"Yeah. So that's why they don't like you. They're afraid I've been fooled by you, that even if you are just a lost human, with no intention of coming back to hunt us, you could accidentally reveal our location to outsiders. They fear for their family's safety, and I don't blame them. Our skins are just as valuable now, but we are safer now that no one in your world knows about us."

"Haven't you told them I'm not like that?"

"Sure I have. That's why they all think I've been completely hoodwinked. They don't appreciate my presence much more than yours now."

Was he saying his friends had all rejected him? That he'd given them up to be a friend to me? Before I could ask, Dyn Meddy called out from a tree on the far side of the clearing. He was perched on a thick branch several feet up.

"My fellow Crivabanians!" he shouted. "The time has come for another Divinado Legendelor. I can't wait to hear what you all have come to share tonight. Please begin forming a line to share your stories."

Bits of gray detached themselves from the masses and hurried toward his tree, forming a line up one side on it.

"Bee, of the Marin Family!" Dyn Meddy announced, welcoming another, slightly smaller Crivabanian onto the branch.

"I've never seen this kid before. Must be his first telling. I wonder what he'll tell?" Veri whispered.

Bee had his tail wrapped around himself and was wringing it with both hands. A nervous habit? Seeming to have just noticed he was doing that, he threw his tail down, squared his shoulders, and began.

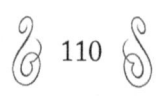

Long our people feared
The fiend, the dragon fiery
Who stamped upon our lands,
Killing many nightly.

He smashed and burned
And ate and maimed
The lives of our ancestors
And the great trees he claimed.

Eyes of lightning,
Breath of flame
The doom of all
From his claw came.

Then at last we rallied,
Our forces small but strong,
Every able-bodied one.
Our fighting knew no wrong.

We all leaped upon him,
Flying over his hide.
One alone not mighty,
Together a force unified.

Bee dropped to the ground and scampered away the moment he was done telling his poem.

"Was that one true?" I whispered.

Veri scrunched up his nose. "Yes. Though his poetry was terrible. But he'll learn eventually. I hope."

"Forget his *poetry!*" I shot him an eyebrow. "So there *are* fire-breathing dragons?"

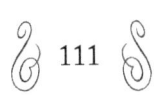

"Yes. At least there *were*, a really long time ago. That's the oldest story we know about ourselves. And even though it isn't always told well, the point is still there. Alone we are strong, but together we are mighty, as the young one said. A force to be reckoned with."

"Whoa."

After what Veri explained to be an appropriate pause, cheers and applause burst from the audience.

Then another took the stage. This one looked slightly older, though I was too far away and too unaccustomed to their features to be sure. He didn't share a poem, but the story was just as moving. It was about a young Crivabanian female whose husband died protecting her and their family. The enemy wasn't eradicated, but the next time he returned, weakened by his fight with the husband, the wife killed him, protecting her children. She never loved again.

There were several more poems and more descriptions of beautiful things than events that had happened. I did regret that none were told in song, though. That would've been a highlight for me. Even so, everything I heard was beautiful. So pretty that I closed my eyes to focus on the words themselves.

"Oh, not this one!" Veri slapped his face and drooped dramatically.

My eyes snapped open. "Why? What's wrong?"

"She tells the exact same story every time. It used to be really cool. But she ruined it."

"What's it about?"

"Just wait."

An ancient race,
The Arkensilvers.
Teeth in the night,
Eyeshine glimmers.

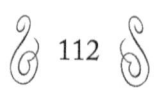

Fleet of foot,
Swift and clever
At fighting magic.
None were better.

Of all their weapons,
The greatest bane
To seal one's fate
Was the arkencain.

Projectiles of stone
And poisoned magic
Would end one's days
With pain most tragic—

"Blah blah blah, on and on. Basically they were great with magic weapons."

"Shut up! I want to hear this one."

"Boring!"

"Shh!"

And then it was over.

"You made me miss the ending!"

"Trust me, you didn't miss anything. You know how I told you about arkencains? Well centuries ago, getting shot with an arkencain meant you would be in tremendous pain for days, unable even to find relief in death until the weapon's magical process completed. There's even a legend that says everyone in your family would feel it when you died. Can you imagine? Horrible. But she tells it every single time, so it's lost its edge."

"Well it's the first time *I've* heard it. I thought it was interesting."

"Whatever." He waved my opinion away. "Hey, this is it! Dyn Meddy's going to tell the story about the helicopter crash."

"Oh!" I straightened, eager to hear what he had to say.

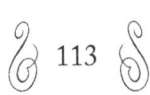

"Listen closely, children. I am about to tell you of the Night of the Greatest Roar. The night that more of our people were lost than ever died in battle, and the reason we keep the crash site sacred."

He bowed his head, steepling his fingers in front of him.

"In the realm of Odan Terridor live the Gwythienians. Once a great people, now an ignorant and thoughtless race. Many, many years ago, the Four Realms chose them to be the guardians of the rocks, and for one of their race to be the Keeper. But nearly two decades ago, they failed. A greedy Gwythienian wanted the rocks for himself, to have power over all the realms."

I stifled a gasp. They were talking about Ferrox. But what about Geneva? Wasn't it both of them?

"He found the Keeper's hiding place and stole the rocks, fleeing with them in the night.

"But something went wrong with his plan. Another Gwythienian came upon him as he fled, and the two of them fought over the rocks."

Was that one Geneva?

"When the second Gwythienian struck a mighty blow, the rocks went flying. And then the first interaction in years between a human and one of the Four Realms took place.

"A human, a soldier in their army, found the stone and took it for himself. Whether he knew what it was we'll never know. But one of the Gwythienians saw him in their witch's water, their way of seeing how they shouldn't. And so he went after the human."

My heart pounded in my ears. A soldier in the humans' army?

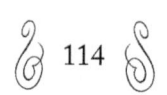

"But the human had a whole army on his side, and they sent a helicopter to fight the beast and save their comrade. One of the Gwythienians took the human in his great hands and flew into the sky with him. The helicopter pursued them and managed to cut off part of the second beast's tail, causing him to fall from the sky. He grabbed and kicked at the other Gwythienian and at the helicopter, but his actions only served to send them all crashing into our realm, killing many of our people including my parents, my wife, and my daughters.

"Then a third Gwythienian arrived after the second left. When this one, with two crossing marks on his face, saw the broken body of the first Gwythienian, he made a great roar, the likes of which has never been heard before or since. Though overwrought with grief at the loss of my family, I ran with our best soldiers to fight him, but the beast was out of control and nearly wiped us out with the massive sweep of his tail. He killed many of my friends. Before we could gather ourselves to retaliate, he'd lifted the broken one from the ground and flown off with it. And that is the last we have ever seen of a Gwythienian.

"The morals of the story are these: First, treasure those closest to you more than your own life, for you never know how long you will have with them. And second, never trust a Gwythienian. They are a greedy, murderous race, too big to notice what life they extinguish beneath their feet as they pass by. One day, we shall have our revenge. But for now, remember we've had bigger problems than a couple of visiting humans. And as soon as they are healed, they will be on their way. Until then, do not make of them a bigger problem than they are, I beg you."

But what happened to the human?

I probably knew. But I wanted to hear their side of it. And I suddenly remembered where I'd seen that image from the helicopter's tail before: plastered all over my father's hospital room. That was the shape he'd drawn over and over. He really had been attacked by a dragon-like monster! Even if he was crazy, he wasn't wrong about that. If only I could get him out of there, away from all the medications and treatments, maybe he could be normal again.

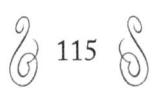

It was true. My dad had found the rock. The rock so close to being right back where this whole thing had started.

And I'd lost it. Lost it right to Tukailaan. Gaedyen could be fighting him for it right now. Would I know if he died? Weren't you supposed to be able to sense if someone was still alive if you loved them enough?

And it had all happened right here! That meant the other missing rocks could be nearby.

Just then, something ripped inside my chest. It felt like I was imploding and exploding at the same time.

I wrapped my arms around myself, shocked and confused, and I lost my balance. For one horrible moment, I swayed on my perch. Then there was nothing but the strange pulse in my chest. An awareness of Gaedyen pulsed there. It felt… powerful. And bad? Had he died? That would be more horrible than falling from the branches several stories into a crowd of Crivabanians. And as wind whipped my face, I realized that was exactly what I was doing.

As the ringing in my ears transformed into the dim crash of destroyed branches, I had less than a second before I squashed a few Crivabanians between myself and the ground. I closed my eyes, wishing to be invisible.

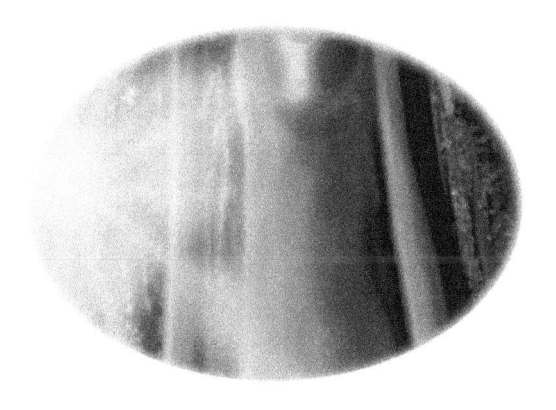

CHAPTER FOURTEEN

Small somethings bounced over my shoulders. I opened my eyes and saw brown earth stretching away from me into a tree trunk. Gray things scampered past. Crivabanians. The strange feeling on my arms and back was their feet as they ran over me. Were they trying to trample me? I lifted my arm and tried to push myself up. Was my brain broken? I felt my arm move, but I couldn't see it. But I also saw and felt a Crivabanian bounce off my arm into a leaping glide.

No way had I managed invisibility in that instant... But they weren't trying to kill me; they were running over me, gliding past me, as if I weren't there. I was on my stomach on the ground, and I lifted my head to look around.

How had I done it? Why had I...? *Oh.* My whole body ached as I suddenly recalled I'd fallen a very long distance from the top of a tree. I didn't know how I was still in one piece, but it should definitely hurt more than it did. Maybe I was in shock and the pain would hit me any second. *Does my body even still work?* I knew my right arm did... I tested the other. *Yep, left one too. Feet?*

Nothing. I tried to wiggle my toes but got no response. From either foot.

The Crivabanians were no longer bouncing around me. I could hear them, but they weren't close enough to see. Could I risk moving my leg without them seeing? Well, I was more concerned with whether it worked. Once I was assured of that, I could worry about witnesses.

I told the muscles in my left leg to tighten and pull my foot up. They didn't obey. Right leg: same.

Oh no.

"Enzi!" A sharp whisper. "Enzi! Where are you?"

"Veri?"

Another pair of little feet landed on me, hopped off, then turned toward me. The gray fuzzy body took a tentative step toward me, reaching out both arms like a mummy.

"Enzi? Are you there? Oh no, are you stuck?"

He couldn't see me. He landed on me and knew generally where I was, but he couldn't see me. How was I still holding on to the invisibility? Shouldn't I have dropped it when I passed out for a sec? I should let go of it now.

I tried to loosen that mental fist that kept a death grip on the invisibility.

"Wait! Don't move. Are you invisible? Don't show yourself yet."

What? He knows? Sluggishly, I tried to grab hold again. Somehow, I managed it.

"Good! Keep that up as long as you can. You must've leaned on a dead branch, because it went down with you. Knocked out a couple of Crivabanians."

"Oh no! Are they okay?" Not only was I not supposed to be here, I'd also announced my presence as loudly as I could, hurting some of them in the process.

Because something happened to Gaedyen!

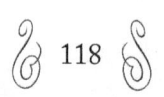

I closed my eyes and tried to focus on him. A tear rolled over the base of my nose, toward the ground. Something was wrong.

Had Tukailaan injured him? Killed him?

Horrible possibilities rampaged through my mind until Veri stirred me.

"Okay, most of them have left, but several look like they're staying to investigate. You have some serious explaining to do, but it'll have to wait."

I groaned. Oh yeah. I also just totally gave myself away. So many things went wrong so close together.

"Enzi? What part of you is under the branch? Stay invisible." He laid a gentle hand on my hair, bending slightly to peer into where he thought my eyes were. He was staring up my invisible nose, but it was the thought that counts. It would've been funny if I wasn't worried about Gaedyen.

"Branch? Is that why I can't move my legs?"

His brow furrowed as he leaped onto my back. "I think it's lying across your back. It's so big the others will notice when I move it. On three, I'm going to hoist it up and you're going to crawl out, okay? And then we're going to run for it because they'll know right where we are."

"I can't feel my legs."

Veri paused. "Let's see what we can do."

The sound of cracking wood rang out, and distant Crivabanian voices quieted.

"Three!" Veri ground out, and a moment later the limb crashed to the ground a couple of feet away just as Veri scooped me up and took off running like crazy.

He ran toward the infirmary. Shaun! Shaun would be there. Maybe he would know what had happened. They had some crazy way of communicating, right? Not that I really wanted to face him right now…

Just as Veri leaped up the steps, he froze, tottering to regain his balance. Voices came from the bright crack between the door and the wall. The injured Crivabanians! We couldn't go in there. I craned my neck for a glimpse of Shaun, but his hammock was empty.

Empty? Was he already rushing to Gaedyen's aid? And it looked like more Crivabanians were in there than just those few, all of them yelling about something.

"Change of plans," Veri muttered, ducking into the shadows. "Remember those berries we saw by the creek? He will likely need some for what he'll make for you. We'll go there."

Water trickled over rocks as Veri laid me down in the grass. "I'm so sorry we had to make a run for it like that. Absolutely unacceptable way to handle back injuries. I hope I haven't made it worse. But staying there…some of them were hurt more badly than I thought with all the falling limbs—I saw them in the infirmary. The more volatile would have had their excuse."

He tapped a foot on my spine. "Can you feel that?"

"Yeah."

"How about that?"

"Mm-hmm."

"And that?"

I hadn't felt anything that time. I was too stunned to reply.

I didn't feel him leap away, but the next thing I knew he was standing in front of me again.

"You need Dyn Meddy. This is beyond my skill, and I've already done enough damage."

"But that will get you in so much trouble."

"We're already in plenty of trouble. What's a little more?"

The sound of many small roots ripping apart met my ears as dirt landed on my face. I winced, turning away. "Veri, what are you doing?"

"Just in case you can't stay invisible as long as you need to. I've got to get Dyn Meddy, and I obviously can't take you with me."

"But he's in the infirmary with a bunch of Crivabanians I just injured! How're you going to get him out of there?"

"I don't know. I'll figure it out. Just stay here and don't move and don't make any sounds. Are you in any pain?"

"No. I'm just numb. It's like I don't have a bottom half. Veri, am I paralyzed?"

A pause in the rustling of leaves.

"Veri?" My voice had a shrill note of panic.

"I don't know. Dyn Meddy will know. I'll be back as quick as I can." And he was gone.

The moment he left, everything came swirling back. My rock started here. This was where my father had found it. Was this where he'd lost his sanity? If he actually had lost it. Was he normal until then? And Gaedyen…something was different. Something had changed. Something must be terribly wrong. And what to say to Veri?

A long while later, two dark figures glided into view and landed next to me.

"Where does the numbness begin?" Dyn Meddy wasted no time as the two of them cleared away the branches.

"Enzi, can you turn visible again? That would really help us."

"Oh, yeah, I think so." I focused on letting go of whatever my mind had been clenched around. "Did that do it?"

"Yes. We have to roll you over now, okay?" Veri gently put a paw on my shoulder.

I nodded, and the two of them rolled me onto my stomach. "Can you feel this?"

"No." My voice shook.

"Tell me when you can feel it."

A few beats later, "There."

"Hmm."

That didn't sound good.

"And this happened how, Veri?" There was a note of anger and suspicion in Dyn Meddy's tone.

Oh crap!

"She fell…"

"And ended up with a gash on her back as well? And nerve damage? Veri, what were you two doing out of the infirmary after dark? You saw the Crivabanians. They want to know why the two humans weren't where I promised they would be! Why they've just been crushed by a branch that…"

He stopped. I couldn't see his face, but I practically felt his eyes narrow at Veri.

"You let them come to the telling? You allowed her carelessness to endanger your own people's lives?"

Veri didn't speak.

"Where is the male human?"

"I don't know. He wasn't with us. We left him at the infirmary."

"I am mortified. And extremely disappointed in you, Veri. This is my reputation on the line here, not just yours. How could you be so foolish?"

"I—"

"Don't speak now. Go collect my mixing utensils from my home; it's closer than the infirmary. Just in case, you must be quick, and you must take a roundabout way back here—I imagine you might have an extra tail. I will gather the other ingredients here and stay with the girl. You must hurry. Our chance of returning her to full normality shrinks with every wasted minute. Fly!"

There was a clipped pitter-pat of tiny feet and then a slight flapping as he glided away.

My heart ached for Veri. Had I just cost him his apprenticeship? His place in the society here? Just how much trouble were we in?

Pains from my waist up began making themselves known to me. Assorted bruises. Some scrapes. I'd probably hit several branches on the way down, besides the giant one that had crushed my back. Lacerations?

Dyn Meddy ambled in the bushes, collecting berries. "How are you feeling now?"

"I can't feel below my waist. I'm worried."

"Veri will be back soon, and we will do everything we can for you. Do not worry now. It does nothing to help."

"Will it hurt?"

"There can be pain associated with restoring nerve damage—if we are able to. We will know soon."

It was hard not to worry when I had so many things to worry about. Questions tumbled around in my head, torturing me. Where was Shaun? What had happened to Gaedyen? Would I be able to walk again?

Before long, glass clanked together as Veri arrived with all the items. Dyn Meddy ran to him and laid out each piece of equipment, dropping bits of leaves and berries and who knew what else into different containers. There was shuffling, pouring, and grinding.

I remained still. I didn't want to mess anything else up. I tried again to shift my legs, just out of habit to see if I could feel anything wrong with them. My mind hadn't caught up with the situation, apparently.

"At least you managed to remember everything." Dyn Meddy growled. "How many came after you?" A mortar and pestle ground together, muddled by wet squelches. Were they grinding up bugs, too? If they were, I didn't even care. I just wanted not to be crippled. And I wanted to know what had happened to Gaedyen.

"Four, I think."

A small splash, then the clanking of a spoon on glass as it stirred liquid.

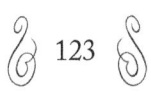

Two sets of small feet pattered toward me, then they were at my side. Dyn Meddy knelt in the dirt behind me, Veri right in front.

"Enzi, chew these berries and swallow them, fast as you can."

I opened my mouth, and he dropped a handful in. They were so bitter my eyes squeezed shut involuntarily as I chewed. Finally, I swallowed them, gagging.

"Good. Now, drink this. It won't taste good, but it's important to drink it as fast as you can, okay?"

"Just give it to me." I reached toward his voice with one hand. My fingers found a small glass vial, and I chugged.

A spluttering cough erupted from my throat at the taste. There were no words for the chalky, pukey nastiness.

Veri grabbed the glass from me, patting my head. "It's okay, just breathe."

I inhaled a deep breath, hoping to calm my convulsing throat.

A moment later I gasped. "It's tingling! I can feel it down my spine…it's traveling toward my legs!" The trail of pins and needles reached my knees, then my feet. Even my toes tingled. I tried wiggling them, but I still didn't have control. "Oh, that feels weird." It was the kind of pins and needles that hurt if you moved.

"What do you feel?" Dyn Meddy put a little hand on my shoulder.

"It feels like there's a stone inside my knee. My left knee. It's like…a lot of pressure building up. Now it kind of hurts—ow! Now it *really* hurts."

"The berries will help dull the pain, but this is an imperfect recipe. This is not something we have dealt with enough to have perfected the treatment. Your knee is out of joint. I wish we could've set it before giving your feeling back, but we couldn't risk jostling your injured spinal cord further. We must wait until it's completely healed before we set it. I'm sorry." Dyn Meddy laid a little hand on my shoulder. "But we are here with you; you're not alone."

I held in the scream that wanted to rip out of me. "But why can't you give me the stuff to fall asleep so I can just be unconscious for all this?"

"My people disagree with my choice to keep you here. While they thought you kept to yourself near the infirmary, they were willing to accept your presence, albeit temporarily. After tonight, however, they are ready to take action. They don't want to risk you two sneaking around, learning things about our home that could be used against us. And they have every right to be concerned, no matter how much I may have been willing to argue for your side. And by now, they've probably put together what really happened tonight."

What had we gotten ourselves into?

"So we must keep you awake because it would take too long to recover from the sleeping draft if you needed to leave on short notice. I'm afraid this is for your safety."

Oh boy. Just what I need. A whole realm of tiny hyper muscles coming for me. It's not like I have anything else to worry about right now.

"Okay, well I can really feel it now. Does that mean it's fixed? Can you set it?" I wasn't brave enough to risk trying to move a leg.

"Not quite."

My fingers clawed the ground as I held my breath, trying not to cry or scream.

I lost track of time. Everything whirled in my head. Eventually Dyn Meddy said, "Veri." Two sets of small, strong hands supported my left leg, and then a *pop*, and the pain doubled. I couldn't stop the shriek erupting from my lips.

Caleb pinned me to the sawdust floor, punching my knee when I squirmed. It hurt, so I stopped trying to escape. But I couldn't stop the tears.

I wanted to make the rymakri appear like I had before. To threaten him, to stop him from haunting me. But I was naked and weaponless, and so I remained.

"Stop crying!"

It just made the sobbing worse. He punched my knee again. The pain was so intense I could hardly stand it.

The pulsing pain amplified. Then my whole leg exploded into a million pieces. Bits of it hit Caleb in the back, distracting him for a moment. I exerted every scrap of energy to break free of him. But he caught me by the shoulder. Pulling me back under him, he grinned at my tear-streaked face.

"Enzi!" Something vigorously rubbed my shoulder, creating burning friction. A hand slapped my cheek multiple times. I blinked, trying to back away from the annoying contact. "Enzi! We have to run. They're coming for us *now*."

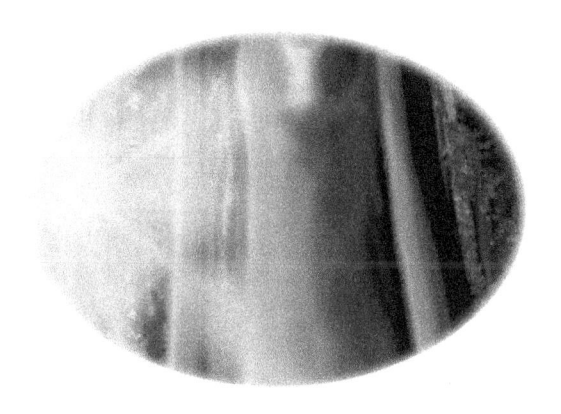

CHAPTER FIFTEEN

"I will hold them off as long as I can," said Dyn Meddy.

I exhaled, relieved he was willing to help us but also worried he'd be in danger because of our mess.

"But, Dyn Meddy, you will lose your position. They'll demote you…"

"I know. Now go!"

"Dyn, I'm so sorry. I never intended any of this…"

Dyn Meddy put a rough hand on Veri's shoulder. "I know, Veri. All there is for you to do now is run. Take the girl. If I find the male, I'll send him to you. But you must hide now! You're out of time."

Veri seemed unable to move. He just stared at Dyn Meddy as if he had something desperately important to say he just couldn't get out.

"It's okay, Veri. You made a stupid mistake, but it hasn't made me doubt what an excellent healer you'll be. I'm proud of you. Now go!"

Veri hauled me up and pumped his little legs faster than ever before.

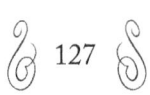

Every step jostled my back and my knee, and I fought hard against tears. Those berries were crap at pain control. Part of me wished we wouldn't have gone, but after what I heard…I needed to hear the story of what had happened to my dad. Yet there was still so much I wasn't clear on. Was it Gaedyen's father who attacked my dad and made him lose his mind?

Dozens of small beings crashed through the trees behind us, coming to an abrupt halt. "Dyn Meddygaeth," one of them called, "where are the humans?"

I woke up to roaring pain in my knee and the same uncomfortable pins-and-needles feeling all over my bottom half. When I opened my eyes, metal surrounded me. And it was at the wrong angle. Like I'd been in an accident with a flipped car. The helicopter?

"About time. It's been half a day. What is it with you and oversleeping?" Veri swung by his tail from the upside-down controls, fists on hips. His swoosh of bangs hung down comically from between his ears.

"Nice to see you too." I moaned, rubbing my eyes. *Gaedyen. Shaun. Angry Crivabanians.*

"How do your legs feel today? Can you move them?"

I tried lifting the one with the knee that had stayed where it belonged the whole time. And it obeyed my command. "Whoa! It works." I tried the other one and got the same result, though it was much more painful. "Gah!"

"All right, good. Now spill it."

"Huh?"

"Why can you turn invisible? What else have you been hiding from me?"

I glanced away, unsure of how much to say.

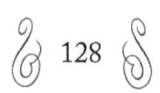

"Come on. I know something's up, Enzi. Rymakri, invisibility, gasping whenever I mention the Gwythienians. And you totally recognized the bow. And you both smelled like Gwythienians when we first picked you up. You might as well just tell me. I'm clearly on your side here. I just ruined Dyn Meddy's life and my own to save you, so you owe me the truth. All of it." He crossed his arms, pinning me with a glare.

He was right. And deciding what to say and not say was really more than my brain could handle at the moment. So the whole truth it was.

I sighed. "I'm the Possessor of the Gwythienians' rock." *Yeah, you know. Just gonna throw it all out there.*

Veri's eyebrows rose practically right off his head. For a moment he was speechless. He dropped down and crouched, arms still crossed. "Do. Tell." Leaning forward, he placed his elbows on his knees and his head in his hands, eyes sparkling. "And make it good. You owe me a story from last night, too."

So I told him how I discovered my old necklace was actually a relic from another world. How I was able to turn invisible with it and how Gaedyen had found me. How we traveled across the country and down into South America to find the Adarborians. And how Tukailaan attacked me and stole the necklace while Gaedyen was speaking with the Rubandors. How Gaedyen and Shaun were somehow able to communicate over a great distance and how Shaun had come here to keep an eye on me while Gaedyen continued adventuring without me.

Veri whistled. "Now that's the best story I've heard in a while. I'm going to put it to rhyme and tell it one of these days."

"Is that all you can think of after I tell you all that?"

"Well it's a darn good story!"

I rolled my eyes. "So anyway...about you guys not liking Gwythienians...is this going to be a problem? For us, I mean." Would it turn even Veri away from me?

"No. I've been thinking about how I'd handle something like that, since you've been so suspicious from the beginning and I didn't know what to expect. I'm not entirely unprepared. I'm just glad to finally know what's been going on."

"I'm sorry I had to keep it from you. I just…I didn't know if it was safe to tell you."

"And Shaun knows everything too, doesn't he?"

"Yeah."

"Hmm. I wonder where he is."

"I hope he's okay."

"Well, while we're on a roll with your spilling all your secrets, how about you tell me what's up with you and Shaun?"

I was silent, unsure how to explain any of it or how much to divulge. Scanning my surroundings for anything but Veri's face, I found Aven's bow leaning against the inside of the helicopter. I blinked. "What's that doing here?"

"I grabbed it on the way to you from Dyn Meddy's house. Seemed like we might need it. Changing the subject?"

I rolled my eyes. "Remember how you told me about Shimbators a few days ago?"

Veri sighed. "Yeah. If you want to change the subject that bad, then I'll just drop it. No need to distract me with crap about mythical creatures."

"Well, they're not actually mythical. Tukailaan is one."

Veri's jaw dropped. "Are you serious?"

"No, Veri. I'm making it all up just for funzies." I raised an eyebrow. "Of course I'm serious."

He made a face at me. "Well, that's concerning."

"Yeah."

"Hmm. But you *do* have a thing for Shaun?" He grinned at me.

I rolled my eyes. "All right, well, fine. If you must know, I'm attracted to Shaun. But I care about Gaedyen, too. It's complicated. And it doesn't even matter, because…some stuff happened a few years ago. Something I'm not going to explain. But I can't handle going through something like that again, even though it would be different."

"But you do like him."

"Yeah, I guess so."

"And he likes you too."

"I'm not sure. If he did, I ruined it the other day."

"Oh, he does. I can tell. But something or someone from the past is standing in the way of it?"

"Sort of."

Very smiled and cocked his head. "You're hopeless. He's a cool guy, and I bet he'd be good for you. Even though he ate a snail. You *will* have to break him of that habit, Enzi, seriously."

"Ha ha ha. Yeah, I'll get right on that." *If I ever see him again.*

"Good. I'm glad to hear it." Then with a huge grin, he said, "Enzi and Shau-un sittin' in a tree, K-I-S-S-I—"

I swatted him so hard, there's probably still an indent of him in the metal wall of that helicopter.

Laughing, Veri hauled himself up. "Touch-y!"

I glowered at him, crossing my arms.

"Well, dang. It must be more serious than I thought if you're this ridiculous about it." He kept his distance—a smart move—but he wasn't one to be discouraged. "Well, I'd offer you dibs on the first round of archery practice, but it looks like we're sort of stuck in here. Best to stay hidden till bright daylight, given the circumstances."

I huffed, glaring at him. "I'm done talking about this."

"Cool. Let's talk about our escape plan, then."

Dropping my face in my hands, I sighed. "Right. What did you have in mind?"

"I mean, if it was just me, I'd just fly from branch to branch as fast as I could until I was a safe distance away. But you can't do that."

"Nope. You're not Superman either. You couldn't glide nonstop. You'd have to take a break."

Veri threw a playful punch at my shoulder. "I'm just giving you a hard time, Enzi. We'll get out of here just fine once it's lighter out and everyone else goes to bed." His eyes narrowed as his grin widened to an epic smirk. "But seriously, think about it. You've never seen me and Superman in the same room. Just saying."

"Enzi?" A puff of warm breath brushed my hair into my face.

My heart stopped as my eyes widened. I knew that voice. My head snapped up.

A huge red dragon face peered through the open helicopter door.

"Gaedyen?"

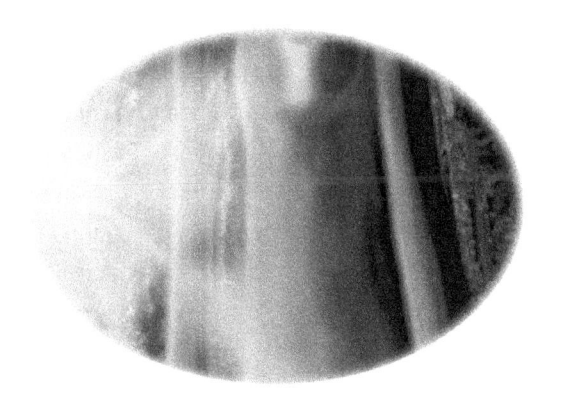

CHAPTER SIXTEEN

My heart resumed its erratic thudding in my chest, drumming in my ears. He was here. He was safe. He was alive. He'd come back! I felt so giddy I wanted to dance. An overjoyed smile lit up my face as I turned toward him.

He smiled back at me, and it touched my soul.

I wanted to go to him, to hug him hard, to know he was really physically there. But then reality came crashing back.

I've never seen you and Shaun in the same room at the same time.

If he was a Shimbator, and he and Shaun were the same, then he'd lied to me an awful lot. He'd only needed me because I was the Possessor. He only ever needed me for that, so of course he would only tell me what he thought would get me to do what he wanted.

Well then, I'm not telling you I've figured you out. I'm going to wait and see how much more of a hole you dig yourself into.

The smile melted off my face.

I crossed my arms. "So you left, and you didn't even bother to let me know you were alive." I glowered at him, lifting an eyebrow when he didn't respond. "Well? Why?"

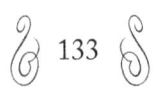

His eyes widened, and his mouth dropped open before he could control his features into his expressionless mask.

Out of the corner of my eye, I could see Veri standing a safe distance away, eyebrows raised.

"Well?" I repeated. If I had any patience for him left in me, I wasn't spending it on this moment.

"Do you not remember anything? How hard did you hit your head?"

A sarcastic bark of laughter escaped me. "That's what you have to say to me right now?"

"I saved you from Tukailaan, Enzi. He tried to kill you when he stole the rock, and I caught you before you could get hurt."

"You caught me before I could get hurt?" I couldn't believe him. "Like I wasn't passed out in the infirmary here for days and on medicine and treatments ever since. Good thing I had you to *save* me. Why couldn't you wait until I woke up? Why'd you leave me with *Shaun*? How the heck did he get here so fast? Huh? What is it with you two, anyway?" *Let's see he what has to say to that.*

"You were injured, so you needed to stay somewhere safe to rest and heal. But I could not leave you alone. I knew a renowned healer was in this realm, so I got you as close as I could. That was the best I could do for you."

His story matched Shaun's one hundred percent.

"Where even is he then? Your favorite human."

"He left. He will not bother you anymore." His face looked so beyond sad when he said that. It ripped at my heart a little. But I shut it off.

Yeah. Look all sad. You are *freaking Shaun.* "I don't have anything else to say to you." I spat. How could he lie so much about this?

"What more do you want!? You missed me, so here I am, and now you are ticked off I showed my face! You did not want Shaun here, so I made him leave, and you are pissed about that too. How am I supposed to give you what you want when you cannot even decide what that is?"

"Seriously? So everything's *my* fault?" *You chose not to be honest with me.*

I grabbed the side of the helicopter and hoisted myself over the edge. So what if a Crivabanian saw me and called all his friends to take me down. I had so much frustrated energy boiling around inside me that I'd welcome the fight. I could take them all.

"Enzi!" shouted Veri. "Where are you going? They might see you!"

I stomped farther away, ignoring Veri's plea and the throbbing pain in my back and knee. A few moments later, he alighted on the ground at my side and hurried to keep pace with me.

"Leave me alone."

"I care too much about you to do that, even though you are clearly an idiot."

I whirled on him. "What? How could you say that? I thought you were on *my* side."

"I *am*. That's why I'm telling you to stop right now and lie on the ground."

I paused and faced him. "What?"

"You're undoing everything Dyn Meddy and I did to your back. Do you want to be paralyzed for life? Because I don't know what happened to Dyn Meddy, but he won't be able to help you again. And I don't have the skill. So stop doing everything you're doing and lie down on your back so your spinal cord isn't irreparably damaged. Your body still needs rest. That's the only reason we're still in Sequoia Cadryl."

Scowling, I knelt and eased myself to the ground. Closing my eyes, I crossed my arms over my chest and hoped Gaedyen wouldn't see how stupid I looked.

"Enzi, listen to me," Veri began. "Gaedyen's right about one thing. You miss him, and you want him back. Then he gets here, and you are so pissed at him, he might as well just leave again. Then you'd be even more unhappy. You need to give the guy a break."

"Sexist!" I accused. Surely he was only siding with Gaedyen because he was a guy. No other reason.

"Seriously, Enzi?" He frowned, and I glowered back. "Look, if you don't go back and talk things out with him, he really will leave. I would if I were him. And then you'll be miserable again. That's why I'm telling you to get your sassy butt back out there and face him. Because I want you to be happy."

"Going back to talk to him would just make everything worse," I said, flinging one hand in Gaedyen's general direction. *He'll just keep lying to me.*

"I don't care. Do it anyway. You'll regret it if you don't. I'll be here for you if it comes to that, but I wish you wouldn't let it. For your own sake."

His eyes pleaded with me, and my determination swayed.

"Please, Enzi. It's not like you can stay here forever. We're on the run, remember? You need to leave, for your own safety, and here's your chance. It would be safer to ride on his back than to walk out of here. And I can't carry you for an unlimited amount of time. I'm strong, but I still get worn out." He whispered the last words, urgency on his face.

I sighed. "What am I supposed to say?"

"Tell him the truth. That you're mad at him, and that will take time to get over. But you're relieved he's alive and okay, and you'll listen to what he has to say. And then leave with him as soon as it gets lighter, because it's not safe for either of you here."

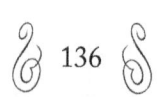

My fists clenched at the thought of listening to anything Gaedyen had to say. All I wanted to do was yell at him for what he'd put me through. To punch him in the face. But I had to admit, there was some truth in Veri's words. If Gaedyen left, I'd regret that. Even though I couldn't trust him.

I took a few deep breaths to calm myself. Why did this have to be so difficult? It hurt my pride to go back and be nice to him. It was more than he deserved. But I didn't want him to leave when we'd just spoken like that. I would end up feeling worse. Eventually.

So I swallowed my pride. Shooting a glare at Veri that turned into a look of concern and discomfort, I slowly got to my feet.

Veri scampered to my side. Taking hold of my hand in his tiny black ones, he whispered, "You're doing the right thing, not letting him leave. If someone's important to you, no matter the hurt, you should do whatever you can to keep them in your life. I didn't do that, and I didn't get the chance to make it right. But *please* take it easy on your back."

He caught me off guard with how serious and...*mature* he sounded. He must be talking about whoever he'd lost in the accident. How old was he anyway? I'd have to figure that out later. I had a Gwythienian to face.

I nodded at Veri and gently tugged my hand from his. I traced my steps back to the helicopter, mulling over and rephrasing inadequate words and sentences as I went. Why was it so hard to communicate with him? The words just wouldn't come. They were hung up on something, stuck somewhere in my brain, unable to find their way to my mouth.

"Gaedyen?" I called nervously, wondering if he'd still be here.

"Yes?"

I crossed my arms, shielding myself. "Well, what *did* you come back for?"

"I could ask you the same question."

Irritation boiled again. But I held my tongue and reserved my snarkiness for later.

I took a deep breath. "Answer me first, and I might consider answering you."

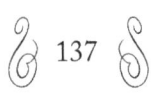

He didn't reply immediately, and I was about to demand an answer when he finally spoke.

"I am returning to Odan Terridor. There are things I do not know, things I need to discuss with Padraig. He is the only one who can help us with our pursuit of the rocks."

"So there's still an 'us,' is there?"

He ignored my comment and continued. "Now that Tukailaan has both the Rock of the Gift of the Gwythienians and the Rock of the Gift of the Rubandors…"

"He has the Rubandors' rock, too? How do you know?"

"Yes, he does. I spoke with the Rubandors, if you remember. That was right before Tukailaan attacked you. I never got to tell you about that…"

I wanted to remind him that was because he'd gone off adventuring without me—if he truly had—but I held in the complaint.

"Okay, so now we know where two of them are. Or at least, that two have been found. And we know who has them, not that it's much help. More disconcerting than anything."

"Yes," he agreed. "And that leaves two more to find."

"Actually, that may be where we are right now. I heard the Crivabanians talking, and they said it was near here the rocks were dropped."

"Exactly. But we do not have time to keep looking for them here. They could be anywhere, under years of vegetation. So I have come to the conclusion that I need to speak to Padraig. There are things I do not understand, and he is the only one who can clear them up."

"Okay. Are you going there now?"

"Yes, we both are. That is, I would like you to go. But that is up to you, of course."

My heart thrilled with the way he included me. I felt like he wanted me, like he needed me with him for the journey. But that only lasted an instant. I remembered I was the Possessor of his realm's rock. He didn't need *me*, he needed *the Possessor*. If he wasn't stuck with me, he wouldn't keep me around.

Why should I go with him, then? If he didn't give a crap about me as a non-Possessor, as just a regular person, then why not stay here, where I had a true friend like Veri? Where I'd been fairly happy for a while? Why inconvenience him with my presence? He knew where to find the Possessor if he needed her. And I would help him then if I could. But what was the point in accompanying him all the way back to Odan Terridor?

"What if I don't want to go?"

He straightened a bit, his face hardening. "You are in too much danger here. Tukailaan knows you fell somewhere nearby, and he will be back for you. Once he realizes, if he has not already, that the rock does not work for him, he will know you survived and will come for you and kill you. He will kill you, Enzi! I *will not* allow that."

My heart may have sung a little. But that didn't mean I was about to let him give me orders. "I'm not asking your permission, Gaedyen. I don't have to go with you if I don't want to, and no 'just trying to protect me' speech is going to change my mind. Why would I go to Padraig of all people? I mean, he's the most likely person to want me dead. He hates humans, remember? Why would I walk right into Odan Terridor to be killed by Padraig, when I can continue living here, hiding from creatures who want me out rather than someone who wants me dead?"

For the merest instant, a crushed, imploding expression filled his eyes, but it was gone in a flash. Now he just looked furious.

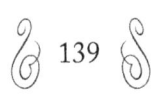

"Enzi, I will not let Padraig hurt you. Do you really know me so little as to think I would take you to him if your life was at risk? Once things are explained, he would know better than to take his anger out on you since I am going to admit to losing the rock to Tukailaan. He will know if he were to kill you, he would be handing Possession to Tukailaan. But if Tukailaan finds you here while I am not here to protect you, he will most certainly kill you. He has a reason. A much better reason than Padraig's revenge on the race who killed his wife. Once he knows the details, he will never consider it. And even if he did, I would fight to the death for you, you stupid human."

My heart swelled. Was that almost romantic? No, that was just me being ridiculous. Just hearing things I wanted to hear. He meant he would do anything to keep the Possessor of the rock alive. He wouldn't let anything happen to me while Tukailaan could Possess the rock.

Gaedyen glanced toward the sky, which was barely visible through the leafy branches. "We need to leave immediately."

"All right. Fine. I'll come with you on one condition."

"Which is?"

"Veri comes too."

Gaedyen quirked an eyebrow. "Why would you want the squirrel to come?"

I glared back with stony severity. "Because he's my friend. He risked everything for me, and I'm not going to leave him here to deal with the consequences. He's safer away from here. If Veri comes, I'll come. If you won't let him, then I'm not going." I crossed my arms.

Gaedyen opened and closed his mouth several times. "I really do not think—"

"There it is! I told you." A voice cut Gaedyen off.

I whipped around, hair smacking my face, to see where it came from. My heart stopped.

It was a Crivabanian, his accusing finger pointed at us as the crowd of Crivabanians behind him rushed forward. "Stop it before it takes off!"

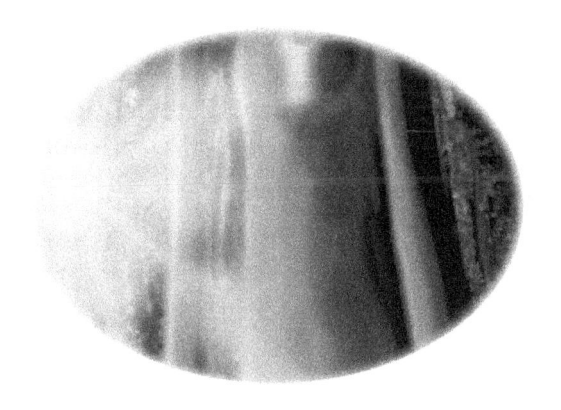

CHAPTER SEVENTEEN

*M*y world shifted as Gaedyen grabbed me by my Crivabanian clothes and flipped me over his head, like he had when Tukailaan had chased us in the rain storm.

"Wait! Don't leave without Veri." I searched wildly over his shoulder. But Veri had already leaped up Gaedyen's leg and latched on to the back of my shirt, my bow in hand.

"Hold on to me!" Gaedyen shouted as he twisted away from our company and darted forward.

How would we get through all the trees? He didn't have enough space to get a good running start, much less a takeoff.

He leaped ahead anyway, right into the thick foliage.

A pine branch smacked my face, nearly dislodging Veri.

Gaedyen's arm shot out and ripped a branch from a tree. He bit the end to a point and, eying me for an instant, tossed it to me.

"Veer left! And don't hurt the redwoods," Veri ordered.

Gaedyen grumbled, "It isn't as if any of this pine will be any good. It's too soft," and veered left as I fumbled with the rymakri, readjusting to its heavier weight and knife-like shape.

"Not that far left!"

I could imagine Gaedyen's scowl at being told what to do by Veri.

"Good, that's the way. Fast as you can."

"Oh, this is a situation in which I should run as fast as possible? Thank you for informing me. I had *no idea!*" Gaedyen growled.

The angry mob gained. I looked to one side, then the other, and they were already there, leaping from branch to branch. We needed to get out *now*.

"They're closing in, Gaedyen!" But he was already pushing himself as hard as he could. He limped slightly, and I remembered his leg injury from the rogue Gwythienian. *How's he able to run this fast with that?*

Ducking to avoid another low branch, I slipped and crashed against his bouncing neck. I gripped with my knees as hard as I could, hoping I hadn't thrown Veri off too. What had I slipped on?

Mud coated my hand. A wide smear of it ran across a discolored bit of skin on his shoulder. His mark. That he always covered with mud. Why would he take the time to hide it in this situation? It was different than before. Puckered scars slashed through it, and the mark's lines no longer matched up.

"Put that back, *now!*" Gaedyen's voice rumbled, and I smeared the mud back over the mark. Not that it'd do any good, since the mud was a totally different color than Gaedyen's skin.

Same location and condition as Shaun's bandaged shoulder. Same limp Shaun had. Mm-hmm.

A Crivabanian let out a battle cry and leaped from a tree directly at my face. It landed in my hair and pulled so hard my head snapped back.

"Ouch!" I reached back to swat it away with the rymakri, but it bit my hand. "Ouch!" I shrieked again, dropping the rymakri and grabbing at him to throw him off. But he evaded my grasp.

Gaedyen stumbled, and my knees nearly lost their grip around his neck. He overcorrected. I held my place better this time but screamed when the Crivabanian on my head swung hard to one side, yanking my hair with him.

A moment later, wild screechy noises came from behind me, and then I was free. I turned and saw Veri engaging the Crivabanian in one-on-one, dragon-back combat.

Another Crivabanian soared from the trees, but instead of landing on Gaedyen's back, it landed on his bad leg.

Gaedyen growled as it bit the tender new tissue mending his massive wound. The creature sank his claws into it next, ripping at the new skin. Gaedyen floundered, trying to kick the animal off while maintaining speed. I swerved, and the first Crivabanian gripped a tiny fistful of my hair again to avoid flying off. I winced as several strands were ripped out.

"How could you betray your own people? You'll never be welcome here again, Veritamyk. You will be an outcast forever!"

"Only Dyn Meddy has the authority to banish me. And I'm not betraying my people! I'm choosing to find out things for myself instead of accepting old prejudices."

"Liar! Cheat!"

Gaedyen roared, and I glanced down at his leg. I gasped as I took in the swarm of Crivabanians digging at the scars. What vicious little monsters!

"Say what you want, Prinspur, but I won't reject humans or Gwythienians because you say so. I will decide for myself."

"Where am I going, squirrel?" Gaedyen kicked out again, managing to shake off about half of the ever-growing swarm of furry beasts.

"Just a little farther! The twisted trees—*oof*."

I turned back in time to see the other Crivabanian land a punch right in Veri's face. I winced.

"I see it. We are almost there!" Gaedyen sped on.

Veri fell back, thumping limply down Gaedyen's back.

"Veri!" I twisted toward him, my knees letting go of Gaedyen's neck. Reaching as far as I could, I knew I'd be too late. He was too far back. Behind him a horde of angry Crivabanians surged.

I had to catch him! If he fell, they'd kill him. I pushed off Gaedyen as hard as I could, knocking the other Crivabanian off with my shoulder. It gave me just enough *oomph* to catch Veri's foot. A painful twinge shivered through my back, but I had to try to save Veri.

As soon as my fingers closed around his furry toes, my legs fumbled for a hold on Gaedyen. I nearly slid right off his tail but managed to hook one knee on his thigh. The motion pulled me down one side, and I almost fell under him. But with one hand I held on to the other thigh and kept a hold on Veri's foot, just as the two giant redwoods of the portal passed over us and we slid out of Sequoia Cadryl.

As soon as we were through, my body swung uncontrollably from Gaedyen's and crashed into the ground, dragging poor Veri into a roll with me. There was an earsplitting creaking sound, but all I saw was a whirl of ground and sky. And the twinge in my back erupted with such fiery intensity I couldn't move.

I faced the sky, and two giant trees plummeted toward me.

"Gaedyen!" I shouted, reaching for Veri and rolling away from the tree. As I tumbled to one side, I caught a glimpse of red soaring past me. The cracking almost deafened my ears. And then a deep reverberation rumbled through me as the timber bounced twice in slow motion before coming to a stop.

Ears ringing, I slowly sat up, wincing, and searched for Gaedyen. Seeing him running toward me, I turned to Veri.

"Veri? You okay?"

"What is wrong with you? I almost flattened you! You nearly died," Gaedyen hissed as he leaped over a log and tilted his shoulder down for me to climb. Blood trickled from his wounded leg. He grabbed a fistful of branches and bit three into rymakri.

"Pfft! I don't need to be *carried*." Veri groaned as I tucked him into the crook of my arm. "And what did I just tell you about my redwoods?"

I gave him the eyebrow. "Seriously, knock it off. It hurts, but I can walk. Let me carry you for a change. And all the gazillions of other trees in the forest are fine." I grabbed the fallen bow and hoisted myself over Gaedyen's neck.

"Claw their eyes out!" a voice shouted from behind us.

Veri peered out from my arm. "Fly, Gaedyen! Get to the sky as fast as you can."

Gaedyen tossed the new rymakri at me and lurched forward, galloping over the long, fallen trunks.

"I'll fight for you, but I've seen you fight for yourself, too. So quit losing these and put them to good use!" Gaedyen shouted at me.

He was right. I could use these. I wasn't the helpless girl from a few weeks ago. I squeezed with my knees as hard as I could, cradled Veri in one arm, and twisted around.

Angry Crivabanians poured out of the broken portal, and they were gaining fast.

They raced through the trees on either side of us again. There wasn't enough open space for Gaedyen to get air.

"You're going to have to burst through the branches, Gaedyen!" shouted Veri. "The trees don't thin out any time soon."

Gaedyen bounded forward, stretching his wings as much as he could between leafy branches.

Twigs snapped as he ploughed through them. Keeping Veri tucked in one arm, I curled over him and leaned as low over Gaedyen as I could while still keeping an eye on approaching enemies. Little cuts burned all over my hand and arm as they withstood the onslaught of branches.

One Crivabanian—*Prinspur?*—was gaining the fastest. I aimed and threw a rymakri at him. Throwing from the back of a moving Gaedyen was about as easy as thoroughly cooking a chicken breast over a stove that randomly shuts off every couple of minutes. The rymakri veered off course and hit a branch in front of my target. The rymakri flailed in the air and its shaft smacked Prinspur right in the face, toppling him off the limb and knocking him out of view. I smiled, satisfied, and I hefted another, searching for my next target.

Gaedyen seemed to finally take Veri's advice. With a lurch that almost knocked me off, he leaped into the boughs above us and straight into another tree a little higher. Limbs and tall, skinny trunks cracked and broke under our weight.

Gaedyen pushed off above the trees, flapped madly, then finally leveled off. The sun blinded me when we emerged into the bright blue sky. Once again, we soared through midair. I faced its yellow warmth with eyes closed, drinking it in and letting my eyes adjust. The air was fresh and cool.

Veri recovered himself enough to crawl around me and hang on to the back of my shirt. He was still a bit shaky, though, which made me nervous.

My stomach lurched as I peered over Gaedyen and took in how high we were. Angry Crivabanians railed at us from the tops of trees, shaking their fists and screeching.

"That was close!" Veri shouted above the wind.

My stomach plummeted as Gaedyen banked left. I'd have to get used to that again. But the feeling of freedom was worth it.

I wanted to sing with joy for being so free again, but the adrenaline rush blocked lyrics from my head. I focused on hanging on for dear life.

Veri shouted from behind me, "This. Is. Awesome!"

Hanging on with my knees, I turned to see Veri standing on two legs and gripping the back of my Crivabanian tank top. I grinned at him, glad he was enjoying himself. The way the wind blew out his gliding sides made me nervous though—a strong enough gust could blow him right off. But at least he could glide safely if something like that happened. If *I* lost *my* seat, it would be a freefall toward two-dimensional existence.

When we landed for the night, I decided I would volunteer to bring home the meat this time. Frustrated as I was with some of Gaedyen's decisions, he *had* just saved our lives. And I owed him a few meals anyway. Plus, I was anxious to try out my skill at hunting with the bow, since I'd done all right with moving targets in Sequoia Cadryl. I wanted to prove to Gaedyen I was somewhat self-sufficient. At least more so than last time we'd traveled together. And knowing I was better at Arunca Rymakri than Shaun was a plus. *Ugh. Hard to reconcile in my head that they are the same.*

I slid off Gaedyen's back and stretched carefully. My back didn't protest, just felt a little sore. "I should be able to find food for the night. You rest, Gaedyen. You've done a lot for one day."

"Would you like a few rymakri?"

"Yeah, thanks."

He struck the blunt end of each rymakri over one pointed tooth, creating a crevice for the string of the bow.

That was considerate of him. I accepted the weapons and ducked under a tree.

I managed to hit one rabbit—only because its back leg had already been broken. I also managed to frighten a squirrel into falling from its branch. The landing knocked it out hard enough that I was able to finish the job. I speared its neck with one of the rymakri so it would look like I'd shot it fair and square. My stomach squelched with guilt over the lie and remorse over the poor creature as I remembered how I'd felt falling from the tree in Sequoia Cadryl.

At least I was doing my share of providing the food. That was something. It reminded me of the last time I'd hunted for us and caught a single fish. I hauled my prey up by the tail and ears respectively and stomped back to them.

When Gaedyen caught sight of me, he brightened.

"Nicely done, Enzi. You must have spent a lot of time practicing. It shows."

A warmish feeling sprouted in my middle but was immediately squished by the truth of how I'd really managed to catch dinner.

"Uh, thanks," I stammered. "Sorry it's not much..." I clumsily held the rabbit toward him. It was embarrassingly gnarly-looking, with the one leg already dangling and the dried blood smearing into clumps of fur near the wounds I'd inflicted.

But Gaedyen reached out with one giant, reptilian hand and took it gently from me. When his large hand touched mine, the contact made me shiver.

Tossing the raw carcass into his mouth, he chewed, swallowed, and said, "Thank you. That was delicious."

"Sure thing. Thanks for the rymakri."

Veri piped up as well. "Yeah, Enzi, good aim! Remind me not to get on your bad side."

I managed a smile at the ever-cheerful little fuzzbucket. "Thanks. How's your head feeling?"

"Totally fine." He made a broad sweeping gesture with one hand, as if to encompass how perfectly fine he was. The kind of thing people did when they weren't really fine at all.

Shooting him the eyebrow, I made a mental note to keep a close eye on him.

I sat and prepared my catch to roast. Not something I really wanted to watch. "Gaedyen, do you remember telling me the legends in your realm about the Sky Leopards?"

"Yes."

"Well, I asked Veri about the stories and legends among his people, and he spoke of the same beings. But you guys have different stories about them."

"Oh?"

"Yeah. You say they created the rocks and gave them to each of the realms, and the realm's inhabitants took on the gifts that each realm's Cadoumai already had. But Veri says they created many different rocks, and although most of them were lost, each group found one rock each and took on the qualities of the rock's stored ability. So I wonder whether the rocks gave the realms their abilities, or did they get their powers from the realms?"

"It happened so long ago, no one can really be sure what actually happened. But it is interesting to hear another perspective."

"Someone's going to figure it out someday," Veri said, curling up near the fire.

I glanced at Gaedyen's side, wishing I could curl up there. It was cold, and I missed how he used to wrap a wing around me to keep me warm while I slept. But it felt weird with Veri. And wasn't I supposed to still be mad at him about leaving and everything?

Maybe if we could just talk it out, we could put it behind us and things could go back to normal. Maybe?

I hesitated, debating.

Should I go over to him or talk to him across the fire? It's really cold. But I don't know if we're on good enough terms to share personal space. Maybe I should grow up and just go sit right next to him and tell it exactly like it is.

He'd lied to me about Shimbators, telling me they were a myth. He needed a butt-whooping for that. But I missed him. It could never be like I wanted it to be, but it could be better than this.

That's exactly what I'm going to do.

I pushed myself up and rounded the fire toward Gaedyen. He lifted his head and watched me approach, eyes widening slightly as I leaned against his shoulder and slid down. Pulling my knees to my chest, I wrapped my arms around them. No need to be completely open about this bravely-entering-personal-space thing.

"So, Gaedyen." I glanced at him as surprise flickered in his eyes.

"Yes?"

"I think we should talk out our differences so we can be back to normal again."

"Okay. I will do what I can, though it may not be enough. But I would like to be back to how we were."

"Well, let's just lay it all out there, okay? You left me alone in the woods to go on adventuring without me, and stayed gone for a couple of weeks with no communication. I have so many problems with that."

His face drooped, eyes hardening. "I am sorry I was not able to handle the situation differently."

"So why'd you leave me? How were you able to get Shaun there so quickly? Why him? What was so important you had to do it alone?" *Let's see what he says to that.*

"I cannot tell you, Enzi, I am sorry."

I glared at him, hiding how much the rejection hurt. "Why not? What happened to us making this journey together? I needed you, and you needed me too. But then you just left."

"I did not have anything to write on, and I could not leave word with the Crivabanians. They do not appreciate my kind, as you just discovered."

"Why does it have to be a secret, though? I know about the rocks, Tukailaan—heck, I was almost killed by him! I am as invested in this thing as you are, Gaedyen. Why can't you explain?"

"I just cannot. Please stop asking."

I dropped my head into my hands. Why did he have to be so secretive?

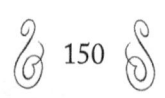

Well, either way, it was cold. I was staying right here for the night.

When he slid his wing out from behind me and gently laid it over my shivering body, my heart lurched, and I squeezed my eyes shut. *Why does he keep pulling me one direction and then pushing me the other? I wish this didn't have to be so hard. What in the world do I really want?*

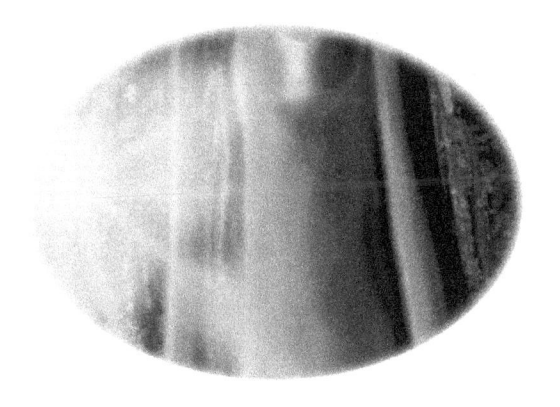

CHAPTER EIGHTEEN

*L*eaning over the stream early the next morning, I stared at my reflection. Getting visibly stronger was cool, but I wished it didn't have to mean feeling more afraid of catching Caleb's eye. I needed to get a lot better at defending myself before going back to my regular life.

Touching my cheek, I pulled the skin back a bit, making it taut. It contorted my face, so I let it go.

Something rippled under the surface. I focused on the water through my reflection, and an image seemed to flicker there. Remembering how I'd thought of going under the wall to see through water before my embarrassing conversation with Shaun, I gave it another try. The something became a little clearer.

Oh wow! Am I finally seeing through the water? How do I look for Mom?

But it wasn't a scene that rippled into focus. It was feline-shaped whiteness. With eyes. My jaw dropped. A Cathawyr?

She nodded at me, then reached out one paw and beckoned.

Was I going insane? It seemed like she wanted me to go into the water. Could I trust her?

She beckoned again, then looked beyond me, over my shoulder. I turned to see what she was looking at, but there was nothing. When I looked back, just blue sky remained in the reflection.

Had she really been there?

"Someone is approaching!" Gaedyen called, pacing toward me. I followed his upward gaze.

Three little green shimmers appeared, heading past us. But suddenly they changed direction and flashed toward us. A moment later they grew into green-winged humanoids.

Adarborians?

"I should strike you down immediately, Gwythienian!" one of the females yelled from the sky.

That doesn't sound good.

Gaedyen positioned himself in front of me, tossing two rymakri over his shoulder. It was nice of him to protect me, but it was even better that he trusted me with rymakri to fight for myself, too.

"Why would you wish to do that?" Gaedyen snarled, muscles tensing.

His tone seemed more confrontational than I'd expected. "Shouldn't we be nice to them so they don't feel the need to strike us down?" I hissed.

They landed, assuming fighting stances, but they remained several yards away.

I glanced around for Veri and found him observing from a tree branch nearby, ready to jump into action.

Good, they hadn't seen him yet. Maybe he could surprise them, if necessary. Or at least get away alive.

"Tukailaan has an arkencain. He hit Aven with it and fled shortly after you left. You would not happen to know anything about that, would you?"

"No, I certainly would not! I thought the arkencains were all destroyed? How is Aven?"

The female scowled at him. "No one can survive the poison of this weapon. Aven is dying as we speak. And even worse, Tukailaan may have our rock! When Aven dies, Possession could pass to him. I supposed he hasn't gotten yours?" She glared at Gaedyen.

"Unfortunately, he has. He took ours soon after Aven left us at the entrance to Ofwen Dwir."

The Adarborian tore one hand dramatically over her face and through her hair. "How could you let that happen? How many other rocks does he have with him, just waiting to be Possessed? Thanks to you and your parents, the Betrayers of the Realms."

"Gaedyen doesn't deserve blame for what his parents did." I stepped forward and stood by his shoulder. "What's being done about the situation? What are all of you doing here? Shouldn't you all be with Aven in Maisius Arborii?"

She scowled at both of us. "As if it is any business of *yours*. We are going to Sequoia Cadryl to seek out their Possessor and healer, Dyn Meddygaeth. Our healers have done all they can, but she is beyond our skill now. Dyn Meddygaeth's healing is renowned throughout all the realms.

"If it were not for the urgency of our mission, I would subject you both to further questioning. I have good reason to believe it was one of you who told Tukailaan how to get in. How else could he have known? But we must continue. There is no time to waste. Aven is coming behind us with a transport of Adarborians. We must hurry to retrieve Dyn Meddygaeth and meet Aven before it is too late."

The female glared at me for a moment, then Gaedyen. "I warn you both that should we meet again, you'll not escape my wrath so easily."

With a glare, she launched toward the sky and stretched her glorious green wings to the sun. An instant later her whole escort was in the air, pumping their wings to gain altitude.

They all shrank to fairy-size, disappearing on the breeze.

Gaedyen sagged. "I cannot believe he has an arkencain. It just keeps getting worse. It is really happening. He is killing Possessors now. Now he has our rock, the Rubandors', and probably the Adarborians'. For all I know he has the Crivabanians' rock too. We were too late."

Veri stared down at us from leafy branches. "I don't think there's anything else Dyn Meddy can do. I've seen him do a lot of things, and I know how he does a lot of them with herbs and all that, but I don't think an arkencain wound is something he can fix."

If only there were some other way to heal her. A magic healing for a magic wound. That gave me an idea.

"Gaedyen, you said the Cathawyr may still be alive, right?"

His brows furrowed. "What does that have to do with this situation?"

"Veri, you really believe in the fifth rock, don't you?"

He glided from the tree to land on my shoulder. "Yeah, absolutely. So?"

I hoped they'd give me a chance even if I sounded like a complete lunatic. "Right before the Adarborians approached, I was able to see into the water."

Gaedyen's tense features loosened a little. "That is great news, Enzi. Well done!"

"Thanks." I winced. "But what I saw was *not* what you'd expect."

He watched me expectantly.

"It was a Cathawyr."

"What?" Veri leaped closer to me, a huge grin on his bright face.

"It sounds crazy, but what if we were able to find the Cathawyr and get that rock of healing from them? What if we could bring it back to save Aven? Or if it has a Possessor, we could get the Possessor to come heal her."

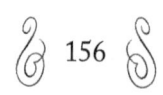

156

"It *is* farfetched, but it might be the only chance Aven has and a great way to hold Tukailaan off a little longer. But we must go to Odan Terridor first."

"Why?" Veri challenged.

"Because Tukailaan knows how to enter Odan Terridor, so he is probably headed there next. And he has a huge head start. I do not mean to be insensitive, but Aven has already been struck and is at great risk of dying. Padraig has not yet been struck as far as we know, and if we are wrong about the Cathawyr and the fifth rock, we are better off saving him instead of letting him get struck with the same fatal wound Aven already suffers from."

Why did my mind have to agree with him? It was too logical, too cold and calculating. I didn't want to think like that, like they weren't even people with feelings and fears. Like they were just livestock and it was better to let the wolves have one than risk losing another.

Disgusted with myself, I nodded.

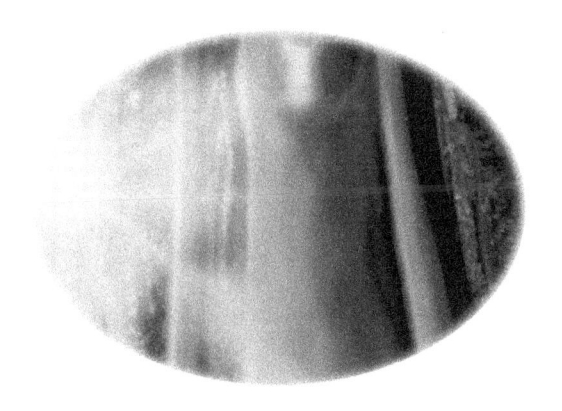

CHAPTER NINETEEN

We stopped late that night, and this time Gaedyen caught a deer. He must've been pretty hungry after my one pitiful rabbit. He tore off a few bits for me to roast for myself, then he ate the rest raw. Veri satisfied himself with some berries.

"Veri, want to try some of this?" I held a piece out to him.

He hopped over and gave it a long, exaggerated sniff. "Nope. Vegetarian."

I shrugged and bit off another chunk. Veri popped another berry into his mouth, a drop of purple juice sticking to the fur around his lips.

"Gaedyen, how far are we from Odan Terridor?"

"About a day and a half."

A day and a half, and I would be in the same state as my mom again. Would I get the chance to ask her about Dad or about her fear of water?

"I found out what Aven was talking about," Gaedyen said.

My eyes flashed to him. The secret she'd whispered to him that he'd refused to share with me. Was he finally going to explain it?

"Remember the part about the fire water from the liryk she gave us?"

Oh, that. How could I not have thought to ask him about the Rubandors yet? Well, we *had* been a bit busy since he'd come back.

"Oh my gosh, Gaedyen. Tell me everything about the Rubandors. What's the fire water?"

"The Rubandors have a network of bright-red gills floating around right outside their heads. Their shape and color are what make it look like the water is on fire when they are all swishing around."

Fascinated, I scrunched my nose. "Weird."

"Yes. Anyway, once I finally got into the realm, they found me with their sonar abilities. I had been so long without oxygen that I had passed out."

I gasped. "Oh no!" He really had almost died!

"But I was fine. They took me to an atmosphere chamber, and I woke shortly after they bound my legs. They told me another Gwythienian had visited, bearing a mangled tail and claiming knowledge of their rock. He warned them a Gwythienian Possessed it now, one who would be coming to terrorize them soon. So naturally they assumed the terror was me. They finally released me once I convinced them of my quest's importance."

"Tukailaan. No surprise."

"Indeed. It seems he may have killed the Rubandor Possessor. So I assume he must have taken Possession of their rock as we feared. But more disturbing is the murderous wound. According to them, from an arkencain."

"He's out to kill us all now." Until the words tumbled out of my mouth, I hadn't identified with the other Possessors. Yes, I was the Possessor of the Gwythienians' rock, but not one of the Possessors. I was outside the group. On the edge.

But Tukailaan didn't make the same distinction. He needed to end my life with the arkencain, too.

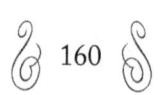

"He always has been. The difference now is he has a formidable weapon."

I didn't want to die. But I especially didn't want to experience the slow death of arkencain poison running through my veins.

Gaedyen landed heavily, his bad leg still troubling him.

We entered near a different opening than the one we'd left through, just in case Tukailaan still monitored the blocked-off part.

"Do not be afraid, Enzi. I promise to defend you no matter what happens."

Yeah, I came, so you'd better. I stepped into the tunnel's opening. "Thanks, Gaedyen. Let's go."

"Wait." Gaedyen's huge hand brushed my arm, halting me.

I turned to him. "What?"

He reached up and ripped a branch from a tree. Breaking the limb in two, he bit one end of each to a point and passed them both to me. "Just in case. Since you know how to use them now."

Gratified, I took the rymakri with a small smile.

With Veri on my shoulder and Gaedyen in the lead, we ducked inside. The moist earth smelled rich and warm, and the strange light shone blue.

This tunnel led to a root ceiling instead of the dirt-and-stone floor I was expecting. Gaedyen guided us through the roots to another opening in the stone. We followed it at a sharp decline until it opened to a dirt floor. A high wall continued from the tunnel around a curve, like a room we were outside of. Two voices argued on the other side, one male and one female. I realized I'd never heard a female Gwythienian before. It was a nice sound. But the male sounded a lot like Padraig.

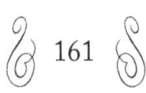

Gaedyen closed his eyes and took a deep breath, then stepped around the wall.

"Padraig, Soroco."

The arguing ceased. The female gasped as Padraig sputtered, "Gaedyen?"

I peeked between the wall and Gaedyen.

Padraig ground out, "I thought I was never to see your face again."

"There are more pressing things right now than our disagreements."

"True enough."

"Truer than you know. Tukailaan has finally emerged. And he has dealt a mortal blow to Aven. With an *arkencain*, Padraig." He paused, allowing the weight of the situation sink in. "She is dying, and I have reason to believe he has her rock."

Good thought, Gaedyen. Make sure he knows why he shouldn't kill me.

"Oh, no." Padraig's voice sounded like his essence had just sagged away. "When did this happen?"

"We found out two days ago, but her injury happened days before that. She has little time. Her people are transporting her to Dyn Meddy as we speak, but…someone with knowledge on the subject doubts he will be able to help."

Padraig sounded suspicious. "How did you learn of this?"

"I was on the way back here to question you about my parents when the Adarborians crossed our path. But we will come back to that. There are other developments."

"Other developments?"

"I found our rock."

His eyes widened, and the suggestion of a smile graced his reptilian lips "You did? Gaedyen, that is incredible. Well done."

"But it is Possessed by someone else."

"Oh. Yes, about that…"

Gaedyen lifted a brow. "You knew? How is she able to Possess the rock while you are still alive without a Possessorship Ceremony?"

"She?" Padraig wrinkled his nose. "You mean he...?"

Frowning, Gaedyen cocked his head. "I am one hundred percent sure she is female."

Dropping my head into my hands, I sighed. *Yep. He sure is. That was a memory I could happily forget. Ugh. But why does Padraig think I'm a guy?*

"Enzi?" Gaedyen beckoned.

I swallowed hard, holding the rymakri behind me.

Veri patted reassurances on my shoulder. "We've got you," he whispered.

With a wince, I stepped out to face Padraig.

Instead of contorting with rage, his brows crinkled in confusion, contorting the crossed scars over his face. "Who is this?"

"This is the Possessor of our rock."

Padraig frowned. "What makes you think that?" He dropped his gaze to me. "Human, show me the rock." He turned to Gaedyen. "You really should not have brought her down here. That will only cause us trouble. And is that a *Crivabanian?*"

Veri waved, grinning like he wasn't staring into the face of something big enough squash his whole family under one foot.

Padraig's frown deepened. "We will deal with that once we have settled this nonsense." Looking down his long dragon nose at me, he repeated, "Human, the rock?"

"I don't have it. Tukailaan stole it from us."

The crossing scars warped as his confusion turned to fury.

Ah. There's the rage. My hands tightened around the rymakri behind my back. I knew they wouldn't last much longer.

"You let Tukailaan steal our rock? How did he find you? He has been underground for decades."

But I kept going. "I don't have it with me, but I can do *this*." And I disappeared.

Gasping, Padraig faltered a step. "No. No, no, no!" Grief cracked his voice.

I flickered back into visibility. *Come on, is it really worth getting that dramatic over?*

Apparently, Gaedyen was also confused. "Padraig? Why are you acting like this? Surely such a reaction is unmerited."

"How long have you been the Possessor, human?" His voice was thick, as if with tears. Could Gwythienians cry?

"I don't know exactly. At least a few years."

Padraig dropped to his haunches, one huge hand covering his face.

"Padraig, what is wrong with you?" Gaedyen reached out to steady him.

"Oh, Gaedyen. The reason someone other than me is able to Possess the rock is because…because I was never its Possessor."

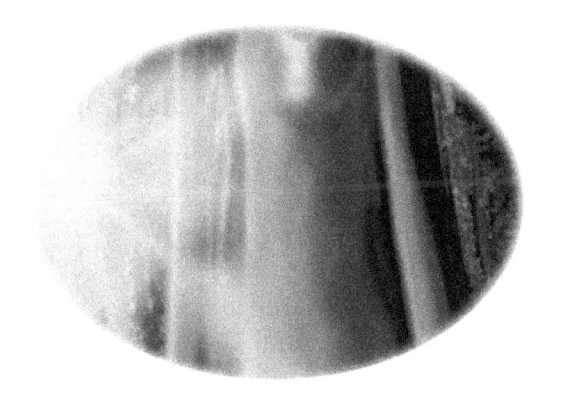

CHAPTER TWENTY

The rymakri clattered to the floor as I stared at Padraig. Gaedyen's mouth hung open, the bruises still shading spots on his skin. "You mean to tell me you have been lying about that too, all my life? How are you the Keeper without being a Possessor?"

"I never said I was not *a* Possessor. Just not of the Rock of the Gift of the Gwythienians."

Scowling, Gaedyen remained standing. "Explain yourself."

I gently scooted the disintegrating rymakri behind the wall with my foot, glad Padraig had been too distracted to notice them. But we weren't out of the woods yet.

"I will in good time, but is Aven's life not more important? I promise to explain, but we must prevent her death before Tukailaan can claim the Cadoumai abilities of the Adarborians. I know who he is working with, and I know of a couple of places they might be hiding. I must search for them. Perhaps I will get the chance to take on Tukailaan alone. Perhaps I can defeat him."

"Who he is working with?" Gaedyen asked.

Padraig eyed Gaedyen. "The person who turned him evil in the first place."

Gaedyen glanced at me and Veri. "You can explain that later as well. If Dyn Meddy cannot save Aven, the only chance she may have is the fifth rock—the healing rock. Do you know where we can find it, if it is real?"

I watched Padraig's eyes for a reaction. One pupil flared ever so slightly, but otherwise he guarded his expression well.

"We would like to search for it, and we hope you can tell us where to start. Did you ever learn anything of the Cathawyrs? Anything that might be true?"

"I did learn a few things in my travels. In fact, I cannot help but believe in their existence. I have seen them. Or one of them, at least."

"What?" Gaedyen's voice went up an octave or two as his jaw dropped.

"The one who created the rock of healing, the fifth rock we know of. I came upon her as she was dying. It is because of that I fear Tukailaan may also have that rock. But there is not time to explain now. You must go to the Cathawyr and find out if they ever got it back. You will find them in the eastern mountains. And I will go in search of Tukailaan."

Stopping in a town this close to home wasn't the best idea—I didn't want to run into anyone I knew. Especially Mom. Should I call her? Maybe. But see her in person? I wasn't ready for that. But Gaedyen insisted on getting me some warmer clothes before traveling to the mountains, so we agreed to make a quick stop.

We flew over several little towns, the trees too thin for my comfort. When we finally reached another little grove near a shopping center, Gaedyen and I turned invisible, and Veri appeared to hover a few feet above the ground.

I became visible again once we were safely covered. "Gaedyen, you'll have to stay here. There's just no way you'd fit, even if you were invisible. I'll be fine with Veri."

I looked down at myself and realized how strange I would look to everyone in these Crivabanian clothes, but I had no choice. I would grab the first things I could find, change into them, and run for it. Not forgetting some kind of jacket for the mountain journey.

"I do not like it, but I will be nearby and listening if you get into any trouble."

"How exactly are we going to sneak *me* in? I might freak some people out, and pets probably aren't allowed."

My eyebrows furrowed. Our options were Veri in plain sight or Veri in…not so plain sight. But I wasn't even wearing enough clothes to hide him anywhere. It would have to be plain sight.

"You could sneak in and hide in the clothes racks or something."

"Clothes racks?"

"Yeah, the things the clothes hang on. They're either in a long line or little circles. Plenty of places to hide."

"Okay, that should work. But you'll have to stay within my sight the whole time, okay? Because if I can't see you, I'm coming out." Veri eyed me.

"Yeah, sure. Just remember not to talk to anyone. Because *that* would really freak some people out."

"Pfft!" Veri smirked. "I've dealt with people plenty. Sometimes freaking them out works to my benefit. Such as scaring the doughnut shop guy into throwing the chocolate-sprinkle ones to make me leave him alone."

I lifted an eyebrow. "So that's how you know about sprinkled chocolate doughnuts."

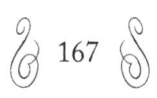

"Of course." Grinning, Veri hopped onto my shoulder. "All right, let's do this."

Ten minutes later, I walked into the clothing store in a Crivabanian green tank top and shorts, no shoes.

Veri approached from the back of the building, went over the roof, and scrambled down to follow me. I hid my wince as gazes lingered on my getup. When I reached the woman's section, I grabbed a couple of jeans, a loose black tank top, a pair of tennis shoes, and an oversized sweatshirt. And a sports bra and three pack of underwear.

Staring straight ahead, I approached the dressing room, half expecting Shaun to show up out of nowhere as he had last time.

But of course I know where he is now. He's outside in Gwythienian form, with no idea that I know his secret.

Ten people were in line in front of me, and the employee was taking one person at a time and unlocking the door for them, after counting their clothes.

Shoot.

I ran back to the woman's section and nabbed a few other random items. If I had a big enough stack of stuff that "didn't fit," hopefully I could sneak out in the things that did.

"How many?" The employee reached for my stack of hangers, her bright-pink nails glittering.

"Six."

Before she could check, a nearby clothes rack crashed to the ground. I thought I might have seen a gray tail whisk out of sight just as she turned to the mess.

"What the heck?" Without looking away from the mess, she unlocked the closest door.

Two doors over, a "lock out of order" sign hung on the handle. *Hmm...*

Hanging up the pile, I pulled the things I wanted off the hangers. I stripped out of the Crivabanian clothes and dropped them on the chair. Sliding into the new pants, I hopped to get them on. Movement caught my eye, and I turned, throwing my arms over my chest.

But it was a mirror. Dropping my arms, I looked at my reflection in an actual mirror for the first time in years.

I turned this way and that, the ever-present scars leering at me. But I was stronger now. There were muscles under those scars. The scars still hurt to look at, but I didn't despise my reflection anymore. It wasn't just a reminder of my powerlessness anymore. It was a sign of my new strength.

I slid on the bra and the tops, ripping off the tags.

I grabbed the other hangers and piled them over one arm, leaving the two empty ones on the hook behind the door.

Opening the door, I stepped out and glanced around for the employee watching the dressing room. She was gathering loose clothes that had fallen off hangers.

Guilt curled in my stomach. She had that mess to clean because of me. "Need a hand?" I grabbed a hanger on my way over.

"Oh, sure. Thanks." She smiled at me and passed me a shirt.

I draped the shirt over the hanger and hung it on the rack. A few moments later, the mess was cleaned, and I was getting lost trying to find my way back to the front.

Veri whistled from between two black sweatshirts. I jumped, not expecting him to show up like that. He winked at me, then hopped out and landed in my sweatshirt hood. He weighed it down so much, it started choking me. I pulled on the sweatshirt's neck, trying to be stealthy about it, then found the sign that pointed to the exit.

I hurried toward the door, Veri bouncing in my hood.

A phone rang nearby, and I turned to see where it was coming from. Half of a desk was visible through an open office door across from the checkout station. The phone rang again, but no one answered.

This is my chance.

I veered toward the office, hoping I didn't look as conspicuous as I probably did.

Pulling the door closed behind me, I locked it and stepped toward the desk. The phone was quiet now. My stomach squirmed. It'd been so long since we'd talked. And she'd yelled at me last time. Did I really need to call her?

I grabbed the phone and punched in the numbers before I could talk myself out of it.

"Tennessee's best logistics comp'ny! Jer'my speak'n."

I rolled my eyes. "Lisa Montgomery, please."

"Just one minute."

"Hello?"

"Mom? It's Enzi."

The choking sob was abruptly muffled, her hand probably shoved over her mouth. "Enzi? How are you? Where are you? Are you okay?"

"I'm fine. I'm sorry it's been so long since I called."

There was silence, then, "Do you hate me?"

"What? No, Mom. I just had some stuff I needed to do."

"Enzi, will I ever see you again?"

I wasn't sure, but I thought there was a pretty decent chance. As long as we didn't get murdered by Tukailaan. "Of course, Mom."

"Well, just in case…I need to tell you a couple of things."

I remained silent, listening.

"Enzi, when you left, you were upset I hadn't told you your father was alive."

My anger at her betrayal boiled back up inside me, stiffening my muscles. I frowned. "Yes."

"I understand your being so upset. I lied to you about something very important. But I wasn't always lying, Enzi. I *thought* he was dead. For years. The military told me themselves. They said he'd died serving his country in some classified situation. No details. That was all I got. And they shipped me his belongings, and that was that. I called, emailed, snail mailed, and harassed them in every way possible for years for more details. To find out where he was buried, but nothing.

"Eventually I accepted I couldn't get more information about it. Did they do experiments on him? Make him do bad things? Why all the secrecy? I hated I would never know. I still don't know."

Knock, knock, knock. Someone jiggled the handle.

Oh crap. Not now.

"The next time I talked to them, they contacted me. About my long-dead husband being alive. It was…"

"Hey!" An angry voice shouted from the other side of the door, pounding against it. "Who's in there? Let me in!"

"Mom? I couldn't hear you. What was that again?"

"I said I…"

"Get out now!" the man screamed.

I plugged my other ear with one finger, trying to focus. "Mom? Can you hear me?"

The door burst open, and a red-faced man glowered at me. "Who are you? Put my phone down immediately."

I ignored him. "No! Not now. Mom? Mom?"

"Get out or I'm calling security." He pointed toward the main doors.

"Mom?"

He marched toward me, yanked the phone out of my hand, and began dialing a number.

Shoot. He really is calling security. Time to go.

I rushed out of the store, Veri a dead weight in my hood.

So Mom hadn't been lying to me for forever? And the government had been lying to her. Well, yeah, they had! There really had been dragons. How much did Mom know? Part of me yearned to go straight home and find out what she was trying to say. I needed to know. But we were in a hurry. I had to finish this first. Then I would find out. As soon as I could.

Mountains finally appeared on the horizon. Once we were close enough, Gaedyen rose above the clouds despite the cold.

Shivering, I was glad for my new sweatshirt and grateful for Veri's warmth at my back.

We soared for hours above the clouds, scanning the misty sky for some sign of the strange, legendary civilization of the Cathawyrs. Eventually, evidence of civilization appeared. A stone hut with crumbling walls, cut from the mountain. A well-worn path with no weeds. We passed many rocks and caves, half-shrouded in mist.

A rocky plateau emerged swiftly from the mist right in front of us, and Gaedyen had to strain every muscle to avoid a crash. The moment we rose above the ledge, there they were. Three huge beige cats covered in unusual brown spots of all different shapes.

Gaedyen flapped madly to slow down and avoid sailing over them. Landing heavily in front of them, he carefully folded his wings and made a respectful bow. They returned the gesture. The middle one gestured with a large, spotted paw for us to advance. I slid from Gaedyen's shoulders, Veri still clinging to mine, and kept pace with him as he followed the trio.

The cold wind in the mountains chilled my skin, and I walked as close to Gaedyen as I could without touching him, soaking up his heat.

The middle one called over her shoulder. "You have come here on behalf of Aven, Possessor of the Rock of the Gift of the Adarborians."

It was a statement rather than a question, and the accurateness of it took us all by surprise.

"Yes." Gaedyen affirmed. "How did you know—if I may ask?"

The left one spoke, ignoring him. "Our Possessor wishes to speak to you. There is not much time. If you want to save Aven and prevent Tukailaan from succeeding, please follow us." And they padded away in synch toward a large, dark hole in the mountainside.

I looked at Gaedyen. Nodding at each other, we followed.

We entered a large cavern, or at least I thought it was. The ceiling was so high I couldn't see it. A ray of light glowed dimly before us.

"They have arrived." The third one spoke in the direction of the light.

Slowly, gingerly, another unusually large paw emerged into the light. But this one was pure white, as if the light had made it from itself, not beige and brown and gray like the spotted fur of the other three. It was followed by an equally snow-white feline leg and a majestic ivory face.

This must be the one I saw in the water.

This great cat—was this a leopard also?—wore an expression much like that of the other three, but hers was even more ancient, even more knowing. Majesty and wisdom emanated from her in silent waves. I glanced at Gaedyen, wondering if we were supposed to bow, but he didn't meet my eyes.

"Gaedyen. Veritamyk. Mackenzi." She stared into our eyes one by one. Her gaze landed on Aven's bow and remained just a moment longer. "You are here to help the Possessor, Aven. And to prevent the conniving Tukailaan from succeeding in his plan to Possess all the rocks."

"Yes…ma'am." Gaedyen faltered.

"I have many names, young one. You may call me Kymri."

"Then yes, Kymri, that is why we have come. We are in search of the fabled Rock of Healing and Life. We have been told its Possessor is here. Can you help us?"

"We will certainly do what we can. We have stakes in this game as well, young Gaedyen. Reasons for wanting Tukailaan stopped, just as you do. It is in the interest of all who live in this world."

"Very well then. Will you show us the fifth rock? The orange rock of healing?"

Kymri's bright-white ears drooped as her eyes drifted to the ground. "It is not here, Gwythienian, I regret to say. But the rock you are seeking is not the orange one. It is purest white, like the soul of its creator. There are many myths of how the rocks came to be, but the truth is I created the orange rock, and its power is far from that of healing. The white rock of healing was created by another."

There's another rock? How many are there?

When Gaedyen's exasperation peeked through his carefully controlled expression, Kymri held up one large white paw.

"Please allow me to explain. The white rock of healing was created by our people's greatest healer. Her birth name was Caranyla, though she also had many other names. When the time came for her to choose what to study, she chose magic, as I did, though her preferences quickly turned toward healing. She was an exemplary healer. If it had been discovered and recorded in any form, she knew everything there was to know about it. If it could be discovered, she made the discovery. She wrote many books."

The majestic glow had returned to the white leopard's face, but something more was there now. Some deep joy perhaps? I couldn't tell.

But the shadow returned as she continued. "Alas, though she was vastly more skilled than any other healer in history, her skill could not save her own life. She was killed, murdered by another of your kind, Gaedyen. And in the end, her murderer got what she deserved for it. She also lost her life to someone who wanted the rock. That Gwythienian's own son took her life in exchange for Possession. And it is he who Possesses it still."

Gaedyen bristled. "Where is this Gwythienian? If you know so much about us, surely you know of his whereabouts. Tell me, and I will bring him to justice for this Caranyla's death! And save Aven before Tukailaan gains Possession of her rock."

"Be careful, Gaedyen of Odan Terridor. Do not be so hasty to leap to conclusions. There is much you do not know. Caranyla's death can never be undone, never made to be less painful. And the only justice of which you speak—a life for a life—has already been done. Another greedy Gwythienian has already killed Cara's murderer."

Gaedyen frowned at being spoken to like that, as if he were a child, but he held his tongue.

"If you do not want me to kill the Possessor, how does any of this information help Aven or stop Tukailaan?" Gaedyen demanded, losing even more of the respectful tone he'd started with.

"I did not say not to kill the Possessor. I merely warn that you may not be so eager to do so when you find him. He is a very important player in the game, Gaedyen, though he does not know it. Cara told me of this rock's extraordinary properties before she died. While the other rocks only work on the Possessor—to make him or her stronger or invisible, etc.—this rock also works on other individuals, healing two at once. But the Possessor is already healing more than just himself with it."

"What does that matter? We must heal Aven."

Kymri stared sorrowfully at him, as if willing him to understand. But he wasn't getting it, whatever it was.

"I will tell you where to find him. Once you do, it will be up to you to decide who to heal. I do not envy your choice."

He would have to decide *who* to heal? He would have to choose Aven. Her life was vastly more important than anyone else's. But who was the other choice? *I* didn't want to die. And I couldn't bear losing Veri. He was such a shining sun all the time. Maybe it was someone else.

While I selfishly hoped for that, I didn't really believe it. Tukailaan had my rock, and we only had the Adarborians' word that he had hers. Was it more terrible to save myself or my closest friend at the expense of all else?

"Enzi." She breathed my name as she turned her bright eyes on me. "You are the greatest surprise of all." Her eyes flitted to the bow and quiver again. "When the rocks were made, to keep peace among the realms, humans proved themselves unworthy to be included. They were not given a rock, and they had no Possessor. It should not be possible for a human to be a Possessor. I have studied magic for years, so I can say with complete confidence that you should have felt nothing when you touched it, or you should have died as your essence tried to take Possession. But you survived. Do you remember when it happened?"

"No." I really didn't.

She scrutinized my face. "Enzi, how far back does your knowledge of your lineage go?" she said, eyes wide and bright.

"Uh, my mom was a foster kid, so I don't have any grandparents on her side, and I knew my other granddad's name, but I never met him. I don't know any further back than that. Why? Tukailaan asked about my grandparents, too."

"You say Tukailaan asked about them? What exactly did he ask?"

I scrunched my eyebrows, trying to remember. "I think just their names. But why does that matter?"

She didn't answer immediately, seemingly lost in thought. At last her mystified expression changed to amusement.

"So he sees a resemblance as well?"

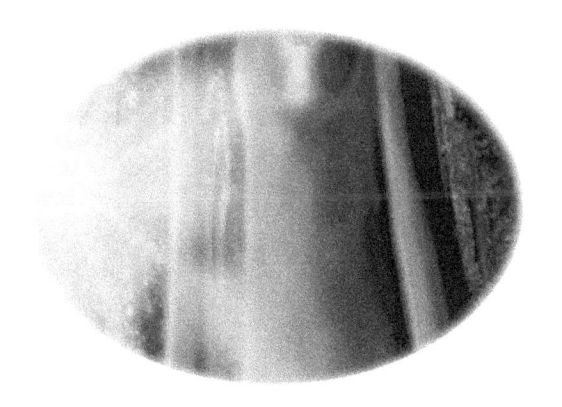

CHAPTER TWENTY-ONE

"What resemblance?" What in the world did my *lineage* have to do with anything?

"Enzi, no one here can prophesy the future, but we can see more of the present than most. We have been watching the present for long enough to know a great deal about the past, which may allow for some idea of the future."

I frowned, lifting one eyebrow. "What?"

"The answer to your question will require some thought. And a good deal of reading. And perhaps some discussing and reminiscing...but this goes much further back than your grandparents, if I am correct."

"What are you talking about? I can't go on another whole journey with all these questions buzzing around. Just tell me!"

But she didn't. *Shocking.*

"You both heard the story in Sequoia Cadryl that recounts why the Crivabanians hate Gwythienians. As a result, you learned things about both of your fathers. And you acquired a few more questions about them as well, am I right?"

I nodded solemnly, wondering how they could possibly know so much. Gaedyen nodded too.

"We want Cara's"—she cleared her throat—"the rock of healing back. Bring it to us, and we will tell you what really happened. In addition to what your ancestors may have to do with all this, Enzi."

"What of the one who is now in Possession? You said there would be a choice?"

"Save Aven if you can. But it is of utmost importance that you bring the rock back to me."

"But can't we just ask him to use his Possession to heal Aven?" I asked.

"I wish you the best of luck. It will be challenging, but not impossible."

Wow. So helpful.

How could they know what happened to our parents? But oh man, did I want to know! I needed to know. If I knew, I would know exactly what to do next. And how to help my dad. And what was all that about my ancestors?

"We will bring it to you," Gaedyen stated solemnly. "We will find a way to get it here. Just tell me, how can we be sure you will not cheat us out of the rock and have no truths for us when we come back? How can we be sure you will honor your word?"

"You will have to trust me, Gaedyen. I cannot tell you how we know, only that we do, and we will tell you if you return with our rock." She glanced at the bow and quiver yet again.

I could tell Gaedyen didn't like it. I didn't, either. But what choice did we have?

"Very well then. We will do it. Tell us where to find this other Gwythienian."

Kymri flowed from the dais to the floor and led us outside. "South of Odan Terridor, halfway between there and the southernmost end of Florida. Aven's escort is likely to pass near there in two days' time. Find her people and tell them the other Adarborians said to listen to you in order to give Aven her best chance. Tell them Annwyl sent you, and I pray they will listen.

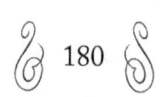

Then take them to the Possessor of the Rock of Healing and do what you must. And Gaedyen?"

"Yes?"

"Padraig was so grieved because the Rubandor whose death allowed Enzi to become a Possessor was his best friend, and they spoke rarely thanks to the demands of their Possessorships. He did not get to say goodbye. But do not hate him. He is not so guilty as you think. He gave up much for his realm and worked hard to make life easier for you, knowing how difficult it would be. He is well worth your respect and love, even though he may not go out of his way to explain himself."

Gaedyen looked into her blue eyes. It was impossible not to believe their truth. "How do you know so much about everything?"

She stopped at the edge of the light, remaining in the cave as we walked on. "That is my people's secret, not mine to reveal."

With a stiff nod, Gaedyen turned back toward the cliff and spread his wings.

I hopped onto his back and turned to find Kymri's eyes on me. "Wait. What do you know about this bow? Why do you keep looking at it?"

A brilliant smile lit up her face, glowing almost as much as when she talked about Caranyla. "That is a good story. You certainly must hear it, but I am afraid there is not time to tell it properly. Aven—oh, Aven—she and our rock are your priorities now. You must hurry. Every moment counts."

Unfurling his wings, Gaedyen leaped off the cliff. I watched as the white leopard faded in the misty mountain air.

We headed east from the great mountain barely an hour after arriving. The day was drawing to a close, and we searched for a safe place to spend the night.

At last we found a scrap of forest on the side of the mountain and landed to make camp for the night.

Gaedyen caught a mountain goat while I shot at smaller prey. I didn't hit a single one, but I tried not to sulk too much about it. We had more important things to worry about than who was the best hunter.

Veri finished off the nuts he'd gathered while Gaedyen and I settled by the fire.

"What is it about Shaun you dislike so?" Gaedyen asked.

I held back a wry smile. I knew his secret, but I wasn't ready to confront him about it. Maybe it would be entertaining to pretend I didn't know.

"I was hurt you'd left me. And left Shaun to babysit me."

"So you were upset at me, not him?"

"I guess."

"What about the day he stopped those girls from trying to steal your necklace? You seemed to like him well enough then."

"You were there, huh? I guess you could've been hiding in the woods or the sky, invisible. Well, yeah." I eyed him, but he kept staring out into space. "That was nice of him. Nobody'd ever stood up to those two before. No guy could resist their disgusting gorgeousness. Yeah, I appreciated him helping me out that day. It was really nice to be put above them like that." I smiled at the memory of their shocked and outraged faces.

"They were not beautiful. They were very…unpleasant. They look nothing like you."

My heart throbbed almost painfully with the wistful desire to take his words as more than he meant them. No, I didn't look anything like them, of course. Even now, with my stronger body, in so much better shape…still not like them. But it was nice to hear him say they weren't beautiful.

"So you liked him then, but you do not like him anymore?"

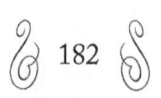

"I don't know why that matters to you, Gaedyen. I like some things about him, I guess."

"What things?"

Crap. Why'd I say that? I should've known it would get me in trouble. But I couldn't come up with anything that seemed remotely believable.

"Just things."

"Enzi, do you think…that is…is there any chance that maybe…he might have a, well…uh…a chance…with…with you? Should that someone from your past not work out, that is."

My eyebrows probably shot right off my forehead.

Gaedyen backpedaled quickly. "Sorry I asked. Never mind, just forget it. He just thought he probably did not…I was trying to find out for him. That is all. Just forget it."

This doesn't seem like something he would joke about. Could he really mean that?

"Um…"

Gaedyen sighed. "Look, Enzi, he thinks quite highly of you and cares about you. He wants you to be happy. He wondered if perhaps *he* could make you happy. He likes that idea. He thinks you are interesting and would like to get to know you better. And he thinks you are…much better looking than those other two females he met."

"He said all that to you, huh?"

"Whether you choose to believe it or not, it is true. I think you should give him a chance. Get to know him a little better. You might find you like him."

He focused away from me throughout his speech, but his eyes flicked in my direction more than once.

"It doesn't matter," I whispered, staring at the ground. I wanted to believe him, to know that what he was saying was true. But…everything with Caleb…if he knew, things would be different.

"How could you say that?" he growled, anger and frustration in his tone.

I frowned. "Because if he knew more about me, he wouldn't think so well of me."

"What could you possibly mean by that?"

"Do you really want to know?"

"Absolutely."

"Fine!"

If he really did feel something for me like I did for him, and if he really was Shaun, who was a human form of himself, it couldn't work. I was too damaged. He might as well know. Maybe it would be less embarrassing to tell him as Gaedyen than as Shaun.

"It's because of my scars."

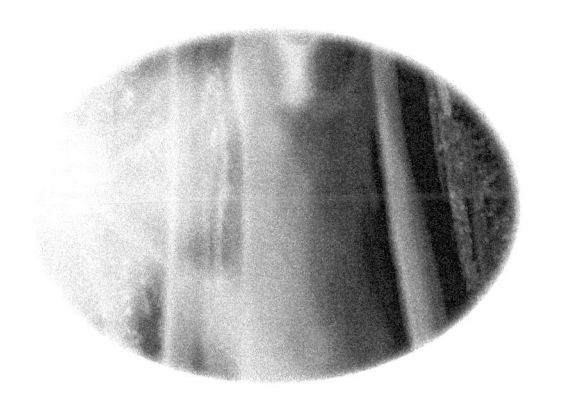

CHAPTER TWENTY-TWO

I hugged myself, trying to cover them. I stared at the ground for a long minute, but when he didn't demand further information, I looked up to see if he'd even heard me. Maybe I'd whispered too low.

To my surprise, his face dropped closer to my level, his brows knit in concern rather than frustration. He didn't speak, waiting patiently for me to continue.

"You remember the scars."

He nodded almost imperceptibly.

I dropped my face into my hands. "Of course you do." Forcing myself to meet his eyes, trying to forget what else he might remember, I continued. "When you reacted the way you did to them, I didn't realize you didn't know what they were, that they looked like other things in your culture. I thought you knew and were making light of it.

"You see, these marks are what's left of wounds from when I was attacked. What happened to me that day…it scared me. So bad I still have nightmares about it sometimes…all the time. What I'm trying to say is—I can't be in a normal relationship. I'm too broken."

Had I really just said that out loud? To Gaedyen?

"Someone attacked you?" His voice sounded strained.

"Yeah, but it was a long time ago—"

"What happened?" he whispered.

And before I knew it, I was telling him the whole story.

"There are people called child molesters and sexual offenders. Do you know what those are?"

He nodded again, his eyes tightening around the edges.

"That girl with the blond hair, she was my best friend when we were kids. One day she told me about some kittens in the old barn on her property and we made plans to go play with them. We weren't supposed to go outside without adult supervision, but that made it even more fun.

"I finished my homework first, and I was too excited about the kittens to wait for Jillian. So I went to the barn without her. She was supposed to come right after me."

My voice was getting thick, and I could feel the floodgates preparing to well over. I shoved the back of my hand over my face, trying to calm down enough to keep going.

"I ran into the barn, calling for the kittens. It was dark. The only light came from uneven spaces between the old planks. I remember the swirly dust floating in beams of light. I thought it was cool.

"Once my eyes adjusted, I saw a pile of something on the floor. And blood. I bent to look closer, and it was the kittens. Some of them were dead, and they were all bloody. The remaining ones yowled in pain. I jumped back, horrified, and was about to run back to the house when someone..." I took a deep breath. I could do this. "Someone else was there. But it wasn't a stranger. It was a guy I'd seen before, the older brother of another girl in my class."

I couldn't stop the sobs any longer.

"I, uh...I remember him cutting my clothes and being on top of me and yelling at me and...he raped me and it hurt, and

I as too young to understand what was happening, but knew it was wrong. I wanted to leave, I screamed for help, and he cut me and told me to be quiet or he'd do it again."

I traced the scar that peeked out of my shirt at the base of my neck.

"I screamed, so he cut me again. I tried to stop screaming, but I couldn't help it. I couldn't stop screaming and crying.

"Finally, I heard my friend and her mom calling my name. I tried to shout, but I was losing my voice. And then his weight was off me. I wanted to run, but I couldn't make my arms and legs lift me. Maybe I was in shock. He must have kicked my head or something because I passed out, and when I woke up, my head hurt.

"I heard them calling my name still, but I was ashamed. I was so ashamed for what'd happened. My clothes were torn; I was bleeding. I didn't want them to see me like that. And they would make me go to the hospital, and Mom couldn't afford it.

"Somehow, I got to my feet and stumbled all the way home, terrified he would find me.

"When I got home I scribbled a note that Jillian's mom had brought me home and I was sick. Then I went to bed early. I wanted to hide what had happened so she wouldn't take me to the hospital. I was too young to know I needed to go anyway. The next morning, Mom came in to check on me. Only my face protruded from the covers, so she checked my fever and didn't see the blood. She let me stay home.

"By the time she got home that night, I was worse. I couldn't sleep, and when I did, I had nightmares, which resulted in me kicking off the covers. When mom came in to check on me, there was no hiding the evidence.

"She found me shaking and sweating, lying on sheets smeared with blood. She called an ambulance. So much for saving money.

"I was out of school for two weeks, surprised my best friend hadn't come to visit me once. She must've known what'd happened. But when I returned to school, none of my friends would speak to me, not even her. At first I thought no one knew who I was because I wore baggy clothes and hid my face, instead of the bright, cheerful clothes I used to wear. But then I realized they were all staring at me. Judging me. Could they know what'd happened?

"Jillian passed me on her way to class. I grabbed her arm and asked why she was ignoring me. She smirked down at my hand, then shot me a venomous glare. 'Get your kitten-killing hands off me, Mackenzi.'

"I let go of her in shock. She must have been playing…I barely remembered the kittens…hadn't thought of them. Not since…How could she think I'd done that?

"As the rest of my classmates spurned me, I realized what'd happened. Jillian and her mom had found the kittens. Kittens that'd been killed. And I'd run away. They thought I'd murdered the kittens and ran out of guilt or something. They thought I was some kind of psychopath who would hurt animals, and they thought I'd given myself injuries for attention.

"And that was the rumor Jillian spread around school. Everyone thought I'd been in some kind of psychotherapy for those two miserable weeks. I never had any friends after that. Got used to avoiding people. And, well, you know how Jillian turned out."

I heaved a deep breath, rubbing tear trails away.

"So now you know my secret. Now you know why Shaun wouldn't want me, why no one would. And after what happened, I don't want to be with anyone that way. I don't think I could handle it. Every time I think about it, memories of him bombard me. His nasty face, the smell of his sweat, blood mixed with the musty smell of the barn. The worst part is his weight, being so helpless. Having absolutely no say in what happened to me. No control."

I couldn't meet his gaze. I'd just bared the deepest part of my soul to him. Why had I told him that many details? What was I thinking?

"How old were you?" he whispered.

"Ten."

"Oh, Enzi. I am so sorry you had to go through that. I could murder him right now."

"I wish you would. Then maybe the nightmares would stop."

Silence weighed heavy between us, and when I brought myself to look into his face, he peered cautiously into mine.

"That is what happens to you in your sleep? The same thing over and over?"

"Yeah. It sucks." *Understatement of the year.*

"I am sorry, Enzi. More sorry than I can say."

I sniffled, wiping my eyes. "Thanks."

"For what it is worth, I do not think it would change Shaun's mind. It is not your fault, nothing to blame yourself for."

Shivering, I wrapped my arms around my knees to hold myself together. *Not blame myself? And is that really what I want? I don't even know.*

"Thanks, Gaedyen." I stood and brushed off my pants. "I'm going to bed."

It was cold, but I needed space from Gaedyen after telling him all that. But he needed to hear it. And it was easier to tell him this way rather than say it to him in his Shaun form.

Now it was over with, and I wouldn't have to do that ever again.

I sat in a vast field, no trees in sight. As I turned to get my bearings, I saw the old camp gear store, where I'd gotten supplies for the journey, back when Gaedyen still insisted on walking the whole way. I leaned back and found something there, supporting me.

Turning, I expected to find a tree, but it was Shaun. He smiled at me, then into the sun. He leaned back on his arms, his hands braced in the grass.

I looked at how close I was to him and found no space between my shirt and his. I was sitting in his lap. For a moment I thought how nice it would be to lean against him and soak up the sun rays with him.

But what did this mean about our relationship? I wasn't…we couldn't…what expectations did he have?

Launching myself forward, I pushed myself to my feet and stood still, unsure of what to say.

"Enzi?" Shaun asked. "Are you all right?"

"Shaun." His name was nice to say, but I was nauseated with nerves. "I can't…"

He rose and stepped toward me, brows knit. "Was it something I did?"

"No! No, Shaun, it's just…" How was I supposed to explain this?

His fingers brushed my shoulders as he stepped in to hug me. I closed my eyes, confused with my wanting to be held by him and the association with wrong and terrible. And then Caleb's shaming grin flashed in my mind, and I shoved Shaun away.

The hurt on his face mirrored the day he'd tried to say something nice to me. The last time I'd seen him. My heart ached. I wanted to take it back, but could I?

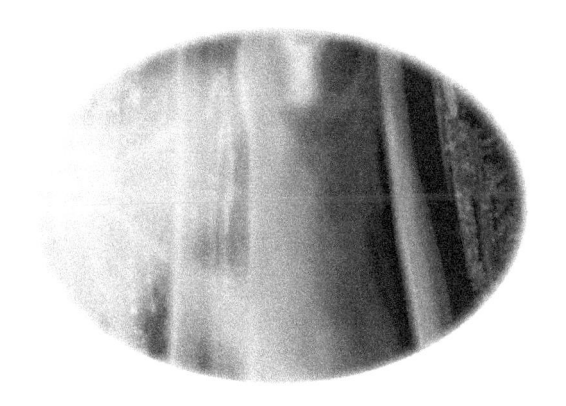

CHAPTER TWENTY-THREE

After not enough sleep and zero breakfast, we rushed toward the mysterious Gwythienian who Possessed the rock of healing, hoping we'd intercept Aven and her transport on the way. If we missed her, the chances of saving her with the rock, if we could even find it, were that much slimmer.

A few hours in, Gaedyen's earflaps perked up. Had he caught a whiff of their trail? He angled his wings, tilting us into a slight turn. He must've caught the Adarborians' scent. Less than an hour later, we caught up.

A line of guards whirled and sped toward us. "Stop! I warn you, do not come a step closer."

An Adarborian greeting if I've ever heard one.

"It is Gaedyen and Enzi, the Gwythienian and human who visited you just a few weeks ago. We have been sent by the leader of the first Adarborian division to bring you to a different place to meet Dyn Meddygaeth. In case he cannot help you, there is another who might have the ability."

"How can we trust you?" one of the female guards demanded.

"Annwyl told me herself. It is of utmost importance."

"We should go with them." A raspy voice emerged from a wooden platform carried between four of them. *Aven.* "I have a very strong feeling about this." Aven's voice shook.

The guards looked at each other, then to Aven's sickly form. Were they wondering whether she was herself enough to follow her orders? Then one of them stepped forward.

"Show us the way to this other healer. We will follow."

I wasn't looking forward to what would happen when Annwyl learned we'd lied to her mother and her transport.

We were about to take off when Aven weakly waved me over. I went to her, hoping she was still all there enough to talk to.

"How are things going between the two of you, little human?" Her accent flavored the raspy voice.

"What do you mean?"

"Oh. If you do not know yet, you will soon."

"What did you whisper in Gaedyen's ear when you left us last?"

"He didn't tell you? Well, that is something only he can share with you, Enzi. It is not my place to say. But trust me when I tell you it is a good thing. Life has precious few good things to offer. The two of you should take care not to waste this one."

Was she losing her mind? What did she mean, precious few good things?

I stored her words away for later. I was really getting concerned about Gaedyen. He was going to have to fight this other Gwythienian. Would he be bigger? Stronger? A more experienced fighter? I didn't doubt Gaedyen's skill, but I still worried about him.

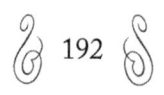

We would have some Adarborians on our side, maybe, but could we count on them? Their first priority would be to protect Aven, not necessarily to help Gaedyen. If it was safer to flee with Aven instead of fight, they would leave us. And they might be a little suspicious when they discovered how antagonistic this "healer" was likely to be.

Soon after correcting course for this mysterious Possessor, he found us.

"You!" a distinctly Gwythienian voice bellowed from above.

We all froze, staring up into the sun.

"You leave her alone and abandoned for twenty years, with not a single indication that you care whether she lives or dies, and then come waltzing in here, after I nearly killed you once, and expect me not to do the very same again?"

His voice sounded oddly familiar. Had I heard him speak before? I'd only ever met Padraig and Gaedyen, and sort of Tukailaan, but no others except…the one who beat us up in the woods! That was when I'd been the one to literally stomp Gaedyen's hip bone back into joint. *Not pretty.*

The other Gwythienian landed hard in front of us, his face too close to Gaedyen's. I was impressed by how big he was. Standing a good two feet taller than Gaedyen, he had to stoop to look him in the eyes. Which he did with fiery intensity. I couldn't help but respect the look in his eyes, as well as fear it. There was something more than mere anger at being disturbed by bothersome company.

"How dare you…" His angry voice dropped off into confused silence. His eyebrow ridges shot up in surprise, and then drew together again in suspicion.

"Who are you, Gwythienian? You are not who I thought."

"My name is Gaedyen."

"Gaedyen? I do not know anyone by that name. You look young—perhaps you hatched after I left Odan Terridor. What are you doing here? As I said, you are not welcome. You may not be who I thought, but I still do not desire your presence."

"We are here about the rock of healing," Gaedyen answered.

The other Gwythienian's face froze as he stumbled backward. He looked at Gaedyen, then at me, and then back to Gaedyen.

"How do you know of this?" he demanded in a hoarse whisper.

"Many lives are at stake. A Gwythienian named Tukailaan is out to murder all of the Possessors and to gain Possession of all of the rocks."

The other Gwythienian's earflaps twitched.

"If that happens, he will be unstoppable," Gaedyen said. "He will do much damage to all the realms, not to mention the humans. And he has an arkencain. He used it to mortally wound Aven, the Possessor of the Adarborians' rock." He gestured to Aven, and she squinted at the other Gwythienian as if confused. "And if she dies, he will gain Possession of that rock. We have reason to believe he has Possession of at least one other rock, and he could have more, just waiting to take out their Possessors as well. We need you to heal Aven to prevent him from gaining Possession of at least one rock. I have no idea of the condition of the other Possessors. Will you help us?"

"I am not on Tukailaan's side. He has done me great wrong, and I would very much like to see him fall. But let us be clear: that does not put me on your side."

"Well helping us would definitely be hurting him!" I piped up for the first time, hoping to use his negative feelings to our advantage. His eyes narrowed on me, clearly even less pleased than before. He was probably one of those anti-human Gwythienians. *Shoot.*

"Why are you against him, if I may ask?" Gaedyen drew his attention away from me. "What did he do to you?"

He stared at Gaedyen for a long moment, and then stated, "I am Bricriu. He is my father."

There was a long pause as we took in that little nuance. Tukailaan was this dude's father? Wow. That meant, he was, like, Gaedyen's second cousin or something. *How weird!*

"If you wish to take your revenge on him, here is your chance. Use your Possession to save Aven before she dies and Tukailaan

Possesses her rock. Hers is probably not even the first one he has Possessed."

Bricriu sighed. "If only I could. I would do anything for revenge, anything except that."

"But why? It will not cost you anything! In fact, it will benefit you."

"Not cost me anything? You are wrong, young one. It will cost me something much more valuable than revenge, even revenge on the one person who has wronged me more than any other."

Gaedyen glared at him. "What in the world could be more valuable than stopping the person who is trying to hurt everyone in every realm? Someone you dislike so strongly?"

"There is only one in the world I care about. One soul, only one. And this rock is keeping her alive."

Is that the one Kymri warned Gaedyen he would not want to kill?

"But we are not asking you to stop keeping someone else alive! Just to share some of its power to save a dying Possessor's life."

Bricriu's eyes blazed, his nostrils flaring as he shoved his face into Gaedyen's personal space.

"Thanks to you, I am now more aware than ever of the limitations of my Possession. When you nearly killed me, I drew healing power from the rock to restore my strength. Once I was healed, I returned to my soul mate. And her state had declined. Because of me. Guilt stabbed me for what I had unknowingly done to her. I will not do such a thing again. She is the only thing that makes this world worth living in, the only bright star in a dark sky. I will not risk her life."

"Is her life more valuable than the lives of everyone else in the world?"

"Her life is worth more than all the others."

As wrong as that statement may be, it was beautiful. She was worth the world to him, literally. I wanted to be worth so much to someone. How indescribably wonderful to mean so much to another person.

Gaedyen considered, cogs turning. "How far from her were we when we fought that night?"

"Perhaps forty miles."

"Then consider this. We know your rock is different than the other four. What if the rock's power is affected by distance? What if the harm was only done because you were so far away?"

"But for all of the other rocks, once you have Possession, you are able to control the powers without being close to the rock at all. It doesn't matter how far from it you are. That is why we were able to make the Keeper," he argued.

"Yes," Gaedyen agreed, "but your rock allows the Possessor to affect someone else. The other four are not affected by distance because the powers only affect the Possessor him- or herself. In your case, the farther you and the rock are from the other person receiving power from it, the less effect it has. But what if you and the rock were close to the subject—or subjects—in need of healing? If there was no distance between you, I think it would still work. Then you can have a safe and healing soulmate, Tukailaan can be foiled, and everyone else in the world will be safe."

Did Gaedyen feel as awful as I did about all the lies he was telling? Would this mysterious other creature die when we took the rock from Bricriu to return to the Cathawyr?

"You make an interesting point. However, the fact that you *think* it could work is hardly enough evidence to gamble her life on. As tempting as that may be, the risk is simply not worth it. She is above all else in this world."

I could almost see the steam blowing out of Gaedyen's frustrated earflaps. Personally, I was impressed by his suggestion. It sounded like a real win-win. He was so much better than I was with words, with convincing people to do what he wanted. It had worked with me, Aven, Padraig. Why couldn't it just work now?

Suddenly Bricriu's head flashed to stare into the distance behind him. Gaedyen tensed as well. Something their Gwythienian senses could pick out that my lame human ones couldn't.

Bricriu bounded toward the disturbance and swiftly took flight, Gaedyen only a few beats behind him. Annoyed grumbles from behind us alerted me that Aven and her transport were following as well. We soared for less than two minutes before I could glimpse what had caused this reaction in the Gwythienians: another something was flying toward us, descending toward some point on the ground between us and them. Both Gwythienians hastened their already-straining wingbeats.

The Annwyl half of the Adarborian transport approached. *Oops.*

When they landed first, Bricriu let loose a bone-rattling roar.

We landed hard, the impact probably killing Gaedyen's injured leg. The moment he reached the ground, Bricriu bounded the two leaps to get between the newcomers and a tight little grove of trees.

"Stop! Do not move another inch, or I will finish you. What do you want with her?"

The shimmering greens, reds, purples, and blues of the Adarborians caught my eye. But where was Dyn Meddy? Wouldn't he have come even if he didn't think there was anything he could do?

"What is the meaning of this, Gwythienian?" Annwyl snarled at us.

"We met the transport carrying Aven and diverted their path here. This Gwythienian is the Possessor of a previously unknown rock that has healing properties. We just discovered its existence and brought Aven here to see if it would help. In case Dyn Meddygaeth was unable to." Then turning back to Bricriu, he said, "If you do not use the rock on her, she has no chance! The rest of the world may have no chance. Think about this, please."

"How could he not come?" Veri whispered, searching among the Adarborians in vain for Dyn Meddy.

"Apparently Tukailaan had another projectile, and he struck Dyn Meddygaeth with it. He is gravely ill, and his people would not let us see him. I fear we shall lose two Possessors soon unless we find a way to heal them."

Gaedyen turned to Bricriu. "Please. Don't let him get away with this!"

Bricriu just stared at Aven, fury frozen on his face. Was he considering it? I hoped he was wracked with indecision and would choose our side.

"If you let Aven die," Gaedyen prodded, "allowing Tukailaan to gain Possession of her rock, you doom the whole world to his hatred. Is that the kind of world your beloved will want to live in once she is healed? Do you think she will thank you for letting that happen? For allowing Tukailaan, your father, to destroy everything? She probably has parents. Friends. How will she feel when she learns you allowed them all to be enslaved or killed because you were too afraid to try?"

"All right!" Bricriu roared. "But I am taking every possible precaution, and you must agree to my terms. And I make no guarantees. I only agree to try briefly to see whether it will negatively affect her. If it does, then we are done, and I will kill you all. If your theories prove correct, however, then I will consider proceeding."

Aven's head lolled back, and she let out a pitiful groan.

Gaedyen's eyes were bright with adrenaline. "All right. What are your terms? We must hurry."

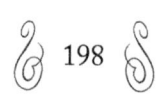

"You! Human. Get down." He glared at me, pointing to the ground.

I leaned over to slide down, but Gaedyen rotated his body the other way, preventing me.

"Hold on just one minute," Gaedyen stormed.

I hastily resituated myself on his neck, trying not to shake Veri loose.

"I will not hurt her. But I will not have anyone dangerous near this female. My terms are these: the girl comes alone, only to carry the Adarborian Possessor. She will take her next to the bed of my charge, as close as possible, and I will attempt the healing. I have already told you what will happen from there."

"You must allow me to see her the whole time," Gaedyen said, surprising me with the fierceness of his demand.

Bricriu started to balk, but Gaedyen interrupted him.

"I will not come near your female. I just need to see that Enzi is safe. Just move the trees a little so I can watch her. That is all. I agree to the rest. Do you agree, Enzi?"

"Yes."

Bricriu's nostrils flared at the demand, but he assented. "Fine. I will break some of the trees. Girl, come down here and pick up the Adarborian."

"Her name is Enzi," Gaedyen growled.

Bricriu ignored him, focusing on me as I dismounted and sprinted to Aven, Veri bouncing on my shoulder.

"Without the squirrel," Bricriu demanded when he caught site of my little companion.

Veri sighed, rolled his eyes, and then leaped from my shoulder. I stood with my feet apart, trying to balance as the Adarborians carefully placed their leader in my arms. She was heavy, but I was strong enough to carry her. Many eyes bored into me as I took their precious leader toward Bricriu and the other Gwythienian.

I faced Bricriu, hoping I could carry Aven all the way. When I reached him, he jerked his head, indicating I was to follow. When we entered the grove, he reached up with his forelegs to break off the tops of several trees. I was glad Gaedyen had made that request, that he had my back.

There was a platform, kind of like a bed, in the middle of the grove. On it lay another Gwythienian, asleep and clearly sick. The shape of her face was slim—feminine like Soroco's. Her eyes were bigger, her neck a little longer. Her eyes were also sunken, and hollows were all over her face, places that should be much more filled in. And her skin was the wrong color. Faded, grayish.

Bricriu's voice drew me from my reverie.

"Set her down here," he whispered softly, to avoid waking the sickly Gwythienian.

I doubted that was necessary, but I played along for his sake, laying Aven's body right next to the base of the platform, kneeling to place her head on my lap.

With one hand over Aven and the other touching the sick Gwythienian, he closed his eyes and took on a look of deep concentration.

"Stop!" Gaedyen bellowed, bounding toward us.

What was he doing? We were almost there! After how hard we'd worked…

"Who is this female?" he demanded, staring at the shrunken body with mystified eyes.

Bricriu glared at him, showing his teeth and positioning himself between Gaedyen and her. "Her name is Geneva. What is it to you?"

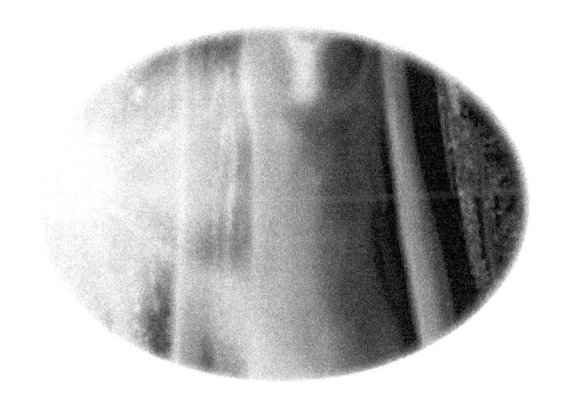

CHAPTER TWENTY-FOUR

Bricriu glowered at Gaedyen. "Geneva, the daughter of Thadaheen and Feldema. She was in an accident, and I brought her here many years ago. I have been trying to save her ever since."

Geneva? Wasn't that Gaedyen's dead mother's name?

"You…you are not Ferrox, son of Padraig, are you?" Gaedyen asked, a strange look of wonder on his face.

Oh my gosh! Did we just find his parents?

I searched Bricriu's face, just as eager as Gaedyen to hear his answer. His face soured.

"What? That bastard? No! I am not him. That is who I thought you were at first. But no, I am Bricriu. And as I told you, I am the son of Tukailaan."

"But, this is Ferrox's wife…?"

Bricriu's eyes narrowed to slits. "She is not his wife. She was always meant for me. She was only with him for a short time before he ruined everything for her with his greed. But she is with me now, where she is safe. I have protected her all these years, and I have healed her to the best of my abilities."

"But she looks like death! How is this *healed?*"

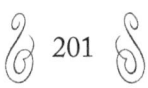

"She has been in a coma. I have done everything I can for her—"

"Yes, you mentioned that. But then why does she look so horrible? She looks like she has not eaten in years. Or seen sunlight. Is she even alive?"

"Yes, of course she is," the other growled. "Healing her has proven difficult. The rock does not work well when you have... when you have inflicted the injuries yourself." Bricriu hung his head, ashamed.

"*You* did this to her?" Gaedyen bellowed.

"Yes, I did! And I regret it every moment of my life. It was all Ferrox's fault. He ruined everything. He was supposed to fly out first. When I grabbed her and tried to incapacitate her, I thought she was him."

"What? Flew out of where? What are you talking about?"

"Why does it matter to you?" His eyes were hard now. "What significance is she to you, other than she is standing in the way of stopping Tukailaan?"

Before Gaedyen could answer, Aven whispered something.

"What?" I asked, bending my head closer to hers.

"Falbane, at last." Her whole body spasmed, then went limp.

"Gaedyen!" I shrieked, terrified. Had she just died, right before my eyes? *Oh no, no, no!*

Gaedyen rushed to me, Bricriu only showing mild annoyance. Several Adarborians were there a moment later, making him much more uncomfortable.

"Gaedyen, I can't see her breathing! What do I do? I don't know what to do!" I was hysterical. There was nothing I could do. Or was there, and I just couldn't see it? *Please, no!*

"Do you know how to feel for a pulse?" Gaedyen asked calmly. I reached for her wrist, placing two fingers under the base of her palm. Nothing.

"I'm not feeling anything!" I shrieked again. I tried the other wrist, and then the base of her neck. Nothing there either. At last I put my ear to her mouth and listened hard, barely taking a breath myself. Nothing.

"Oh no," I whispered. "Gaedyen," I looked at him, tears pooling over. "She's gone." I choked on the last word, not caring if anyone saw me sobbing.

Annwyl appeared in front of me and snatched Aven's body from my lap. "No. No!" She sobbed, dropping to her knees and wrapping her arms around her mother.

Gaedyen hung his head, defeated. Bricriu didn't speak or move. For the first time, I could hear the slow, wheezy breathing of the female Gwythienian.

Aven was dead. Tukailaan was the Possessor of her rock now. Did he have Dyn Meddy's? How long until Dyn Meddy died too? And Padraig and me? *Oh, Aven…and who is Falbane?*

"I am sorry the Adarborian is dead, and I do admit to a good deal of concern over my father Possessing her rock, but as there is nothing I can help you with now, I must ask you all to please leave us in peace."

Gaedyen whipped around to face Bricriu, a snarl on his face. "Do you know who this female is?" he asked coldly.

Bricriu scowled. "You forget you have already asked me, and I have answered. She is Geneva—"

"She is the wife of Ferrox, thought dead for many years but alive all this time! The daughter-in-law of the Keeper, and you have kept her hidden here, for nearly two decades." Anger rippled from him.

"What does it matter to you?" Bricriu bellowed back. "You are nothing but a youngling, too young to have ever known this female! What is her life to you?"

"I am the grandson of the Keeper." Gaedyen replied in a slow, cold voice that sounded ready to explode. "You were right to say I was too young to have known her. I hatched the night she supposedly died along with her mate." A pause, and then,

"Ferrox was my father. And Geneva, she was—is—my mother. I am her son."

Bricriu's face slackened, his breathing increasing as he flicked his eyes back and forth between Geneva and Gaedyen.

Gaedyen continued. "You stole her from me! Whatever wrong she may have done, whatever she and my father conspired to do, however horribly it may have affected all of the realms, she is still my mother. I still wanted to know my parents, despite it all. I was meant to be raised by her! And you kept her from me my whole life. I never got to see her when she was young and healthy. Only here, now, rotting away behind some trees so you can live out some sick fantasy."

Bricriu's face warped into a murderous scowl.

"Gaedyen…" I tried to warn him to cool it. "Maybe now isn't the best time for this…"

But he ploughed on. "Why is she not healed then? Hmm? What did you say the reason for that was? Yourself?"

"Leave now!" Bricriu roared, entering Gaedyen's personal space. With as mad as Gaedyen looked, I wouldn't have put my nose anywhere near his.

Annwyl snarled at Bricriu, her dark features contorting with rage and grief. "None of us are leaving until you have paid for what you have done. You killed her, Gwythienian. May your name live in infamy, and may you suffer a loss as grievous as that which you have inflicted on me and the whole world today!"

She launched into the air. At first, I thought she was flying at Bricriu, but she veered toward Geneva at the last second.

A blade appeared in her hand, pointed at Gaedyen's mother. My heart stopped.

"You'll kill Dyn Meddy too!" Gaedyen shouted.

I pulled the bow from behind me and had an arrow flying at her in half a second.

Gaedyen and Bricriu lurched toward her, but giant Adarborians suddenly materialized and restrained them.

Annwyl's feet had already landed on Geneva's huge limp neck, dagger raised and falling as the rymakri flew by her shoulder. She whirled on me with a snarl. I'd missed, but I bought Geneva a few more seconds.

"If you kill her," Gaedyen pleaded, "Bricriu will not save Dyn Meddy either, if we can get him here. And then Dyn Meddy will be lost as well. The loss of Aven is inconceivable, but how much worse will it be to lose another Possessor to Tukailaan?"

Her chest heaved, hand held high but thankfully still.

"Instead, threaten to kill Geneva unless Bricriu gives us the rock. Then we will fly to save Dyn Meddy while you and yours return to Maisius Arborii to give Aven the burial she deserves."

Annwyl trembled. She faced away from me, her back heaving with sobs.

"Aven wouldn't have wanted you to let Dyn Meddy die to satisfy your anger, however justified. She would tell you to do what you could to save him, to stop Tukailaan. Would she not?"

Annwyl screamed and kept screaming.

My heart lurched.

Then she leaped into the air, hovering just over Geneva's body, and brandished the dagger at Bricriu. "Do as they say, Gwythienian. Give them the rock, or I will kill her."

Bricriu moved, and Annwyl shot toward him, shouting again.

"I am merely moving to retrieve the stone, Adarborian. Please, a moment."

The knife had paused mere breaths in front of his face. It was a mark of Bricriu' self-control that he managed to stay still.

Bricriu took a slow, measured step behind Geneva's bed, his giant Adarborian over to make sure he wasn't retrieving a weapon.

He held up a closed fist, then slowly opened it in front of Annwyl's grief-stricken face.

Annwyl snatched the white rock, hurled it at Gaedyen, then grabbed Aven's body and launched into the air. The Adarborians restraining Gaedyen and Bricriu took flight after her.

Bricriu's eyes landed on Gaedyen, and I knew what he was thinking: We had much less manpower on our side without the Adarborians.

I whirled and sprinted toward Gaedyen, jumping onto his shoulders at the last second. He launched into the sky and flapped so hard it nearly knocked me off. I checked that Veri was holding on to something, and finding him safely at my side, focused on keeping my seat.

I expected to hear angry wing beats chasing us, but nothing. I dared a look back and was shocked to see Bricriu sitting exactly where we'd left him, his hand on Geneva's back, eyes following our escape. Slow seconds passed, but he continued to get smaller and smaller. And then he was gone.

Why hadn't he tried harder to get the rock back?

We flew fast that night, only stopping to rest after hours and hours of straight flying. Gaedyen stretched his arms and legs one at a time, then both wings and his tail. He drank some water from the brook, shook himself, and told us to mount again.

Gaedyen flew hard for several more hours. I barely held on, and Veri was blown right off in a sudden descent as Gaedyen landed on a startled deer and dispatched it instantly, devouring the front half in one bite.

"What the heck? A little warning next time?" I glowered at him.

Veri glided down and landed on my head.

"I just sacrificed my mother—just after finding out that she'd been alive all this time. It is unlikely she will survive without the rock of healing now. Forgive me if I have too much on my mind to think of warning you when I see the chance to grab a meal."

Gaedyen tore off a hunk of meat. Handing it to me, he popped the rest of the carcass into his mouth.

"I'm so sorry, Gaedyen." That wasn't enough to say, but I didn't have any better words.

Veri drooped down to my shoulder as he whimpered. Turning to look at him, I caught a squeamish grimace on his face. He stared at the blood running from the fresh meat. Was it dredging up horrible images of what condition Dyn Meddy might be in?

Ashamed of Gaedyen's insensitivity and mine, I swung the bloody meat behind my back.

"Hey, Veri. Why don't you take a little walk? Just some time to yourself…it might be a nice break for you," I suggested.

"Yeah, okay." He sighed, sliding off my shoulder and sulking off toward some bushes.

"Poor guy," I whispered.

"I hope, for his sake and my own sanity, that Dyn Meddy survives and can stop Tukailaan. Losing another Possessor would be worse than unfortunate, but for my mother to die for nothing, or for Veri to lose the person who taught him everything he knows and who he looks up to so much…" Gaedyen's voice trailed off as I stared at him in surprise.

"I thought you didn't care for Veri," I countered.

Gaedyen shrugged. "I cannot thank him enough for all he did for you in Sequoia Cadryl. He was there for you when I wasn't."

"Yeah." What else was I supposed to say to that?

"Hey, Aven whispered a word, *Falbane*, right before she died. Do you know what or who that is?"

He scrunched up his face. "It sounds familiar. I feel like it is associated with someone going missing. Or a scandal of some kind. But I am not sure. We will have to ask Padraig next time we see him."

I bit my lip. There was something about that name. What was it? It must have been super important for Aven to have said it with her dying breath.

"Enzi?"

"Yeah?"

"There is something I need to tell you."

"What?"

"About Shaun."

Oh. He's going to confess now, is he?

I crossed my arms and tried not to look down my nose at him. "I'm listening."

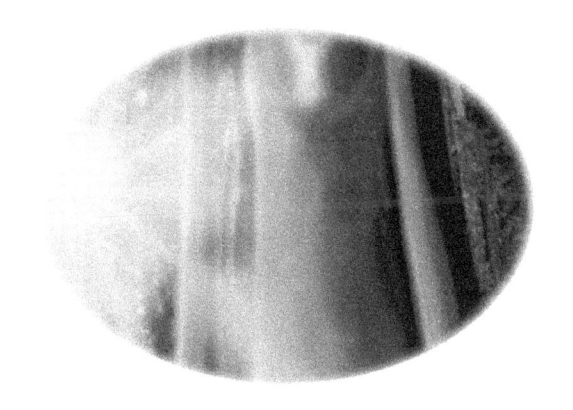

CHAPTER TWENTY-FIVE
Through Veri's Eyes

Maybe I'm not cut out to be a healer after all.
Dyn Meddy was going to die, and I couldn't do a thing to stop it. All my training, all my hours practicing. For nothing.

I couldn't save Enzi without Dyn Meddy, and now I can't save him either.

I sulked, dragging my feet and looking for something to kick. A fallen leaf wafted into my path, and I kicked it hard. It twisted two feet in the air and then dropped to the ground. I scowled at it. That was very unsatisfactory. My foot itched to kick something hard that hurt.

A breeze tickled the fur on my back. It smelled like…bad breath?

I whirled to see a huge Gwythienian that wasn't Gaedyen looming above me.

"And what's a raggedy little Crivabanian doin' in these woods, so far from home?"

Then I saw the mangled tail.

"Tukailaan?" I shouted in surprise.

"Well, ya seem t'know me, but I ain't never met ya, have I, Crivabanian?"

"No, you haven't." I glared, my fur standing on end.

"Didn't think so. My apologies, but I ain't got time to deal with ya, and I can't be havin' ya screamin' and alertin' everyone else to me bein' here. Nothin' personal, but I gotta give you the boot." And he lifted one large foreleg and slammed it where I'd been only an instant before.

"Enzi, Gaedyen!" I dodged another stomp. "Tukailaan's here. Run for it!"

I couldn't tell whether they'd heard me or not, so I shouted again, desperately hoping I was close enough for them to hear, before veering off in another direction. No sense leading Tukailaan right to them. If I couldn't get away, that would suck. But he didn't need to have them, too.

"Hurry, guys! Get out of here!"

Trees crashed to their deaths behind me as I leaped and glided from one branch to another, hoping to throw Tukailaan off.

But he seemed to follow pretty well. I considered hiding in a squirrel hole I came across, but my scent would lead him right to it. But hiding somewhere back on the path might throw him off my trail. So I scurried forward as fast as I could, then doubled back to the squirrel hole. I found it again, but it would be a tight fit.

And then the next tree over tilted and fell, crashing into the one I stood in and rattling its branches. Tukailaan's eyes swept the trees. I only had a second to disappear before his eyes would land on me. I dove through the sliver of an opening, hoping I would squeeze through before he saw me.

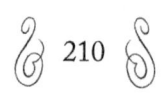

I tumbled much longer than I'd expected, falling for several seconds before meeting the woody bottom. I stared up at the entrance, a cavernous ceiling stretching into darkness above me. The hole was at least a hundred feet up, and it looked big enough to fit an elephant through. As I stared at it, befuzzled, Tukailaan's huge ear flap passed in front of the opening.

It seemed very strange for Tukailaan's earflap to be in proportion to the now-humungous hole in the tree.

Did I land on my head?

A wet, sticky sound drowned out the stomping. It oozed like old, globby paint being smeared over a wooden surface right by my ear. I turned toward the sound and leaped away from the monster. Four giant, gooey feelers and a floppy gray stalk of a body oozed toward me. A huge round shell rose up behind it.

Oh gross! A giant nasty snail? I rolled out of its way. *What the heck is a malwoden doing here?*

Darting around it, I ran right into a pile of stuff. A huge piece of contorted metal and some other junk. Fumbling around those, I made a gliding leap for the wall and clung to it when I landed. I was surprised it was easier to hang on to than I'd expected. I reached the hole, pulled myself through it, and gazed at the forest.

Everything seemed to have grown a ton while I was in the strange cavern. The twig I'd been standing on stretched out for a mile in front of me. A fallen leaf drifted past, the size of a human canoe. A hairy green worm inching alongside me was taller than I was. Every detail competed for my attention.

I heard a noise and ducked back into the hole.

Stuffing my anxious hands into my pouch, I felt for the trinkets I kept there. But my pouch was nearly empty. Frowning, I fished around and still came up short. Only two small objects remained in my pocket. I pulled them out.

It was the two stones I'd found at the helicopter crash site once.

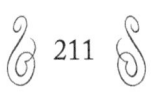

I'd forgotten about them. They were very pretty—one green, the other red. I looked closer. They didn't look like two forgotten bits of rock that hadn't seen the light of day in years. They weren't even dirty. Light glimmered off them as if they'd just been picked up from a stream, and the sun couldn't even reach in here...

With widening eyes, I stared first at the red one, then at the green, then back again. A red rock and a green rock? Both shining like they were covered in a layer of water...

No way. No way! They've been in my pouch this whole time? The last two rocks that are supposed to be with Tukailaan...and I've had them with me this whole time? Enzi's gonna kill *me!*

Wow, my realm's rock. The red one was definitely more beautiful.

And the Adarborians' rock. And...I was the size of a bug. I'd been holding the rock when Aven passed away. Did that mean...? I dropped them into my pouch and hoisted myself up the wall, realizing it was a piece of metal, realizing the whole pile of junk was mine—things I'd taken from the helicopter and kept in my pouch—but they hadn't shrunk with me like the rocks had.

I crawled up the wall again, emerging into sunlight. I needed to test this theory, and the sounds of Tukailaan searching for me were getting harder and harder to hear.

I stood and shook out my arms, preparing to try using the green rock. It was a good thing I didn't feel stronger. If I were the Possessor of Dyn Meddy's rock, well, that would mean he was dead.

Excited by the idea that I might have the Adarborians' abilities, I gripped the rock tightly and wished to be my normal size again. I squinted my eyes shut, trying to think the right thing. I needed to grow, to be bigger.

But not too much! Not a giant. Just my normal size. Two feet, one inch.

When I opened them again, that branch looked like the proper size under my feet.

I didn't feel stronger, but I needed to be sure I wasn't Possessor of Dyn Meddy's rock. That would be too horrible.

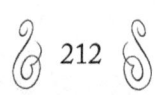

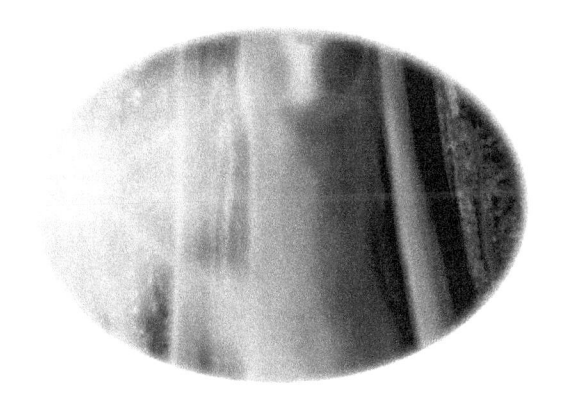

CHAPTER TWENTY-SIX
Through Enzi's Eyes

"Enzi, I am afraid I told you a lie."

"Mm-hmm." I raised an eyebrow, wondering where he would go from here.

"The thing is"—he scraped at the dirt with one forefoot, avoiding my eyes—"I know this isn't the time for this, but I need to be honest with you."

"I'd like that. Go on."

"Do you remember when I told you about Shimbators? How they are a myth?"

"Oh, yes. Yes, I do."

He cocked his head, perhaps confused by my tone. "Well, that is not entirely true."

"So Shimbators are real is what you're saying?"

"Yes." He stared at me, stock-still.

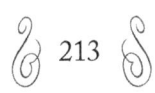

I flung my arms into the air. "Gaedyen, I've known for a while now. Tukailaan is a Shimbator. Remember that weird guy from when we left Odan Terridor? Tony? That was Tukailaan. The whole reason he started following us in the first place was because he saw the stone on my necklace that day. He showed up as Tony before turning into Tukailaan and attacking me. That's why you kept smelling him on the journey down to Maisius Arborii."

Gaedyen's earflaps stood erect as he scowled at me. "Why did you not tell me this before now?"

Crossing my arms again, I glared right back. "Why didn't *you* tell me Shimbators are real instead of lying to me about them? Hmm?"

He sagged, earflaps drooping. "Fine." Dragging a giant forefoot over his face, he sighed. "And there is more."

Is he going to tell me he is Shaun? I knew it! But...I'm not sure how I should react. And after what Shaun said to me the last time I saw him, and when Gaedyen asked the other night if I thought Shaun had a chance with me...

"Shaun is a Shimbator."

His eyes bored into mine.

After a long pause, I said, "Okay."

"You aren't surprised?"

"Once I knew about Tukailaan, I wondered."

"Ah. Well." His brows knit together, and he looked away. But toward the sky, rather than the ground.

What is he looking at?

He sniffed the air, inhaling deeply.

"So...is that all you wanted to tell me?"

"Not exactly—do you smell that? It smells like..."

His eyes grew wide, and my heart plummeted to my toes. *It better not be the strange smell of Tukailaan that somehow reminds Gaedyen of both me and Padraig.*

"Enzi, Gaedyen! Tukailaan's here. Run for it!" Veri shouted.

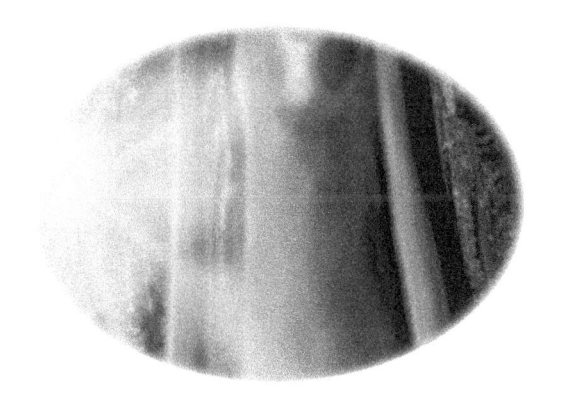

CHAPTER TWENTY-SEVEN
Through Veri's Eyes

Shoving both rocks back into my pouch, I glided to the forest floor, searching for something heavy. I landed on the cover of pine needles, then spotted a large boulder in the distance. I started for it, and then Enzi's voice jolted me back to reality.

"Veri! Where are you? Veri? Gaedyen, I can't find—" She cut off her own sentence with a scream that echoed from the direction Tukailaan had been headed.

I sprinted after her, pushing my legs to run as fast as they could. Couldn't the Adarborians, like, *speed* travel, or something? Apparently I wasn't wishing for that the right way though, because I wasn't traveling any faster than I'd ever run.

"Enzi!" Gaedyen bellowed.

Good, he was on his way. Possible new abilities aside, I was still no match for Tukailaan alone.

I reached a clearing and saw them. Gaedyen and Tukailaan, running toward each other, Enzi between them and running toward Gaedyen. Who would reach her first? It had to be Gaedyen! He *must* do this!

But Tukailaan was faster. Enzi shooed Gaedyen away with her arms, trying to keep him from putting himself in danger for her. But it wouldn't be enough. Tukailaan was bigger, and his body could make longer leaps. Gaedyen was younger and faster, but he was too far away. Then Enzi stumbled, falling in Tukailaan's path. She fumbled for the bow, but she couldn't get the rymakri lined up fast enough.

No! I wanted her to get up, I willed it to happen. But it would be too late. Tukailaan was there, his whole body suspended in midair and falling, forelegs aimed to crush the life out of my friend, out of the next Possessor he wanted dead.

I was nearly to her. One thick tree stood between us, and another one farther off, between her and Tukailaan. If I could shrink, I could grow too, right?

Digging the claws of my back feet into the closest tree, I flung the rest of my body forward, trying to focus on growing long enough to reach the other tree, trying desperately to reach it in time. Two heavy Gwythienian feet slammed into my expanded back. I had a fraction of an instant to get ahold of that tree before he crushed me and Enzi both.

My claws found their mark in the thick trunk, and I strained every last fiber of my paw muscles to keep them there.

I flexed every muscle to stop Tukailaan's from stomping on Enzi. My claws gouged the tree bark—but I had to hold on! Tukailaan bounced off my back. And then something rammed into my stomach, nearly knocking me loose again.

"Gaedyen, seriously!" I shouted. "Watch it."

But victory was not to be achieved so simply. Tukailaan was still there, and he was about to react to what I'd done. And after displaying abilities I shouldn't have, I'd practically just waved the missing rocks in his big, ugly face.

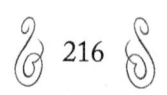

But I was Possessor now. The strength to push back against Tukailaan and Gaedyen…it meant…a *double*-Possessor. Did that mean…? I shoved the fear for Dyn Meddy aside, hardening myself for now. Just for this moment.

I can handle this. For Enzi.

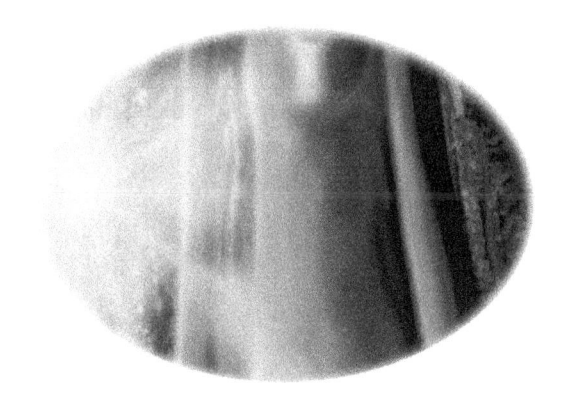

CHAPTER TWENTY-EIGHT
Through Enzi's Eyes

"Veri! Where are you?" I shrieked.

Shades of emerald swirled above me, blurring with pinpricks of sunlight as I spun in all directions, searching for Veri's voice. He didn't reply.

"Gaedyen," I whispered. "Let's split up and look for him, okay?"

He frowned. But I turned before he could protest. We'd find Veri faster if we split up.

"Enzi!" he hissed.

I turned back toward him. "What?"

"It is definitely him—his scent. The one that smells like you and Padraig. He really is here." He tossed me three rymakri, freshly bitten.

I caught them and nodded, appreciating his confidence in me. Confidence enough to give me weapons without being all chivalrous about it. He knew I could shoot, at least a bit. And I sensed some respect because of that. And that was really nice.

"Thank you," I mouthed, holding up the stick before mounting it to my bow.

He nodded before I turned and continued searching for any sign of either friend or foe, weapon at the ready.

And then Tukailaan was in front of me, running me down. I ran away from him as fast as I could, my arms pumping desperately, but my legs wouldn't move fast enough. It was like slogging through molasses, like trying to run in a dream. Gaedyen ignored my wild gestures to save himself and sped toward me almost as fast as Tukailaan. And then my legs completely betrayed me, and I tumbled to the ground.

Would Tukailaan kill me instantly for Possession of the Gwythienian rock? Or would he draw out my death?

I rolled onto my knees, trying to pick myself up. I knew my chances were slim, but I had to try. Then the light from the sun disappeared as something huge blocked its light. I scrambled to line up the rymakri, knowing it would take a miracle to aim and shoot in time.

But the impact didn't come. I was still three-dimensional. I expected to see a Gwythienian, so much bigger than Gaedyen, even bigger than Bricriu, big enough to block the sunlight. I expected to see his face above me, leering.

But it wasn't Tukailaan who'd blotted out the sun. It was...*a blanket?*

And then Gaedyen was there, trying to slow his rampage and careening into the blanket instead. I expected him to sail through it, for the blanket to collapse over his face and billow around him until he came to a stop. But the blanket barely gave way, and Gaedyen literally bounced back from it, looking dazed.

"Gaedyen, seriously," Veri's voice complained. "Watch it!"

"Veri?" I called. "Where are you?" I stumbled, trying to get to my feet while getting the rymakri into place.

Before I could find him, Tukailaan soared over the blanket and crashed into Gaedyen, pinning him.

"Gaedyen!" I screamed, swiping my bow into position.

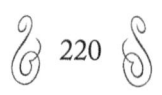

Tukailaan's face whipped around and sneered at me as my fingers fumbled with the rymakri.

"Do not dare use an arkencain on her!" Gaedyen roared.

Tukailaan snarled. Our eyes met, and his hard, warrior expression vanished for an instant before a sneering grin replaced it.

"Human faces. They all look the same! But I ain't gonna waste an arkencain on her when I can just as easily squish 'er underfoot. It's a shame the only creature who ever lit a spark in you is such a weaklin'. If only she were your equal, another Gwythienian. She may 'a been able to help you then. Not that she coulda saved ya, of course. Yer gonna die. I'll finally end Padraig's line today. Interesting though, that you have the same genetic flaw I do, though we ain't close relations."

"Gaedyen's not flawed!" I found myself yelling foolishly in his defense. Technically, that wasn't exactly true. But Tukailaan was *not* allowed to have an opinion. *What was that about a "spark"?*

I glanced back to the furry blanket, wondering if I could use it as a distraction. But it was gone.

"You ain't told 'er, have ya?" Tukailaan sneered.

"Told"—he wheezed under the pressure of Tukailaan's body—"her what?"

"Oh, cough it up. You know what I mean." His piercing gaze returned to me, sneering. "Just the fact that yer a Shim—"

"Stop!" Gaedyen's eyes went wide as he cut Tukailaan off, his face showing fear for the first time as he stared at me. "Enzi, I am a Shimbator. I am so sorry I was not honest with you before. I was afraid—"

Tukailaan landed a punch to his face.

"I will…explain it to you…later, Enzi. A little busy…" He grunted, blocking another punch.

"Hiiiyaaahhh!" Veri's voice erupted from somewhere behind me. The three of us turned just as Veri speed-glided into

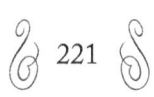

Tukailaan—and half knocked him off Gaedyen. It was enough to give Gaedyen the leverage he needed.

Tukailaan swiped at Veri. It looked like he'd hit him, but Veri must've been too quick. He was gone faster than my eyes could follow.

With Tukailaan distracted, Gaedyen slid out from under him, elbowing him in the face as he leaped to the side.

Tukailaan roared, teetering off balance. He leaped up and poised to take Gaedyen down, and I remembered I didn't have to be totally useless. I raised my bow, but before I could aim, a furry missile knocked Tukailaan off course again. I lowered the weapon, not willing to risk hitting Veri.

The moment Veri resurfaced, I pulled my bow into the air, training a rymakri on Tukailaan's ugly head.

But he moved so fast, and Veri and Gaedyen kept showing up in and out of my line of sight. I was too terrified of hitting one of them. I held the rymakri on Tukailaan anyway, waiting for the right moment.

My heart pounded, confused, afraid, wanting to believe, and full of adrenaline.

A deafening, blinding roar rippled through the air from behind me. It vibrated the whole forest, knocking me to my knees.

The two Gwythienians stopped fighting and backed several paces away from each other, searching the sky.

I followed their gazes.

A dark shape against the sun. Flapping wings. A Gwythienian for sure. But who? *Please, not Bricriu...I'm not sure we can trust him.*

Tukailaan ripped a branch from a nearby oak and bit it into a rymakri. They were too far apart for hand-to-hand combat now, so Tukailaan was going to throw a rymakri at him. Gaedyen caught on and had his own weapon ready in a flash.

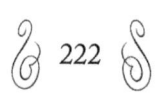

But Tukailaan was quicker. He caught Gaedyen in his good wing shoulder just as Gaedyen threw his rymakri. Gaedyen roared in pain, but so did Tukailaan a moment later. Once more they bit and threw, but this time they both missed.

The dark shape roared again, and he was close enough now that I recognized him.

"Gaedyen, it's Padraig!" I yelled in relief, cupping my hands over my mouth to send my voice over the cacophony.

Tukailaan's head flashed up to stare at the sky, and just as his last rymakri found Gaedyen's previously good wing shoulder, Padraig crashed into Tukailaan, knocking him onto his side and pinning him to the ground.

"You will not touch my grandson!" Padraig roared.

Tukailaan stared, speechless. "What? How're ya alive?"

"A pleasure to see you again as well, brother." Padraig sneered at him, his upper lip trembling like a ferocious dog, just waiting to sink its teeth into its enemy. "It is so nice to find you so… unchanged."

"But how…?" Tukailaan repeated himself.

"When you disgraced our realm and our race with your inhumane practices and I was thrust into your position as the only other candidate for the Keepership, I played a little trick on the realms. They forced me to give up the life I'd always wanted, thanks to your indescribably poor judgment, so I took a little risk. I had been planning to travel to Ofwen Dwir to visit the realm of the Rubandors, to learn about their culture. But as you took that from me, and as I had befriended Gwaltmar, their candidate, I arranged with him to coat our hands with a protective sealant before the ceremony so we could avoid touching the rocks. Afterward, we switched rocks and touched those so we would Possess each other's rock instead of our own. We were not sure if it would work, but it did, in the end." Padraig regarded Tukailaan with a determined but grim expression.

Tukailaan returned his gaze, and Padraig faltered, not having expected such a reaction to that information.

"Ah! Is that so? So that'd be why your friend's rock didn't work fer me when I killed 'em."

Padraig's eyes hardened as he growled. "So it was you? You murdered Gwaltmar for his rock?"

"Oh." Tukailaan chuckled. "Yes, I did." He bucked out from under Padraig. "Yeah, and you ruined my life. You let that monster, Meleena, outta the dungeons, and her foul offspring killed my wife!" Tukailaan lunched at Padraig, but Gaedyen flew into him and knocked him down before he could reach him.

Padraig was there in an instant. He leaped on Tukailaan's forelegs and pinned them down while Gaedyen bore down on his back legs and tried to control the whipping tail.

Padraig huffed, "Your wife...? I thought Meleena *was* your wife. But which Gwythienian...I did not know you had ever committed to anyone else. Who was so unfortunate to commit to you?"

"No one ya knew." Tukailaan scowled, straining against them.

Padraig smiled down at him as if he were a silly child. "You forget, brother, that I am Keeper. I know every Gwythienian in Odan Terridor."

"I assure you, *brother*," Tukailaan snarled, "I ain't forgotten, and ya didn't know my wife. She weren't Gwythienian."

Padraig's eyes narrowed. "Tell me, Tukailaan, why do you speak in this strange manner?"

Tukailaan laughed heartily. "Oh, good ole' Padraig, the one who knows it all! But you ain't ever guessed my secret. You dunno where I been all these years, and what's more is Shimbators ain't just a myth. I'm livin' proof."

Wonder and disgust warred on Padraig's face. "What?"

Tukailaan sneered, relishing Padraig's surprise. "The legends *are* true, brother. The legends of treacherous skin changers, the

Shimbators our dear old father scared us with when we were younglings. And I'm one of 'em now. I've got two forms: what I was born with—and a human."

Tukailaan glanced at Gaedyen. With a wry smile in his direction, he asked Padraig, "And do you want to know the best part?"

Padraig seemed too stunned to reply.

Tukailaan took advantage of their distraction and burst free, pausing several paces away.

"Well then, I'll tell ya. Gaedyen, yer own uppity little grandson, is also a Shimbator."

Padraig's shocked face turned to take in Gaedyen's stiff form.

"Gaedyen?" Padraig breathed his name, but he didn't respond. He only looked away.

Tukailaan grinned at Padraig with such insane, wild delight, it made me shiver. And then his form quivered and shrank, changing color as it did so. In his place stood the human—and disgustingly naked—Tony.

"Yes, Padraig. I'm still Tukailaan, just in human form. Do ya believe me now?"

"But…how…?" the mystified Padraig stammered.

Tony—Tukailaan, I mean—grew angrier and swelled back into his Gwythienian form. "How? How should I know? It just *is*. I didn't choose it. And the first time I turned, I couldn't find a way to turn back. For years, I thought I'd doomed myself to that human life forever."

Padraig struggled for words. "Is that what happened the night you escaped?"

"Indeed. A human woman found me in the woods. Alone and darn near starved. She hauled me all the way back to 'er house and nursed me back to health. She became my wife. And then you let Meleena out, and she killed her! You took my family from me." Tukailaan trembled with rage. "But getting my revenge was a cinch."

Padraig glared at his brother. "What do you mean?"

"I took from you what you took from me."

The scars crossing Padraig's face wrinkled as his eyes widened. "Tafli was killed by humans…I saw the evidence myself."

Tukailaan let out the biggest bellow of laughter yet. "Yeah, she was killed by humans. But I helped, usin' both forms. But the point is, I planned her death. When you're cursed with a human form, you tend to make human friends. I helped with the death of Ferrox, too. So you would begin to know the pain you dumped on me."

It was Tukailaan who killed Ferrox—his parents hadn't fought each other to the death. And Geneva's still alive. Is anything Gaedyen knows about his parents true?

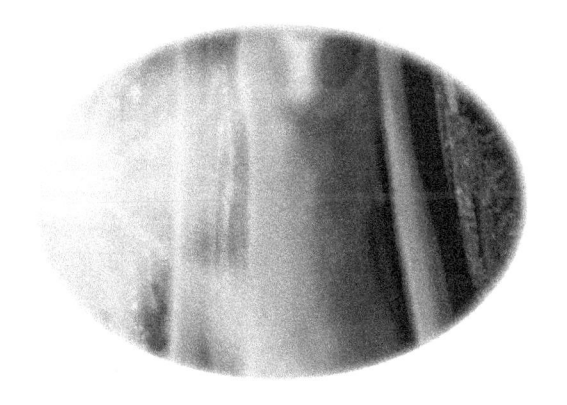

CHAPTER TWENTY-NINE

"So for your...revenge...you took away the life I wanted, and then stole those I loved as well? But Tukailaan, I did not release Meleena. She was never released at all."

Tukailaan's exultant smile drooped at the edges. "What d'you mean?"

"She escaped the same night you did. I have not seen her since. I thought the two of you escaped together."

"Liar!" Tukailaan leaped at him.

But Padraig was ready for him, a rymakri in hand. Glowering at Tukailaan, he pitched the rymakri at him. It ripped through his shoulder, and Tukailaan bellowed in pain.

"She was the Possessor of the Rock of Healing decades ago," Padraig said. "I could not help but assume it was still so, and the two of you were still haunting human lands with your devilry."

Backing up, Tukailaan glanced at Padraig, then examined his surroundings. When he leaped and retrieved a sturdy branch from a nearby beech, Padraig was quick to mirror his move, and they both stood poised to throw.

"She was no Possessor!" yelled Tukailaan. "Just a miserable blight on my life."

Before either of them sent their rymakri flying, another stick came whistling through the air, narrowly missing Tukailaan's neck. He whipped toward Gaedyen, who was already brandishing another rymakri.

Tukailaan took two giant steps toward Gaedyen, then suddenly whirled and plunged his weapon into Padraig, who had come up behind him to defend Gaedyen. It was a smooth move on Tukailaan's part, and it left Padraig gushing blood.

"No!" I whispered.

"Enzi!"

I turned toward the shout. Gaedyen met my eyes, tossed three more rymakri my way, and then took off to rejoin the fray. He was on them in a flash, pulling Tukailaan off Padraig and trying to choke him. But Tukailaan fought hard, scratching Gaedyen's face with his wing claws.

Coward. I finally had a good, clear shot and took it, but I missed.

Tukailaan was much bigger than Gaedyen and bucked him off quickly. Once free, Tukailaan sprang at Padraig again. I took aim, aligning my stick with where his body would be. Where was the most efficient place to shoot a Gwythienian?

Maybe the heart? I let the stick fly.

I was a moment too late. It did hit him, but I missed his heart. The rymakri lodged in his side, and back under his spine. I was rewarded with an angry roar. I couldn't see whether it penetrated his other side, but it'd been enough of a distraction for Padraig to throw him to the ground.

"Sweet shot!" Veri called as he whizzed past me, heading toward the brawl.

"Thanks!" I shouted back, smiling at my little victory.

Veri soared over them, pulled in his gliding membranes, and dove. My heart stopped—he was headed right for Tukailaan! He landed on Tukailaan's massive head, clamping his feet around one ear flap, and then extended his body to wrap all the way around his face, covering his eyes.

Tukailaan pawed at him, backing up. Veri was dangerously close to Tukailaan's mouth. If he managed to push him off his face, he would be in easy chomping range. I readied another rymakri. But before I could even focus my missile, Gaedyen and Padraig were both leaping toward them.

Gaedyen did a sort of flipping-spinning motion midair and landed with his tail toward Tukailaan. With his good leg, he aimed a hard kick at Tukailaan's middle and sent him skidding into a nearby tree. Padraig performed the same motion as he soared through the air and landed in front of where Tukailaan skidded, giving him another firm kick.

Tukailaan's furious howl shook my bones. Veri slipped, and my heart skipped a beat. But he unfurled himself and pushed off from Tukailaan's head before he could slap at him.

Tukailaan faced Padraig and pounced on him, biting his neck. Padraig didn't make a noise, and I was horrified it may have been the final blow.

That fear must've gripped Gaedyen as well, because he suddenly had new strength and launched himself at the two again. Tukailaan saw him and maneuvered so Gaedyen's weight landed on Padraig instead of him. Gaedyen tried to correct himself, but it was too late. He came crashing down on Padraig, who cried out in pain.

Tumbling off Padraig, Gaedyen glared at Tukailaan, searching for another opening. Tukailaan smiled at him, his head held high in premature glee over the outcome of an unfinished battle. He glanced at Padraig, then leaped toward Gaedyen, arms outstretched.

Gaedyen caught Tukailaan with both forelegs and immediately pushed him away, but Tukailaan was too quick. He'd seen that move coming and wrapped one rear leg around Gaedyen's ankle, pulling him down as he flew backward.

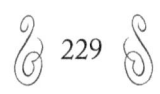

Gaedyen landed hard on his back and didn't move. Tukailaan rose slowly, shaking his head as if to clear it.

"Gaedyen!" I screamed. He had to get up! I hadn't told him how I felt yet.

Tukailaan reared up on his hind legs, rising over Gaedyen's still form. His heavy forelegs plummeted toward Gaedyen's chest. I released the shot I'd been reserving for the right moment. It whizzed through the air, shearing off Tukailaan's right ear flap.

He roared again as he fell to one side, only partially landing on Gaedyen, his eyes searching for me.

Scowling, he growled. "You have been awfully troublesome for one single human. Say, did Padraig ever tell you what exactly they locked me up for? What I did to humans?"

I silently nocked another rymakri.

"Tukailaan! Your quarrel is with me," Padraig shouted, getting shakily to his feet.

Tukailaan laughed. "You are about to die, Padraig. And when ya do, I'll Possess your Rubandor rock. I'll be the first to Possess multiple rocks at once. Then there won't be anything ya can do about it. You won't be able to stop me ever again. I'll truly be free."

"All I ever wanted was for you to be happy, brother," Padraig wheezed. "Back before the Keepership changed. You knew that, back then. You knew I did not want the Keepership. You knew I was happy for you when you were told you would have it, because I knew you wanted it. How could you wish such miseries on me, when I have wished nothing but the best for you?"

"Nothing but the best? How 'bout when you told on me to our father? You threw my whole life away. And then you allowed Meleena to kill my wife. You never wanted the best for me!" Tukailaan spat.

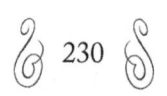

"Tukailaan, it broke me to report you, but what you were doing was wrong. You were murdering humans who had nothing to do with us, and who are just as sentient as us, no matter our differences. And besides that, your actions with Meleena endangered our entire realm. And the Four Realms. It was not for my own devices I reported you; it was for the good of the many. Where is Meleena now?"

Tukailaan scoffed. "Dead, I hope. I ain't seen 'er in decades. And if yer such a kind-hearted one, how'd ya end up with a son like Ferrox?"

Gaedyen snarled.

"How'd ya create somebody who wanted to take the rocks for himself and make himself better'n everyone else? Was that with their best interests in mind? Or was all 'a that fer me again?" He punctuated his sarcasm with a derisive snort.

A slight shuffling on the ground around Tukailaan, and Veri's large, furry leg forward-kicked the base of his tail with considerable force. Tukailaan's back end flipped up over his head and crashed to the ground, bending his neck to an odd angle. Padraig was on him in an instant—the wheezy voice from a moment ago had been fake!

"You dare talk about my son like that?" And he punched Tukailaan's jaw with his sizable Gwythienian fists.

Tukailaan only laughed. "Or maybe he ain't so bad...he coulda had another purpose that day, besides takin' the rocks fer himself..."

Another punch landed on his face.

"Come on, brother. If a body was gonna steal the rocks for themselves, they'd have to frame it on somebody else. Takin''em would be very obvious, too noticeable. No smart Gwythienian'd just go and steal 'em right out from under your nose. They'd need another body to do the job. And if I was gonna kill off the Possessors, as I obviously been plannin' on doin' for a while now, which Possessor'd I wanna do in first?"

Padraig was frozen, two fisted hands ready to pound Tukailaan. "What are you saying, Tukailaan? What do you mean?" He sounded half crazed now. "Tell me!" he roared in his face.

Cackling, Tukailaan swung one arm toward Padraig, slamming a large boulder against his head. Sneering, he said, "Or maybe I just made all 'a that up to distract you."

Tukailaan bucked Padraig off him and was on his feet in half a second, grabbing one branch in each hand and biting both into weapons at the same time.

Gaedyen jumped into the space between them, his own weapon in hand, ready to defend his grandfather.

Tukailaan bellowed and shoved one stick at Gaedyen, but Gaedyen deflected it with his own, knocking it to the ground.

"What you just implied about my father, was it true?" Gaedyen's eyes shone fiercely as he stared Tukailaan down.

"It might be," Tukailaan answered with a maddening grin.

Gaedyen let out a low growl. "Tell me now, or I swear I will kill you!"

Again, he laughed. "Ah, youngling. Ya won't kill me while I hold information you'd like to get yer mitts on now, will ya? But once I tell ya what ya wanna know, you'll strike me down. Not that it'd do much good, of course."

Padraig was up again but shaky. He'd been bleeding from his side for several minutes now, still fighting with everything he had.

"Tukailaan, please."

I hoped he was faking weakness again, but I couldn't tell.

"Do ya think *asking nicely* will get ya better results?" He sneered.

Quick as a flash, Gaedyen scooped up Tukailaan's stick he'd deflected earlier and wielded it along with the other he'd made for himself. He lunged at Tukailaan, but Tukailaan sidestepped him at the last instant and dove at Padraig. Soaring through the air, Tukailaan aimed.

He drove the branch into Padraig's chest.

Tukailaan victoriously bared his teeth. "I've beaten you, Padraig. Yer outta my way now."

"I am sorry it came to this, brother," Padraig whispered.

And he placed one hand on Tukailaan's arm, his grasp like steel. With the last of his strength, he rolled over onto Tukailaan, grabbed a rymakri from the ground, and shoved it into Tukailaan's side. Tukailaan roared, and Padraig stabbed him again as he dropped his weight and the rymakri sticking out from his chest, puncturing Tukailaan's as well.

Tukailaan rolled them both over and pushed himself off Padraig, stumbling to the side.

I nearly screamed when Veri landed on my shoulder and grabbed the remaining rymakri from my hand. Swooping to the ground, he snatched up a still-intact rymakri, then launched himself into the air again.

"You've failed again, Padraig. I'll always beat ya." Tukailaan pulled himself to his full height and raised a rymakri over Padraig.

"No!" Gaedyen launched himself toward them.

And then out of nowhere, a giant Veri was standing directly in front of Tukailaan. The huge Veri glared at Tukailaan, and with a shout, shoved a rymakri into either side of Tukailaan's throat.

Tukailaan stepped back, wobbled, and fell to the ground. Gaedyen stopped pursuing him and ran for Padraig.

I ran after Gaedyen.

"Padraig? Gaedyen, is he okay?"

Padraig seemed to be saying something. I slowed as I neared them, trying to hear what he whispered.

Gaedyen stared down at Padraig, looking like he might cry.

Veri landed on my shoulder. "Tukailaan is dead."

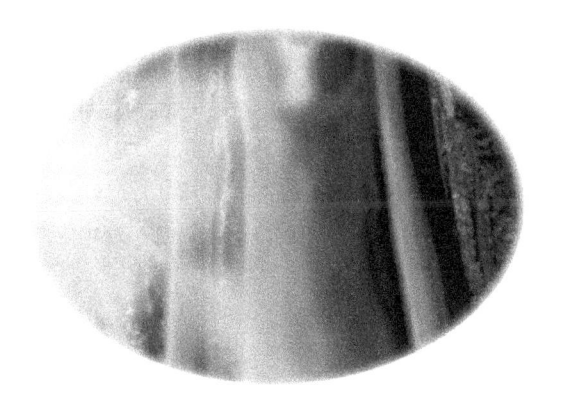

CHAPTER THIRTY

I knelt by Padraig's face, watching Gaedyen.

Padraig opened his eyes and whispered, "May your rymakri stay sharp and your aim ever true. I have always believed in you. Find Meleena and take the rock from her. She would find a way to do harm even with a rock that heals. Then go lead the life you wish to live. Do not let anyone else control your future. You only get one life."

Padraig coughed, turning to face me. "Take care of him," he whispered, and his head fell to the ground, eyes open. His chest rose once, then stilled.

Padraig was dead.

Tukailaan was dead.

"Gaedyen?" My voice shook.

He just looked at me, then at Padraig for an instant, and then at me again. Some measure of emotion broke through the hard mask of his face—he'd just lost his grandfather, the only family he'd ever known, the one who'd raised him.

"Should…should we bury them?"

"I am afraid that would be impossible. They are both bigger than me, and I am not currently at my strongest. Besides, my people would dig up Padraig at least to take him back to our realm for a proper Keeper's burial." He squinted at the intertwined corpses. "Though, I do not want there to be…flies and such…" His voice choked off.

He faced away from me, his body shaking with silent grief.

I slid my arms around his neck and awkwardly patted him. "I'm so sorry, Gaedyen."

His huge hand pressed me closer to him.

A crackling-ripping sound came from behind us, and I turned to see what it was without moving away from him. This was a moment I needed to prolong as much as possible.

Veri was tall again—as tall as Tukailaan had been on his hind legs—and he laid a leafy branch over the fallen Gwythienians and then turned to a different tree and tore another limb loose.

"I suppose that is the best we can do for now," said Gaedyen. "Padraig will get a proper burial as soon as possible."

He dropped his hand, and I held in my pent-up emotions as I stepped away from him.

I dared a look at his face. He stared quizzically at Veri, his eyes following his every move.

"Did I imagine him becoming suddenly stronger?"

My brow furrowed as well. "Not unless I imagined it too."

"And the part where he grew? Did I…*bounce* off him at some point?"

That giant furry blanket that had stopped Tukailaan from crushing me had been Veri. "Yes, I believe you did."

"Veri!" Gaedyen called.

His turned toward us, then he leaped into the air, shrank to his normal size, and glided to my shoulder.

"I'm so sorry, Gaedyen."

"Thank you, Veri. Now explain how you are suddenly able to change your size and be strong enough to hold Tukailaan's head for so long. Even being a Cadoumai does not explain the changing size."

"Oh, that." His face fell.

"Yes, that."

"Yeah, how'd you block Tukailaan from squishing me?" I asked.

He hung his head. "I think I have Possession of the Crivabanians' rock. And the Adarborians'. They've, um, sort of been in my…pouch…the whole time…"

"The whole time? What do you mean, 'the whole time'?" I demanded.

"Yeah…well you know how I collect little things, like that helicopter metal, right? Well, before I collected that, I found these two really pretty, smooth, shiny rocks by the crash site one day. They sort of sank to the bottom of my pouch, and I haven't seen them in a while. Kinda forgot I had them."

He looked warily up at us.

I propped my hands on my hips. "You mean to tell me you had Possession of both the missing rocks this *whole time* and could have been useful every time we needed help?"

"Obviously not!" Veri huffed, jamming his tiny fists on his hips. "I wasn't the Possessor until a few minutes ago. Aven and Dyn Meddy were the Possessors…until today. I'm only a Possessor now because…because of their deaths." And his face grew sorrowful again. "I didn't even get to say goodbye. The last time I saw him…he sacrificed his position for me. And I never got to say thank you." He sniffled, shoving his wrist under his nose.

My stomach sank. I knew Aven had died—she'd passed away in my arms—but I hadn't realized Dyn Meddy was gone too. Poor Veri. And Padraig, the last of the old Possessors, was also dead, just a few feet away. So much death today…so many lives lost. And important ones too!

The last three of the old Possessors, and the twin brother of the Keeper himself.

I was glad Tukailaan was gone. But I mourned the loss of the others. They were important to the Four Realms, and not only that, they weren't supposed to die as Possessors. They were supposed to have been able to give up their responsibilities and burdens to younger shoulders decades ago. But they never got that chance.

"Gaedyen, I'm so sorry about Padraig."

"It was difficult to be raised by him, but he really did put forth his best to fulfill the job he never wanted to have. Never before have I seen anyone so fully live and die for his people. He deserves to be honored."

I agreed, but I couldn't find the right words.

"Come on," I finally said. "Let's finish covering them, and then we'll return to Odan Terridor and bring back some Gwythienians to help us transport them."

Gaedyen rose slowly to his feet and followed me and Veri to finish covering our dead.

Gaedyen ripped off branches and tossed them to me, then I covered Padraig and Tukailaan. Veri pulled off his own branches, swooped over the pile, and let them fall where they may.

As I laid a branch over Tukailaan's ugly head, a pattern on his shoulder caught my attention. It was similar to Gaedyen's—like an eggshell that had been broken open. But I knew the shape of Gaedyen's, and this was different. The marks weren't all in the same place, or the same size. Was this his commitment mark? Like what Veri had said?

We were all exhausted from the fight, especially Gaedyen, but none of us wanted to sleep there, so we traveled a little deeper into the forest before resting for the night.

I offered to get Gaedyen food, but he said he wasn't hungry. And I didn't really want to go hunting just then anyway. Veri was strangely energized, though, as if he'd gotten a high from the fight. He scampered off to find some edible vegetation, while I sat stiffly on the ground, tired but wide awake.

I wanted to ask Gaedyen about what he'd said during the fight—what I'd thought he'd said. But wasn't it insensitive to bring up something like that while he was grieving for the only parent figure he'd ever had?

I'd have to just lay there all night wondering about it... maybe counting the stars would distract me.

"Enzi?"

I closed my eyes. There was something really nice about hearing my name in his voice. "Yes?"

"Do you remember, before the fight, when I told you that... that Shaun is a Shimbator?"

"Yes. I remember that. Kind of a hard thing to forget."

"I am sorry I lied to you. I was afraid."

"Afraid? Right, because I'm the intimidating type." I scoffed. "Look, Gaedyen, I knew." I looked into his eyes. "I figured it out. You are Shaun."

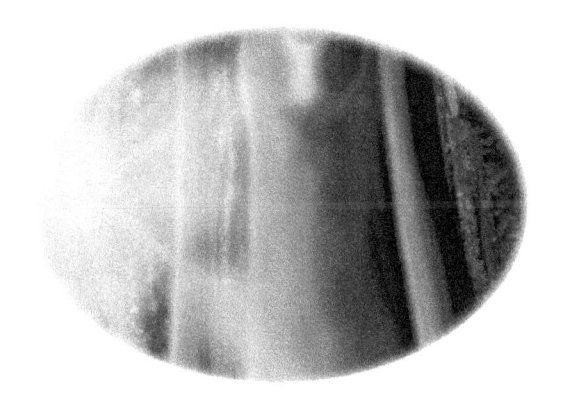

CHAPTER THIRTY-ONE

"But...how...?"

"Gaedyen, think about it. It wasn't that hard. You have identical marks in the same place. And how would you really manage to get a message to someone else in a faraway place to come stay with me in Sequoia Cadryl while you 'went searching for Tukailaan'? For some reason, you decided to be the human version of you while we were there. I'm not sure why you let me keep being mad at you and didn't just explain it."

"I just wanted to make you happy, Enzi. I am sorry I lied to you, but I did not see any other way. I tried to go back to being a Gwythienian after waking up in Sequoia Cadryl as a human, but because I had damaged my mark in the fall, I could not. The mark is a Shimbator thing, you see. That was why I kept it hidden. It would have been dangerous to parade it about among the other realms. But when I was stuck in human form, I was afraid I would not ever be able to turn back. And I did not think telling you the truth would make you happy. I had hoped to make your life better as Shaun."

That filled in the remaining holes. *So do I know it all now? Or are there more secrets? How can I fully trust him if he keeps hiding things from me?*

"Enzi, please say something."

I wanted to say something, but my brain and my mouth weren't functioning just yet.

"Enzi? Is it what I feared? Are you disgusted? Afraid? Appalled? Please, do not spare my feelings. The worst is better than not knowing at all."

He sat on his haunches, his head ducked to my level, eyes vulnerable, questioning.

"What Shaun said the last time I saw him in Sequoia Cadryl…?"

"Yes, that was me too. I meant every word."

I covered my mouth with my hands. Taking slow steps toward him, I reached around his strong neck, holding him tight.

I felt a rumble in his throat—was he trying to say something? I listened, but I couldn't believe what I heard.

"Enzi, I love you."

I couldn't believe it. Why wouldn't my brain tell my mouth what to say?

"Did you hear me, Enzi?"

"What did you say?" My lips trembled as I stepped back and scrutinized his.

"Enzi, I am in love with you. I…" He sighed and looked down. "I wanted to tell you before. I know this is horrible timing, but…well I could not stand to risk another moment of something happening to one of us before I could tell you. I do not wish to make you feel awkward around me; I just needed you to know. And to know I will never lie to you again."

He sounded so ashamed and apologetic, like he was inconveniencing me with his declaration. But I must have been wearing my joy on my face when he looked back at me, because his forlorn face brightened and his ear flaps rose a little.

"Gaedyen, do you really?"

"Of course I love you! You—well—you are you."

"Oh, Gaedyen!" I cried as I rushed to him and held him as close as I could. "I love you too. So much."

And his big arm wrapped around me, squeezing me tight. I could barely breathe for how good it felt. I wasn't even embarrassed at the sigh that escaped my lips at his touch. It felt like getting lost in music. Like flying high above the clouds. And then his large hand covered my back, his long fingers wrapping around my waist.

His hand gently pulled me away from his body, and I regretted the distance between us. Until I saw his eyes. He pulled me only far enough away for me to see his face. He held it at my level and stared searchingly into my eyes.

"Enzi, are you sure? You do not have to say so just to make me feel better about myself. Please, be honest."

"I *am* being honest, Gaedyen." I almost giggled. "I *do* love you too." I was afraid my grin might break my face.

His lit up too, but he still seemed unsure, afraid to believe.

"Gaedyen, seriously."

"Enzi, I am going to switch to my human form, okay?"

My heart thudded. He was going to turn into Shaun—human-Gaedyen. The paradox of both of them overwhelmed me. I wasn't ready for that.

He closed his eyes.

Oh crap. He was going to be naked, wasn't he? Maybe he didn't need to change forms just yet. Maybe he should just stay Gaedyen for a while longer…

I opened my mouth to suggest it, but his eyes were open again, and he looked horrified.

"Gaedyen, what's wrong? What did I do?"

"I was just trying to return to human form…but I *failed*."

"Wait, so you can't turn human?" I tried to hide the relief in my voice.

He closed his eyes again and still looked horrified when he reopened them.

"Enzi, I am stuck," he told me gravely. "I am so sorry." He turned his distraught eyes back to me. "I promise I was not lying to you...I do not know what is wrong with me. Unless..." He eyed his mark. "Enzi, is it just me, or are the lines of my mark not aligned?"

As he bent his shoulder toward me, I touched the mark. It was the first time I'd ever seen the whole thing unobscured. It was like a cracked eggshell a creature was about to emerge from. There were several small cracks clustered close together in the middle, then similar lines spaced farther apart the farther from the middlehey expanded. And many of them were broken. As if the skin had been cut and then sewn back together carelessly.

"Yeah, it does look like the skin didn't grow back together right."

"Oh no. Enzi, I am so sorry."

"Shh, don't worry about it Gaedyen." I smiled, lifting a hand to touch his rough face. "I fell in love with you in this form, and I don't need you to be a human for me. Humans are terribly boring, you know. Gwythienians are way cooler." I beamed up at him.

The ridges where his eyebrows would be if he were human drew together in confusion. He opened his mouth to say something, but we were interrupted.

"Enough of the mooshy-gooshy stuff! Guys, none of that is news to anyone but apparently the two of you. I called it *ages* ago. You must be the two blindest people in existence, seriously." Veri chattered excitedly. "Enzi, if I wasn't slightly afraid he would stomp me into mush for telling you, I would've let you in on it sooner. In fact, now that I'm a double-Possessor, I would've told you today, probably, if he hadn't just done the job himself. And holy crap! Check out this new battle wound." Veri held out his leg for inspection. A deep gash dripped dark blood, matting the fur around the wound.

"We should stop the bleeding." I grabbed the hem of my shirt to rip off a strip of fabric like they do in movies. It was surprisingly difficult—not like in the movies.

Veri alighted on a trunk close by, and I bandaged his leg the best I could.

"Nicely done, Enzi." Veri held out his leg and rotated it back and forth to check out my bandaging skills. "Imagine. Lacerated by a Shimbator in his Gwythienian form. Best scar yet!"

What a different take Crivabanians have on scars. Could it be possible to someday look at my scars the way Veri looks at his?

Gaedyen's sad voice interrupted my thoughts. "I wish I would have had a chance to explain to Padraig, if he had to know at all. I wish he would not have had to die only knowing a little."

That reminded me of my mom. She'd lived for me ever since I was born. It wasn't right, calling her so rarely. But still, she'd lied to me for so long…

Gaedyen saw me brooding. "What is wrong?"

"I'm just thinking about my mom and how I'd like to let her know I'm okay. And the last time we talked, she was about to say something important and then got cut off. I want to know what she was going to say. And I need to check on my dad. I have no idea how he's doing."

"We will do exactly that as soon as possible," he assured me, draping his giant hand around my waist again. "And then I will focus on becoming human again."

I gulped. What exactly did that entail?

But for the moment, I didn't need to worry about that. Or about my mom. For the moment, Gaedyen and Veri were okay, and Gaedyen, well, he finally felt the same about me as I did about him. He had all along, crazy as that was.

Time would bring more challenges, but for now, there was us.

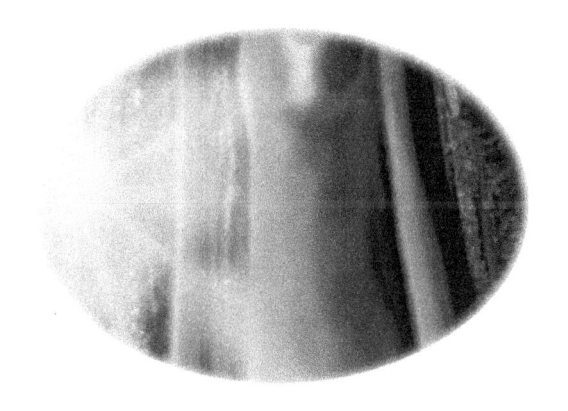

CHAPTER THIRTY-TWO
Through Bricriu's Eyes

"Do not worry, my sweet Geneva. Those nasty people are gone now. They will not bother us anymore."

I stroked Geneva's unresponsive head. I hated her bad days, but I knew she would be better soon. I always made her better. She was lucky to have me, really.

I eyed her coloring, noting it was more red and less beige than it had been recently. "You do look brighter today, Geneva. It must be finally getting rid of that brat, Gaedyen. You are fortunate I was there to protect you, love. And do not trouble yourself with whom that imbecile claimed to be. Of course he isn't your son. You never had children. But we could have children together someday. If you would like to. Once you get better."

What would I have done if she'd been pregnant with *his* child when I saved her? Shivering at the unimaginable horror, I abandoned that thought and focused on stroking her head, hoping she would wake enough to respond.

"Geneva?"

No response.

"Geneva, I just want you to know we are going to be okay. I will protect you, no matter who or what comes after us. I always have."

Squeezing my fist over the object it encircled, I smiled. They were such idiots.

"Geneva, do you know what I have here?"

She moaned a little, but I couldn't be sure it was a response.

Holding my fist next to her head, I unfurled my fingers to reveal my secret.

White fractals shimmered over her face and the stone she rested on as the rock in my hand caught the sun's rays.

"This is the real rock, love. They only have a fake."

I couldn't resist the grin from the thrill of that knowledge. They'd been so eager to leave, they'd simply taken the first rock I'd thrown at them. Had they figured out my little trick yet?

"Don't worry, Geneva, my dear. They will never get close to you again."

A whoosh of air broke around us, ushering in the scent of thorns and loneliness. Terror seized me as memories of Meleena, my mother, assaulted my mind. I closed my fist, tucking it against my chest protectively. I whipped my head from side to side, searching for the source. I knew she was dead—I had killed her myself to take Possession of the Rock of Healing so I could save Geneva. But sometimes her paralyzing scent wafted toward me from nowhere, dancing around me and haunting my nightmares.

But she wasn't still alive. The rock worked for me. I was its Possessor. It was just a bit finicky at times. Healing someone as sick as Geneva was certainly a lot of work.

I was just imagining things. I should rest. With Geneva. If she were awake and knew all I had done for her, she would want me to sleep by her side, of course. She would thank me and smile at me and desire me as much as I desired her.

I would never allow Meleena to ruin that for me, like she had ruined all other aspects of my life to get back at Tukailaan.

I shook myself. *I must keep my senses. Can't let her get the better of me in death as well as in life.*

The rock was hard and cold and small in my hand. I opened my fingers to gaze at it again. Unease roiled in my gut.

Even though she's dead, of course, there's nothing wrong with a little caution. After all, it wouldn't be right if I didn't do everything possible for my love. Negligence is unacceptable.

I glanced at the smashed meat I'd been trying to convince Geneva to eat. The large rock I had used to crush the hunk of meat into tiny minced bits lay on the stone next to Geneva.

I can't be too careful.

I set the shiny rock down and smashed the meat-mashing one on top of it.

It splintered into countless pieces, but I could still see them. If they were big enough I could see them, Meleena could too.

I brought the mallet rock down again and again and again. There would be nothing left of it to take. No one could take it from my love. Not after this.

THE CATHAWYR

Odan Terridor Trilogy: Book Three

COMING SOON

Connect with Savannah!
@savannahjgoins
Instagram | Goodreads | YouTube | Twitter | Facebook
Visit Savannah's website for writing tips and story updates!
savannahjgoins.com

Did you enjoy this book?
If you have a minute, a review would be greatly appreciated!

ACKNOWLEDGEMENTS

If you compare the following acknowledgements to the same section in *The Gwythienian*, you'll see how incredibly blessed I've been with an abundance of writing friends since I first started out. I thank God for giving me the most wonderful friends I've ever had through the writing community.

To my Dream Big Writers group, since finding you guys in October of 2017, you've become a major highlight of my week. Thursdays are always my favorite weekday and I especially love NaNoWriMoing it up with ya'll every November!

To my accountability partner, Cam, thank you for making me feel so welcome in the group that first time I came. I was pretty shy back then and almost didn't go, but I'm so glad I did! Thanks for reserving the conference room for us every Thursday, and for the many writing sessions we've shared, especially when I was working part time!

To my partner-in-shenanigans, Alicia Grumley, I'm so glad I met you that first writer's group night! I've loved every chance we've had to write (and get distracted talking for hours), especially at Books and Brews! I treasure your friendship and I am so grateful to your precious mom for bringing you into the world so I could have the very best writing bestie ever. Lots of love, girl.

To my Writers' Business Mastermind, Brittany Wang, Holly Davis, and Alicia Grumley, thank you so much for all you've taught me. You've given me so many wonderful ideas and listened to all my crazy plans. I'm so glad we get to learn and grow together every week and I am so grateful for each of you!

To Holly Davis, who also can't remember how long ago we first met on Instagram, but who was my very first writing friend, thank you for reading all my blog posts and newsletters when no one else in the world knew or cared about them, and for watching and commenting on all my AuthorTube videos, especially when I first started out and nearly gave up so many times. I COULD NOT have gotten so far without you, and I am so, so glad we found each other!

To Heather VenKat, who along with Holly and I make up the Mischief Managers, I'm delighted to be the Third Twin and so thrilled to have a vet friend in the writing world! It's awesome to have a friend in the same two worlds as me. I can't believe how much fun we all had organizing #BeatingWritersButt and I can't wait to see what other mischief we start! Who's got some no good we can solemnly swear to get up to?

To Michele, the leader of the Heartland Christian Writer's Group and my fellow grammar nerd, thanks for the many lovely debates over how many dots belong in an ellipsis and other wonderful grammar nuances! You made me realize how much I actually enjoy striving toward nerd status on grammar things. And it was your encouragement and support that made me keep coming back to my very first writer's group way back when I was so painfully shy it wouldn't have taken much for me to give up on attending. I am so glad I met you and greatly treasure our friendship! Onward to Realm Makers and more grammar debates!

To Annie Sullivan, thank you for showing me what believing in yourself can do. I am in awe of all the amazing things you've done for your writing career and so inspired by you. Nothing is too big for you to reach for and try to achieve. Much of my growth in confidence and courage have come from you this year. Don't mind me over here totally copying everything you do! I can't wait to see where our author careers take us. Last one to a million-dollar book deal is a rotten egg!

To my Snack Pack, I can't believe I've only known most of you for barely a year. It feels like we've been a thing for ages!

Rachele, thanks for being a rockin' ML for our NaNoWriMo region. You always make NaNo extra epic! Mackenzie, thanks for the many ARCs and for organizing our spectacular trip to Book Expo and Book Con! Your planning skills are the bomb! Kristin, thank you for the business advice that really helped me out and for being a stupendous example of perseverance and a great attitude toward life. Alicia, Michele, and Annie, ya'll already got your own paragraphs! I'll see ya'll next shark week (and hopefully many times between now and then)!

To my 2019 Wander Writers Retreat peeps, thank you Brittany Wang, Holly Davis, Kari Weeks, Becca Douglas, Jessi Elliot, Evie Driver, Destiny Murtough, Keylin Rivers, Bri Leclerc, Mandi Lynn, Meg Latorre, Kate Kavanaough, Jenna Streety, and Brook Passmore for being so wonderful and welcoming in Toronto. I love each and every one of you ladies and look forward to many more Wander Writers Retreats in our futures.

To my incredible Street Team, Heather Sokol, Alicia Grumley, Annie Sullivan, MaryAlice Peoples, Holly Davis, Kahla Leighton, Jill Hackman, Brittany Wang, Kimberly Paterson, Heather VenKat, Jenna Streety, Teresa Beasley, Missy Goins, Stephanie Mirro, Kristin Ungerecht, Dominique Nieves, Katie Nellis, Jessi Elliot, Jessica Bullard, Stephanie Marie, Morgan Cain, Brianna Leclerc, Kari Weeks, and Meg LaTorre, who each read this book early and helped me promote it, thank you all for being such awesome human beings. I love each and every one of you!

To my first and epically fantastic editor, Nadine Brandes, thank you so much for combing through that atrocious draft of *The Gwythienian*. You taught me more than any other individual about writing, and it's only because of you that *The Gwythienian* wasn't a horrible embarrassment. You taught me about info dumping and repetitive writing and all my bad writing habits, while still pointing out where I did well and where you laughed.

If it wasn't for those encouragements, I may have given up under the weight of all the red.

To the primary editor of this book, Sarah Liu, thank you so much for taking on a deplorable draft of *The Crivabanian* and helping me muddle through all the weak bits. Without your devoted attention and thoughtful suggestions, it would be in very rough shape. Thank you for everything!

To my chapter heading illustrator, Rob Costacorta, thank you for making a beautiful illustration of Sequoia Cadryl! I can't wait to commission the illustration for *The Cathawyr!*

To my proofreading and formatting team, Katherine and Jeffrey Collyer, thank you guys for doing a lovely job refining and formatting this book on a crunch schedule.

To my character artist, Ingrid Nordli, thank you for making my characters visible and doing a gorgeous job! I love the illustrations and can't wait to commission more art from you!

To my other half, my husband, Ben, thank you for supporting me in my dreams of pursuing authorhood and for being cool with me spending an exorbitant amount of money on this career that may take many years to start paying back. I love you the most and can't wait to watch our entrepreneurial futures unfold together.

To my biggest fan, my mother-in-law Missy Goins, who thinks even the cruddy things I write are fantastic, thank you for your support through all the hardships and discouragements and mess-ups, and for being the most excited about all the good things. And thank you for always believing that I would make myself an author, even when I didn't. You've always been one of the first to read a new draft, and your encouragement is invaluable. And thank you, Bill, Jenny, Frantzy, and Austin for cheering me on with her!

To my parents, Gregg and Jenny Glass, thank you for giving me a great education. Mom, thank you for giving up your career to teach me and Tori yourself and for doing a FANTASTIC job. I think we turned out pretty awesome, if I do say so myself. And thanks, Dad, for working so hard so that Mom could stay home and teach us.

To my sister, Tori, thank you for listening to my ideas and stories, and for being the first person to take *The Gwythienian* to Italy!

To Grams and Pop, thank you for being awesome grandparents! Ya'll bragged to every single one of your friends about what an amazing author I am, and knowing that is a great feeling. Pop, I'm inspired by your career as a businessman working for yourself and hope to emulate you in that one day soon. Grams, thank you for making "booklets" with Tori and I out of construction paper and crayons, and encouraging us to draw and create with playdough and plastic animals. And for playing house in the sandbox. You made a huge contribution to my creativity and a lot of my "awesome authorness" is thanks to you. And thank you both for being married over 60 years now. What an inspiration that is! Love you guys!

To Noni and Aunt Linda, thank you both for beta reading the early and horrible drafts of *The Gwythienian* and *The Crivabanian*! I appreciate your encouragement and feedback so much. Let's go on another sisters' cruise soon! And Noni, I am so inspired by the story of how you became a businesswoman. I will never forget it and will always use it as a measure of success to reach for. Despite all the businessmen who tried to stop you as a woman in the workforce during that time period, you've risen above them all and I am so proud. I get my ambition from you, and just you wait to see all the great things I will do with it!

To the person reading this book thinking you could never write your own, that's a lie. There is nothing more special about me that enabled me to write this book and would prevent you from writing your own. Talent is mostly an acquired skill. If you have a story to tell, get started telling it.

Here's the secret: sticktoitiveness.

Don't give up when the curser blinks at you from an empty page. Start writing crap. You can edit it later. The only thing you can't do is edit a blank page.

Don't give up when someone doesn't like your writing. It takes time and LOTS of practice to get good at it. Find someone else who's learning and team up to learn together. Check out the bazillions of free resources online to improve your writing. And find the ideal audience who wants to read your story. Few stories are for everyone. Find the people who need yours. Those are your people.

Don't give up when you get rejected by agents, publishers, bookstores, and all the other people who could reject you. Part of being in this business is growing a thick skin and being wise and humble enough to learn from critiques and rejections, even though it isn't fun. With time, they can help you improve. And as long as you keep trying things and keep improving your writing, eventually you'll stop having more rejections than you know what to do with and you'll have more offers than you can handle.

At last, when all is dark and everything is going wrong AGAIN and you don't know how it could possibly be worth giving it any more blood, sweat, or tears, listen to Neil Gaiman's Make Good Art speech. It's on YouTube. That speech has gotten me through many a dark day, and it is quite possible that I'll have a quote from it tattooed on myself by the time you're reading this.

And if you want an incredible writing community like the one I've thanked above, you can totally get one. You can start by following all the people I mentioned above on social media. They're obviously awesome people and great writers to follow and learn from. Then you can google local writing groups in your area. Check the NaNoWriMo website for local NaNo groups. If there aren't any close by, there's probably one worth driving to a few times a month. If you're still drawing a blank, start your own. You can also find tons of great writers' groups on Facebook. And once you've found them, just be your awesome self. Be kind, be encouraging, be willing to listen and lend a hand in order to find people who will reciprocate those actions. And never take them for granted.

They are your people.

VOCABULARY

Adarborian (Ah-dar-bore-E-an)—a humanoid creature with hummingbird-like wings capable of dramatically growing and shrinking.

Amolryn (Am-ole-wren)—a great South American tree that produces a variety of colored flowers, and according to legend birthed the first Adarborians from its blossoms.

Annwyl (Ann-will)—an Adarborian leader, daughter of the great Possessor, Aven.

Arkencain (Ark-in-cane)—a dangerous magical weapon created by the Arkensilvers. Capable of slowly poisoning its target to death over several days.

Arkensilver (Ark-in-silver)—an extinct race of magical creatures capable of intensely weaponized magic.

Arunca Rymakri (Are-un-kah Rim-ak-ree)—the art of knife- and spear-throwing, according to the Gwythienians' traditions.

Aven (A-vin)—an Adarborian, Possessor of their rock, mother of Annwyl.

Bricriu (Brick-ree-oo)—a rogue Gwythienian, whose identity and intentions are currently unknown.

Cadoumai (Cad-oo-my)—any member of one of the four realms whose gift is very strong.

Cathawyr (Cath-ah-we're)—the fabled race of great cats about whom the realms have many legends.

Crivabanian (Cree-va-bane-E-an)—a creature like a large flying squirrel with hidden depths of physical strength.

Coranyla (Cora-ny-lah)—a Cathawyr and the creator of the rock of healing.

Divinado Legendelor (Dee-vin-a-dough Leg-an-dell-or)—a

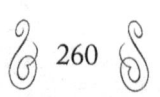

special night of storytelling among the Crivabanians.

Ferrox (Fare-ox)—a Gwythienian, father of Gaedyen and son of the great Padraig, husband of Geneva. One of the Betrayers of the Realms.

Gaedyen (Gay-dee-yen)—a Gwythienian, son of the Betrayers of the Realms, Ferrox and Geneva, and grandson of the Keeper, Padraig.

Geneva (Gin-E-va)—a Gwythienian, mother of Gaedyen, wife of Ferrox. One of the Betrayers of the Realms.

Gwaltmar (G-walt-mar)—a Rubandor, the Possessor of their rock, friend of Padraig.

Gwythienian (G-why-thin-E-an)—a dragon-like creature with the ability to see through water into other places and to turn invisible.

Kimry (Kim-ree)—The leader of the Cathawyr race and the creator of the orange rock. The only Cathawyr to have lost her natural color.

Liryk (Lie-rick)—the directions to one other realm given in the form of a poem from one realm to another many years ago.

Malwoden (Mal-woe-den)—giant snails, found only in Odan Terridor. The favorite food of the Gwythienians.

Masius Arborii (Maze-E-us Are-bore-E)—one of the four realms, home of the Adarborians, located in the jungles of South America.

Ofwen Dwir (Oaf-when D-we're)—one of the four realms, home of the Rubandors, located under water off the coast of California.

Rubandor (Roo-band-or)—a creature like a giant axolotl who can sense their surroundings with sonar-like abilities.

Odan Terridor (O-dan Tare-i-door)—one of the four realms, home of the Gwythienians, located under Tennessee and the surrounding states.

Padraig (Pah-j-rig)—a Gwythienian, the Possessor of their

rock and the Keeper of all the rocks, father of Ferrox and grandfather of Gaedyen.

Parva (Par-vah)—an Adarborian healer.

Sequoia Cadryl (Sec-oi-ya Ca-drill)—one of the four realms, home of the Crivabanians, located within the redwoods of California.

Soroca (Sore-oh-kah)—Gaedyen's aunt on Geneva's side.

Tukailaan (Too-ky-lahn)—a Gwythienian, brother of Padraig and one who wishes to steal his place as Possessor and Keeper and to gain Possession of all four rocks.

Rymakri (Rim-ak-ree)—the wooden knives and spears made by the Gwythienians. They do not last long and must be used immediately.

Shimbator (Shim-bah-tore)—a legendary type of Gwythienian, one who is able to transform into a human and back into a Gwythienian at will.

Veritamyk (Very-tam-eek)—a Crivabanian creature who befriends Enzi on her journey.

Vorbiaquam (Vore-bee-ak-wam)—a cavern in Odan Terridor with walls of waterfalls and pools of water on either side of the strip of land within, a place for Gwythienians to look into the water for other places.